The Author

FREDERICK PHILIP GROVE was born Felix Paul Greve at Radomno in West Prussia (now a part of Poland) in 1879. Raised in Hamburg and educated at the University of Bonn and later at the University of Munich, he began his career as a poet and translator into German of many English and French writers, including Balzac, Flaubert, Gide, Swift, and Wilde. His first novel, *Fanny Essler*, appeared in 1905; his second, *Maurermeister Ihles Haus* (Mastermason Ihle's House), in the following year. He left Germany in 1909 for the United States.

In 1912, under the new name of Frederick Philip Grove, he began teaching school in Manitoba, and continued in that profession until 1924.

Grove's first book in English, *Over Prairie Trails*, is a sequence of seven sketches of his weekly trips through the Manitoba countryside. His first novel in English, *Settlers of the Marsh*, establishes the essentially tragic pattern of his fiction, the heroic pioneers who seek domestic and material happiness but seldom realize their goals.

Grove's autobiography, *In Search of Myself*, begins with a fictitious account of his early life in Europe and moves on to a largely accurate presentation of his life in Canada.

In 1929 Grove left Manitoba to accept a job with a publishing firm in Ottawa. In 1931 he settled on a farm near Simcoe, Ontario, where he spent the final years of his life.

Frederick Philip Grove died in Simcoe, Ontario, in 1948.

THE NEW CANADIAN LIBRARY

FREDERICK PHILIP GROVE

Settlers of the Marsh

With an Afterword by Kristjana Gunnars

The following dedication appeared in the original edition:

To Arthur L. Phelps

First published in 1925 by The Ryerson Press, Toronto
First NCL edition published 1966 by permission
of Mrs. Frederick Philip Grove.
This New Canadian Library edition 1989

National Library of Canada Cataloguing in Publication Data

Grove, Frederick Philip, 1879-1948
Settlers of the marsh

(New Canadian library)
Bibliography: p.
ISBN 0-7710-9961-4

I. Title II. Series.

PS8513.R68S48 1989 C813'.52 C88-094950-3
PR9199.2.G766S48 1989

We acknowledge the financial support of the Government of Canada through the Book Publishing Industry Development Program for our publishing activities. We further acknowledge the support of the Canada Council for the Arts and the Ontario Arts Council for our publishing program.

Typesetting by Rowsell Typesetting Limited
Printed and bound in Canada

McClelland & Stewart Ltd.
The Canadian Publishers
481 University Avenue
Toronto, Ontario
M5G 2E9
www.mcclelland.com

4 5 6 7 8 06 05 04 03 02

Contents

One	*Mrs. Lund*	7
Two	*Niels*	60
Three	*Ellen*	97
Four	*Mrs. Lindstedt*	132
Five	*Bobby*	190
Six	*Ellen Again*	232
	Afterword	267

CHAPTER ONE

Mrs. Lund

ON THE road leading north from the little prairie town Minor two men were fighting their way through the gathering dusk.

Both were recent immigrants; one, Lars Nelson, a giant, of three years' standing in the country; the other, Niels Lindstedt, slightly above medium size, but compactly built, of only three months'. Both were Swedes; and they had struck up a friendship which had led to a partnership for the winter that was coming. They had been working on a threshing gang between Minor and Balfour and were now on their way into the bush settlement to the north-east where scattered homesteads reached out into the wilderness.

It was the beginning of the month of November.

Niels carried his suitcase on his back; Nelson, his new friend's bundle, which also held the few belongings of his own which he had along. He wore practically the same clothes winter and summer.

Above five miles from town they reached, on the north road, the point where the continuous settlement ran out into the wild, sandy land which, forming the margin of the Big Marsh, intervened between the territory of the towns and the next Russo-German settlement to the north, some twenty miles or so straight ahead.

At this point the road leapt the Muddy River and passed through its sheltering fringe of bush to strike out over a sheer waste of heath-like country covered with low, creeping brush. The wind which had been soughing through the tree tops had free sweep here; and an exceedingly fine dust of dry, powdery ice-crystals began to fly – you could hardly call it snow so far.

It did not occur to Niels to utter or even harbour apprehensions. His powerful companion knew the road; where he went, Niels could go.

They swung on, for the most part in silence.

The road became a mere trail; but for a while longer it was plainly visible in the waning light of the west; in the smooth ruts a film of white was beginning to gather.

The wind came in fits and starts, out of the hollow north-west; and with the engulfing dark an ever thickening granular shower of snow blew from the low-hanging clouds. As the trail became less and less visible, the very ground underfoot seemed to slide to the south-east.

By that time they had made about half the distance they intended to make. To turn back would have given them only the advantage of going with, instead of against, the gathering gale. Both were eager to get to work again: Nelson had undertaken to dig wells for two of the older settlers in the bush country; and he intended to clear a piece of his own land during the winter and to sell the wood which he had accumulated the year before.

They came to a fork in the trail and struck north-east. Soon after the turn Nelson stopped.

"Remember the last house?" he asked.

"Yes," said Niels, speaking Swedish.

"From there on, for twenty miles north and for ten miles east the land is open for homestead entry. But it is no good. Mere sand that blows with the wind as soon as the brush is taken off."

They plodded on for another hour. The trail was crossed and criss-crossed by cattle paths. Which they were on, trail or cattle path, was hard to tell.

Once more Nelson stopped. "Where's north?"

Niels pointed.

But Nelson did not agree. "If the wind hasn't changed, north must be there," he said pointing over his shoulder.

The snow was coming down in ever denser waves which a relentless wind threw sideways into their faces. The ground was covered now.

"Cold?" asked Nelson.

"Not very," Niels answered deprecatingly.

"We're over half," Nelson said. "No use turning back. If we keep north, we must hit Grassy Creek, road or no road."

They plodded on. That they were not on the trail there could be no doubt any longer; they felt the low brush impeding their steps.

Sometimes they stumbled; Niels laughed apologetically; Nelson swore under his breath. But they kept their sides to the wind and went on.

Both would have liked to talk, to tell and to listen to stories of danger, of being lost, of hair-breadth escapes: the influence of the prairie snowstorm made itself felt. But whenever one of them spoke, the wind snatched his word from his lips and threw it aloft.

A merciless force was slowly numbing them by ceaseless pounding. A vision of some small room, hot with the glow and flicker of an open fire, took possession of Niels. But blindly, automatically he kept up with his companion.

Suddenly they came to larger bush. Not that they saw it; but they heard the soughing of the wind through its aisles and its leafless boughs; and they felt the unexpected shelter.

They stopped.

"Danged if I know where we are," said Nelson in English; and he began to beat the air with the stick which he had cut for himself, going forward towards whatever gave the shelter.

The stick cracked against something hard.

"Well," Nelson exclaimed, again in English, "I'll be doggoned!" He had stepped forward and put his hand against the wall of a building. "We've hit something here."

Niels kept close.

At the top of his voice Nelson shouted, "Hi there! Anybody in?" And again he beat against the wall.

They edged and groped along and came to a tiny window which was just then illumined by the flicker of a match.

"Hello!" Nelson sang out in his booming voice. "Open up, will you?"

And, having felt his way a little farther along the building, he came to a door which he recognised as such when his hand struck the knob. He rattled it and hammered the jamb with his fist.

They were on the south side of the house, sheltered from the wind which whistled through trees that stood very near.

A light shone forth from the window. Whoever was inside had lighted a lamp. Nelson redoubled his shouts and knocks. They waited.

At last, after a seemingly endless interval, a bolt was withdrawn, and the door opened the least little bit.

Impetuously Nelson pushed it open altogether.

In its frame stood an old man of perhaps sixty-five, bent over, grey, with short, straggling hair and beard and hollow eyes, one of which was squinting. He held a shotgun in his hands, with one finger on the trigger.

"What you want?" he asked in the tone of distrust.

"Let's in," sang Nelson. "We're lost. Caught in the storm."

"No can," the old man replied with forbidding hostility. "Get on." His threatening gesture was unmistakable.

"You Swedish?" asked Nelson in his native tongue.

The old man hesitated as if taken off his guard by the

personal question. "Naw," he said at last, still in English. "Icelandic. Get on."

"Listen here," Nelson reasoned, persisting in his use of Swedish, "you aren't going to turn us out into a night like this, are you? Let's in and get warm at least."

"No can," the old man repeated. "Get on."

"Say," Nelson insisted. "We're going to Amundsen's to dig a well for him. We come from Minor. We don't know where we are or how to get there."

"One mile east and four mile norr," the old man said without relenting.

A draft slammed the door, nearly catching Nelson's hand in the crack. But quick as a flash the giant reached for the knob and held it before the old man could push the bolt into place.

The old man, however, had also reached out; and with unexpected strength he did not allow the door to open for more than an inch. Through this opening he pushed the barrel of the gun right into Nelson's face.

Nelson laughed. "Say," he sang out once more, "tell us at least which way is east."

The old man nodded a direction. "Follow the bush."

When Nelson let go of the door, it slammed shut; and the bolt shot home. Again Nelson laughed his deep, throaty laugh and looked at Niels.

Through the window came the faint glimmer of the little lamp. In its light the two men looked like snowmen. On the lapels of their sheep-skins the snow had consolidated into sheets of ice.

The lamp in the shack went out; and they were left in utter darkness.

For a moment longer they stood, stamping their feet and swinging their arms against their bodies. The mere absence of the wind felt like actual, grateful warmth. They lingered.

But Nelson broke the silence at last. "So much for him. I guess we'll have to try to make Amundsen's. Five miles, he says."

"All right," Niels agreed.

They started out again, in the direction of the nod.

Here the snow fell without that furious, driving force which had made it a blinding torment on the open sand-flats. It fell in flakes, now. Still, progress was slow; for, where the wind found its way through openings in the bush, drifts had already been piled in the lee of the trees. Often the two men found themselves in knee-deep banks and fell. It took them an hour to make the first mile.

Then Nelson exclaimed, "Now I know."

They turned north, crossed the huge trough of a creek or river on a bridge, and were engulfed in the winding chasm of a narrow logging trail.

The darkness was inky-black; but a faint luminosity in the clouds above showed the canyon of the swaying trees overhead.

They went on for a long, long while.

"There we are," Nelson exclaimed at last; and the same moment a dog struck up a dismal howl from somewhere about the yard; but he did not come out to bark or snap at them.

Nelson found the house; and his vigorous knocking soon brought a response.

They were admitted by a scantily-dressed man and entered a large kitchen which occupied half the space of the house.

The man inside accepted the fact that Nelson had brought a partner without comment and donned overalls and sheep-skin to fetch straw from the stable, to spread on the floor of the low-ceilinged room. Then he brought blankets and left them alone.

Amundsen's farm consisted of a quarter-section, heavily timbered except for thirty-six acres which were cleared. His buildings, encircling the yard, were of logs well plastered with clay, the dwelling being, besides, veneered with lumber and not only white-washed but painted.

The house held two rooms, a kitchen which also served as dining room; and a bed-room with three beds. Above the beamed ceiling stretched a huge attic. The stable was large enough for four horses and six cows. There were, further, a chicken house, harbouring also a number of geese, ducks, and turkeys; a granary, well-floored; a smoke-house; and a half-open shed for the very complete array of implements. Whatever Amundsen did, he did right.

Niels slept late on the morning of their arrival. It had been past three o'clock when they lay down.

The kitchen was empty. There was a good fire in the range; and he found all he needed for washing. The adjoining room was closed; but he saw through the window that the door to the stable was open; and since he expected to find Nelson and Amundsen there, he went out.

On the yard, the snow lay six inches deep; more was filtering down. It was pleasantly cold.

Niels found Nelson and Amundsen discussing the work to be done.

"Seventy-five cents a foot, down to twenty-five feet," Nelson said in Swedish. "Beyond that a dollar and fifty. We go on till we get water. Unless you want us to stop . . ."

Amundsen laughed. "I must have water," he said emphatically. "Melting snow is too slow. And in summer I have to haul four miles from the creek. However, whenever I want you to stop, I shall pay for what has been done."

Niels looked the man over. Both he and Nelson had nodded to him.

There was something careful, particular about Amundsen's whole appearance. He might be fifty years old. He did not wear overalls under his sheep-skin but a grey suit, the legs of his trousers being tucked into high leather boots which were well greased. About his neck he wore a neatly-tied, plaid-pattern sateen tie. His head was covered with a wedge-shaped cap of black fur. He had a small moustache, trimmed to a short, bristly brush; his cheeks and chin were freshly shaved. His eyes were small and blue and had a trick of avoiding those of his interlocutor. He shrugged his shoulders when he spoke and gesticulated with both hands. Before he spoke, he thought; and, having thought, he spoke with decision. He seemed to realise with great force and made others realise that thought could be changed and modified, but that a spoken word was binding. Every motion of his showed that he watched jealously over his dignity. But his voice was harsh and loud as if he were trying to give a special emphasis and significance to every word. When he listened, he bent his head to one side and looked at the ground, drawing up his thin brows and lending ear with all his might. That gave him the air of being constantly on his guard.

"If it please God," Amundsen said at last decisively, "we shall find water . . . Well, shall we go in?" And he led the way to the house.

"Mrs. Amundsen still poorly?" Nelson asked.

"It has pleased God to confine her to her bed," Amundsen replied with corresponding choice of words in Swedish. He shrugged his shoulders and raised his hands in a deprecatory gesture. "It is a visitation. One must be resigned."

When they entered the house, Amundsen ceremoniously letting the two others precede, a girl of perhaps eighteen or nineteen years was busy at the range. The bed on the floor had been removed; the table was spread.

Niels looked at the girl and expected some kind of introduction; but none was vouchsafed. Neither did she seem to take any notice of the guests.

She was somewhat above medium height, taller than her father, with wide hips and a mature bust. Her hair was straw-yellow and neatly but plainly brushed back and gathered into a knot above the nape of her neck. Her dress was of dark-blue print, made with no view to prettiness or style, but spotlessly clean.

Her whole attitude, even to her father, spoke of self-centred repose and somewhat defiant aloofness.

It was not till the three men were seated at the table that Niels had a glimpse of her face. Her eyes were light-blue, her features round, and her complexion a pure, Scandinavian white. But it was the expression that held him: hers was the face of a woman; not of a girl. There was a great, ripe maturity in it, and a look as if she saw through pretences and shams and knew more of life than her age would warrant. No smile lighted her features; her eyes were stern and nearly condemnatory. But somehow, when Niels looked at her, a great desire came over him to make her smile.

Amundsen noticed his scrutiny and disapproved of it; for with his loud and matter-of-face voice he cut it short.

"Well," he said, "pray." And, standing up, he spoke with a firm and insistent voice a prayer which sounded as if he were rather laying down the law to his creator than invoking his blessing.

Then, without looking up, he sat down. "Ellen, coffee."

"Yes, father," replied the girl with an unexpected note of obsequience oddly at variance with her preoccupied air.

Breakfast was eaten in silence. The girl did not sit down with the men but ate while standing at the range.

Nelson was the first to rise. "Well," he said, "I guess we better get started."

They went out.

Amundsen remained on the yard, busying himself with the sleighs to which apparently he intended to transfer the box from the wagon.

Soon after, when the two men had gathered their tools, picks and shovels, Niels saw to his surprise the girl, clad like a man in sheepskin and big overshoes, crossing the yard to the stable where she began to harness a team of horses. They were big, powerful brutes, young and unruly. But she handled them with calm assurance and unflinching courage as she led them out on the yard.

"They're famous run-aways," Nelson said.

"And he lets the girl handle them!"

"Yea . . ." Nelson replied. "But they don't run away with her. It's him they smash up every once in a while."

"Does she work on the farm?"

"Like a man," Nelson said.

She tied the horses to a rail of the fence and went to join her father. Between them, the two lifted the wagon-box from the wheel-truck, in order to transfer it to the bob-sleighs.

Niels ran over and took hold of the girl's end; but she did not yield without reluctance. A frown settled between her brows. Without a word she went to get the horses.

Nelson had gone on with his work; and Niels rejoined him while Amundsen and his daughter placed two barrels into the wagon-box.

The girl drove away; Amundsen returned to the stable.

"Better not take too much notice of the girl," Nelson said when the man had disappeared. "Amundsen might show you off the place."

When Amundsen, after a while, emerged from the stable, he was leading a team of older, steadier horses which he hitched to a hay-rack still on wheels. He worked in his slow, deliberate way, without a lost motion, and giving to the veriest trifle an importance and a sort of dignity which seemed laughable or sublime.

Niels watched him covertly till he drove away.

Meanwhile he and Nelson worked silently, with the steady team-work peculiar to Swedes.

Then the girl returned from the creek. As she drove in on the yard, she happened to look at Niels. It was a level, quiet look, unswerving and irresponsive. It did not establish a bond; it held no message, neither of acceptance nor of disapproval; it was not meant to have any meaning for him; it was an undisguised, cool, disinterested scrutiny.

Niels coloured under the look. He lowered his eye and went on with his work, a little too eagerly perhaps: he was self-conscious. In order to shake off his embarrassment, and in an impulse of defiant self-assertion, he dropped his pick, straightened his back, wiped his forehead, and sang out, in Swedish, "A penny for your thoughts, miss."

But he repented instantly; for the look of the girl assumed a critical, disapproving expression; the frown settled back between her brows. Thus she turned her attention to her horses and ignored the men at their work.

Nelson, too, had straightened and looked at Niels, grinning. "You've got your nerve," he said admiringly.

Nelson felt still more embarrassed; but he laughed and fell to work again.

Some time during the afternoon Niels had an occasion to go into the house. When he entered the kitchen, the door to the second room stood open; and he had a glimpse of the bed in which the sick woman lay. Ellen was sitting on the egde of the bed and holding her mother's hand.

The woman's face seemed to be all eye: large, dark eyes in large, cavernous sockets. Ear, nose, and cheek had a waxy transparency.

Ellen was in sheep-skin and tam, as she had come in from the yard. When she heard a footfall, she looked back over her shoulder, rose, and closed the door.

Niels felt ashamed of his behaviour in the morning.

At night, after the day's work had reluctantly been brought to a close, the three men sat in the kitchen. Nelson smoked a pipe; Amundsen partook of a dram; Niels declined both tobacco and "schnapps."

"Done any breaking yet?" Amundsen asked.

"Yes," said Nelson. "Three acres last summer. Too late for a crop, though. I'll clear enough to break four or five more in spring."

"That's good," said Amundsen in his slow, deliberate way. "You've bought horses. Where are they?"

"At Hahn's."

"I know him," Amundsen said with a peculiar smile. "He's German. He used to be a good, steady fellow till last year. Then he went crazy and joined the Baptists. As if the word of the Lord were not perfectly clear . . ." And he reached for a Bible on the window-shelf.

But Nelson forestalled him. "Do you intend to break next summer?"

"If I live and am well." Amundsen's smile was deprecating. "I've brushed and cleared three acreas in summer. So, if it please God . . ."

"You've surely done well in this country."

"Yes," Amundsen admitted. "It might have been better, of course. But I can't complain. God has blessed my labour."

"You came only seven or eight years ago, didn't you?"

"Nine. But when I came I was in debt. I owe no man now."

"Too bad about your wife," Nelson said after a while. "Have you had the doctor in?"

"She is in the hand of God," Amundsen replied sententiously. "What is to be will be. I am a sinner and a stricken man." It sounded as if he boasted of the fact.

"Too bad," Nelson repeated.

Once more Niels looked at the man. There was something repulsive about his self-sufficiency. His wife was lying at the point of death; but he had not even called in what help human skill and knowledge might give. He relied on God to do for him what could be done . . . And his daughter worked like a man . . .

Next day the sky was bright and clear. Not a wisp of cloud was visible anywhere. But it had been very cold overnight . . .

Work felt grateful: this country seemed to have been created to rouse man's energies to fullest exertion . . .

Again the girl was about the yard. She fetched water for the stock and fed cows, horses, and pigs; and when the chores were done, she went with her father to get hay from a stack in the meadow . . .

Without his being conscious of it she intrigued Niels. She was so utterly impersonal. The only softer feature she betrayed consisted in an absent-minded patting of the old dog that limped through the snow across the yard, wagging his tail whenever she came, to return to his lair in the straw-stack as soon as she left.

The place was so utterly lonesome that it reminded Niels of the wood-cutters' houses in fairy tales. Wherever you looked, the bush reared about the buildings: great, towering aspens, now bare and leafless but glittering with the crystals of dry, powdery snow in the cracks of the bark.

Whenever Nelson and Niels were alone, the latter asked questions. Once he enquired after Amundsen's wife. Somehow she reminded him of his own mother; and like his mother she aroused in him a feeling of resentment against something that seemed to be wrong with the world.

"They say he's worked her to death," Nelson said. "I don't know. People talk a lot. Around here the women and children all have to work. I saw her on the hay-stack last year. I've seen lots of others. Soon after, there was a child, born dead. She's never been up again."

"But why not send for a doctor?"

"Nobody here sends for the doctor. He'd charge twenty-five or thirty dollars to come . . ."

The week went by. On Sunday Niels and Nelson were idle.

In the afternoon many people called at the farm in the bush, the women to look in on Mrs. Amundsen; the men, to gossip in the kitchen . . . Where did they all come from in this wilderness?

Some of the callers were Germans, some Swedes and Icelanders, two or three English or Canadian.

The men wore sheep-skins, big boots, and flannelette shirts; most of the women, dark, long skirts, shawls over their shoulders, and white or light-coloured head-kerchiefs. Many of them had babies along which they nursed without restraint.

Nelson knew them all; but it struck Niels that both he and his friend were outside of things. Many spoke German which Amundsen seemed to understand though he spoke it only in a broken way. Apart from the Canadians, one single couple – elderly Swedes – used English exclusively. To Niels it seemed that they were handling it with remarkable fluency. Their name was Lund.

Mr. Lund was between fifty-five and sixty years old: a man who once must have been of powerful build; but he seemed to be nearly blind; and as he walked about, he groped his way as if all his members were disjointed. When he sat down, he either reclined or bent forward, resting his elbows on table or knees. The hair on the huge dome of his head was scanty, grey, straggling; a short, grey beard covered his chin.

His wife was by ten years his junior: a big, fleshy woman of florid features who must have been attractive in the past. She was lively, in a coarse, good-humoured way, not without wit; and she treated her husband with a sort of contemptuous indulgence.

Both man and wife were shabby; though Mrs. Lund wore a glaring waist which would have drawn attention in a city and seemed entirely out of place where she was. Her black hair might have been a beauty if it had been kept tidy.

These were the people for whom Niels and Nelson were to dig the second well.

To Niels it was a foreign crowd. He had no contact with them. He felt lonesome, forlorn . . .

Then Mrs. Lund ran across him.

"So you have only just come into the country, Mr. Lindstedt?" she asked with the air of a lady of the world, speaking Swedish. "And what do you mean to do?"

"Oh, I don't know. Make some money and take up a homestead, I suppose . . ."

"Mr. Lindstedt," she said, leaning over from her seat on a big, old-country trunk, "why don't you buy?"

"Buy?" His tone was vacant surprise.

"Sure. This isn't the old country, you know. Lots of people in this country buy without a cent of money. Crop-payments, you know."

"Well," Niels hesitated, "so long as I can get a homestead for nothing . . ."

"Listen," she interrupted him. "Believe an old homesteader like me. By the time you're ready to prove up, in the bush, you've paid for the place in work three times over. And what with the stumps and stones, everybody is willing to sell out as soon as he gets his patent. Yes, if you could get a homestead out in the open prairie . . . But there the land's all settled. And when a man *has* proved up and owns his quarter of bush, what can he get for it? Two thousand dollars. And that's for six, seven years of back-breaking work; and sometimes for longer. Take a prairie farm, now, which sells for six thousand dollars, let me say. You work it for six years, and you've paid for it in half crops. And you own all your machinery besides. You are worth ten thousand dollars. And meanwhile you haven't been working so's to make a cripple out of yourself. Think it over, Mr. Lindstedt. That's all I say. Think it over. But you want to get married, of course."

Niels coloured. He was ill at ease . . . There must be a flaw in these arguments.

Mrs. Lund rose. "Carl," she called. "Come on. Time we get home."

"Yes, Anna," her husband replied; and when he had slowly raised himself, he adjusted with trembling hands smoked glasses before his eyes. His wife helped him into a series of three or four coats, each being singly too light for the season. She herself donned a man's coat and, over it, a sheep-skin.

Nelson approached. "Came in the bob-sleighs?"

"Yes," Mrs. Lund replied.

"Going straight home?"

"Imme*date*ly."

"We might come along," Nelson suggested, "and tramp it back."

"Why, certainly, Mr. Nelson," Lund said with insincere cordiality. "Certainly, Mr. Nelson. Look the place over."

"Lots of room in the box," Mrs. Lund joined in.

"Come on," Nelson said to Niels.

And both got their sheep-skins and caps.

On the yard there was a great deal of bustle. Four or five different parties prepared to leave. Horses pawed, nickered, plunged. Nelson found Lund's team and backed them out of the row. One of the horses was a tall, ancient white; the other a bony sorrel with elephantine feet.

Assisted by his wife, Lund lifted himself into the box and sat down on its floor, drawing the straw close about him. Mrs. Lund sat on the spring-seat in front; Nelson climbed in beside her, taking the lines; and Niels stood behind them.

"Well," Mrs. Lund sang, "good-by everybody."

It was the first time since their arrival at Amundsen's farm that either of the two friends left the yard. Niels was glad to escape from the crowded house. He felt as if freedom had been bestowed upon him in the wild. Somehow he felt less a stranger in the bush. Though everything was different, yet it was nature as in Sweden. None of the heath country of his native Blekinge here; none of the pretty juniper trees; none of the sea with its rocky islands. These poplar trees seemed wilder, less spared by an ancient civilisation that has learned to appreciate them. They invited the axe, the explorer . . .

The trees stood still, strangely still in the slanting afternoon sun which threw a ruddy glow over the white snow in sloughs and glades . . .

A mile or two from Amundsen's place they passed a lonely school house in the bush. It stood on a little clearing, the trees encroaching on it from every side. Except for Nelson's occasional shout to the horses they drove in silence.

After four miles or so they emerged from the bush on to a vast, low slough which, from the character of the tops of weeds and sedges rising above the snow, must be a swamp in summer. It was a mile or so wide; in the north it seemed to stretch to the very horizon. To the east, in the rising margin of the enveloping bush, Niels espied a single, solitary giant spruce tree, outtopping the poplar forest and heralding the straggling cluster of low buildings which go to make up a pioneer farmstead.

That was Lund's place.

Slowly they approached it across the frozen slough. Taller and taller the spruce tree loomed, dwarfing the poplars about the place . . .

They drove up on a dam; and the view to the yard opened up.

There were a number of low buildings, stable, smokehouse, smithy – none of them more than eight feet high in the front, and all sloping down in the rear. The dwelling at the southern end of the yard was a huge, shack-like affair, built of lumber, twelve feet high in front and also sloping down behind.

The yard was encumbered with all kinds of machinery. Several horses and cows were mixed into the general disorder; and over it all a sprinkling as it were of children was spread out. These struck Niels so forcibly that, for the first time, he took the lead in asking a question.

"All those children yours?" he asked.

Mrs. Lund laughed a broad, hearty laugh.

"We have only two, Mr. Lindstedt. A girl and a boy; and the boy is adopted. Our own boy was drowned in the Muddy River, five years ago. So we adopted Bobby from the children's home."

When they turned in over a rickety culvert of poles bridging the ditch, a number of grown-ups came out from the door of the dwelling.

"You've callers," Nelson said.

"Well," Mrs. Lund laughed, "you know us, Mr. Nelson. We've always callers." Turning to Niels and changing back into Swedish, she added, "This is the general meeting-place for fifteen miles around, post office, boarding house, and news store combined."

Behind the giant spruce tree and the surrounding bluff of poplars a number of teams were tied to the fence-posts.

"Hello," a girl said, coming to meet them in front of the long-extended stable with its low doors which gaped like the entrances into caves, for straw was thrown over roof and back of the building.

The girl was perhaps sixteen years old, fat, overgrown, physically mature; but her face showed a certain baby-like prettiness; and she was gaudily dressed in cheap and flimsy finery. With amazement Niels noticed that her skirt was of black silk . . .

Niels was the first to jump to the ground; and while the others alighted, he looked about. Every one of the five or six horses that stood on the yard had something the matter with it. One was lame; the other humpbacked; and a third was hardly able to move with old age.

Nelson, still holding the lines, shook hands with the girl. Her face bore an almost engaging smile.

"Hello, Mr. Nelson," she said. "And how are you? Didn't it snow up early this year? And how cold it is!"

Mrs. Lund stepped down with the air of a great lady, her numerous wraps gathered loosely over her arm.

"This is Mr. Lindstedt, Olga, a friend of Mr. Nelson's. Now listen, Olga. You and Bobby put the horses in. And give them a good feed of oats."

The emphasis on the word "good" attracted Niels' attention.

Nelson tried to interpose. "I'll put them in," he said and bent to unhook the traces.

"Not at all, Mr. Nelson," Mrs. Lund objected. "You know Olga. She'll look after that. Don't you bother."

Olga shot a glance at him, half shy, half coquettish.

"Hello," a pleasant-faced boy of eleven or twelve sang out, joining the group just when they started for the house.

"You look after the horses, Bobby," Mrs. Lund repeated. "Give them a good feed of oats."

Mr. Lund, as if forgotten by everybody, had groped his way out of the box and was standing helpless, feeling about with his hands for something to support himself by. Niels saw it and stepped up to guide him. But again Mrs. Lund protested.

"Never mind daddy, Mr. Lindstedt," she called. "He is on his yard. He can find his way."

The next moment she had mingled in the group at the door of the dwelling. With an elaborate courtesy which would have been becoming in a duchess she started the formalities of introduction. A dozen times Niels had to shake hands. The names went past his ear in bewilderment.

A single one struck him: that of a woman who formed a rather striking contrast to all other women present. It was "Mrs. Vogel."

She was dressed in a remarkably pretty and becoming way, with ruffles around her plump, smooth-skinned, though rather pallid face. In spite of the season she wore a light, washable dress which fitted her slender and yet plump body without a fold. Her waist showed a v-shaped opening at the throat which gave her – by contrast to the other women – something peculiarly feminine; beside her, the others looked neuter.

But more than anything else her round, laughing, coal-black eyes attracted attention. They were in everlasting motion and seemed to be dancing with merriment. Mrs. Lund was like a great lady, accustomed, no matter what she wore and how she looked, to lord it over every one in her surroundings; but even she seemed to live under a strain, as if she kept her spirits up in an eternal fight against adverse circumstances. Her predominance was a physical one, gained by sheer weight and dimensions and held by sonorous contralto and booming ring of the voice. All the other women were subdued, self-effacing, almost apologetic; as if daunted by work and struggling not to be swamped by it. Mrs. Vogel was different. Difficulties and poverty did not seem to reach her. She shrank from them; she smiled till they vanished. She did not step out and fight; she stepped back, into the protection of her sex; and they passed her by.

All this did not become clear to Niels in articulate thought. It gathered into a general impression of attraction. Her sight roused his protective instincts, the impulses of the man in him.

"Mrs. Vogel," Mrs. Lund had said in introducing her, "the gay widow of the settlement."

Mrs. Vogel's face had lighted up. She had shuddered in mock seriousness. "Widow sounds so funereal," she had said and stepped back. But the look from her dancing eyes had sent a thrill through Niels.

The next moment he found himself involved in a conversation with a short, slight man of thirty-five or so who spoke a fluent English. It went, so far, quite beyond Niels' understanding.

Nelson joined the group.

"Where have you been?" Mrs. Lund veered about.

"Put the horses in," he replied.

"Well," she exclaimed, "what do you know about that?"

And at once Nelson was surrounded by a laughing, hand-shaking crowd of men.

On its outskirts lingered Olga Lund, a transfixed smile on her face and a red mark, as from a lover's kiss, on her throat.

Bobby had run off to join the children.

"Well," Mrs. Lund invited. "Come in, folks."

And she led the way into the house.

"Yooh-hooh," a yodling shout rang out as soon as she opened the door.

And Niels who happened to be next behind her saw three men sitting at an oil-cloth-covered table to the left of the large, low room. One of them was the yodler, a tall, slim man with a merry face and a black moustache, unmistakably German. The three were playing at cards.

"Hello, Nelson," the same voice shouted. "Back again?"

And Nelson, pushing through the crowd, shook hands, long and violently, both men laughing the while. There was ostentation and exaggeration about their meeting.

The card-player raised a bottle. "Here, have a schnapps, boy, on your happy return."

For a moment there was a bedlam of noise, shouts, and laughter. Then, when the confusion subsided, Mrs. Lund who had dropped her wraps pushed through, with a view to the proprieties, and introduced Niels.

But a few minutes later he found himself once more on the outskirts of the crowd, partly on account of his inability to speak either English or German, partly because it was his nature to be alone, even in a crowd.

He looked about, appraisingly.

The house, built of lumber, was unfinished inside: the raw joists showed in the walls. The floor was unpainted, splintered up to an alarming degree, its cracks filled with earth and dirt.

The furnishings consisted of oddly assembled pieces: upholstered easy-chairs, worn down as it were to the bones; and threadbare and ragged hangings. In the south-west corner of the large room stood a plank-table, home-made, and strewn with papers: the post-office.

Niels could not help contrasting the shabby, second-hand, defunct gentility of it all, and the squalour in which it was left, with the trim and spotless but bare austerity of Amundsen's house. It struck him how little there was of comfort in that other home: Ellen's home! And yet, how sincere it was in its severe utility as compared with this! Amundsen's house represented a future; this one, the past: Amundsen's growth; this one, decay. Every piece of the furniture here, with the exception of the post-office table and the oil-cloth, came from the home of some rich man; but before it had reached this room, it had slowly and roughly descended the social ladder till at last, at the tenth or twelfth hand, it had reluctantly and incongruously landed here as on a junk pile.

And suddenly the problem of the woman's and the girl's clothes was solved as well: they were second-hand.

In his mind's eye Niels placed Ellen and Olga side by side: easy-going sloth and what was almost asceticism.

He felt immensely depressed; for a moment he felt he must leave the house never to return.

A commotion in the crowd roused him at last from his contemplation. The callers were getting ready to leave. Across the enormous slough the sun was nearing the horizon.

Hand-shaking. Leave-taking . . .

He looked on. He was not concerned. This, too, was a foreign crowd: he had nothing in common with them.

Slowly all went away, till nobody was left but Nelson and he. They, too, made preparation to leave; but Mrs. Lund protested.

"You'll stay for supper. You'll have moonlight for the way back."

And she began to bustle about, clearing the table and shaking down the fire in the stove which was an ancient range, battered and footless, propped up on bricks.

Nelson had sunk back in his chair, an old cradle-rocker, covered with damask which had once been pink; steel-springs and horse-hair protruded through its rents.

For another quarter of an hour there was coming and going outside.

Mrs. Lund turned to Niels where he stood behind the stove, in the shadows. "That's the way," she said in the tone of polite explanation, "it's with us every Sunday."

"And many a week-day, too," Olga added smiling.

"Not *that* way," Mrs. Lund protested, pushing her sleeves up above her elbows and baring powerful forearms. "You see, Mr. Lindstedt, most of these people come for their mail on Sundays. On week-days nobody has the time." She stepped to the door and, opening it, called in a strident falsetto which could have been heard from half a mile away, "Bob-beee!"

"Yes," the boy answered with startling nearness from just around the corner.

"Attend to your chores, boy," she said. "Get wood in and snow. And do the feeding."

Olga rose. "I'll do the feeding."

"No," Mrs. Lund forbade briefly, "not to-night."

The girl acquiesced with a smile.

"You get the bacon," her mother went on . . .

Thus, in the rising dusk, the preparations went forward.

"Where's daddy?" Mrs. Lund asked suddenly, straightening from the stove.

"Here, mamma," the voice of the man replied from the darkest corner where he lay reclining in a large wicker chair which was unravelling in a dozen places.

"Go and help Bobby," she said.

"All right, mamma," he agreed, raising himself painfully. Then he groped his way along the wall.

"One day," Mrs. Lund went on, addressing Niels, "we are going to have everything as it should be. A large, good house; a hot-bed for the garden; real, up-to-date stables; and . . . everything. And the children are going to learn something. We want Bobby to go to college . . ."

Niels looked at her. Since she had spoken in Swedish, he had understood.

But suddenly he understood far more than the mere words. He understood that this woman knew she was at the end of her life and that life had not kept faith with her. Her voice was only half that with which we tell of a marvellous dream; half it was a passionate protest against the squalour surrounding her: it reared a triumphant vision above the ruins of reality. It was the cry of despair which says, It shall not be so!

Niels was unable to answer. He felt as if he should step over to her and lay his hand on her shoulder to show that he understood. But he knew, if he did so, she would break down and cry.

His eye wandered from her to Nelson and Olga sitting close together and conversing in whispers.

Not knowing what to do, in the intensity of the feeling that had swept over him, he went to the window and looked out into the rising dark.

To his surprise he saw Mr. Lund walking about on the yard without groping his way. His step was uncertain; his back was bent; but on it he carried an enormous bundle of coarse, dried rushes, for litter or feed: and he had no trouble in finding his way.

This sight sobered Niels. Somehow he felt it incumbent upon him to say something.

"It is a beautiful country," he ventured.

"In summer," Mrs. Lund said. "You should see it in summer, Mr. Lindstedt. The flowers and the shrubs! One day," and again that quality rose in her voice, "we shall plant lindens and maples all about the yard and cut all those old poplars down."

Niels looked up. "But the poplars . . . And that wonderful spruce tree . . ."

"Yes," Mrs. Lund agreed, "the spruce tree . . . But if somebody pulled every poplar right out of the ground he'd do us a great big help."

Niels did not reply.

The ruddy glow that was still reflected from the high

clouds flaming in the west of the sunken sun spread its dull warmth over the yard: dusk had wiped out the picture of disorder and litter; and like a giant finger pointing upward, to God, the spruce tree stood on guard at the corner . . .

When Niels looked back into the room, the last glimmer of that light played over Nelson's and Olga's heads. The face of the girl was actually beautiful now as she sat there with dreaming eyes, her cheeks suffused with that ecstatic smile of hers.

She, too, had a dream; but her dream was of the future: it was capable of fulfilment, not fraught with pathos as her mother's. . . .

The whole room was softened into some appearance of harmony by the dark: fit setting for the dreams of the young and the retrospection of those whose dreams have come true: a horror to those in despair . . .

As if she felt it, the woman lighted a lamp.

Again Niels looked out.

There, on the yard, Mr. Lund was slowly walking about with closed eyes, a forked willow-branch in his hands. Thus, while Niels watched, he went from place to place, all over the yard, into the corners, across the open, along the stable, towards the gate at the culvert. Suddenly he stopped, standing in the light of the high half moon; and in evident excitement he called to the boy who soon after brought him four poles which he placed on the snow-covered ground.

To Niels his doings seemed inconsequential and irrelevant; such was the influence of the boundless landscape which stretched away in the dim light of the moon . . .

Life had him in its grip and played with him; the vastness of the spaces looked calmly on.

When Lund came in – his grey and hairy face bore a smile of transcendent rapture.

"Well," he said very quietly, as if he were blessing everything, "I have located the well."

"That right?" Nelson asked without interest.

"Yes," Lund replied. "The rod turned very distinctly. We shall get water.

"We need it," Mrs. Lund said skeptically. And, turning to Niels, she added, "We have been using the water from the ditch . . . It gives the horses swamp fever. . . ."

"We'll get it, mamma," Lund repeated. "I know. Don't worry."

The table was set. Mrs. Lund called for supper.

Niels sat between her and Bobby; Nelson, between Olga and Mr. Lund. No grace was said.

For a while the meal proceeded in silence.

Then Nelson spoke. "Going to school, Bobby?"

"Yes," the boy replied with a grin on his frank and humorous face. "Not very regular."

"We send him whenever we can," Mrs. Lund explained. "It's nearly four miles to go; in summer the swamp can't be crossed; then it's more; and in winter the snow is often up to his hips. It isn't work that's keeping him, Mr. Nelson; don't you believe it. We want our children to get an education."

"Yes," Lund agreed, still with the smile on his face. "If we can only send him to the Agricultural College. Have you ever seen it, Mr. Nelson?"

"No, I haven't."

"Why, it's grand! That is farming, I often say to mother. I have been to the college myself, for three years. Did you know it?"

"Don't talk nonsense, daddy," his wife interposed good-naturedly. "What shall the people think of you?" And, turning to Nelson, she added. "He was at the college all right, but feeding pigs."

Lund sighed. A sullen expression settled on his face. Everybody except his wife felt embarrassed.

"We've seen better days, that's true," Mrs. Lund went on. "When I was a young girl, I was a trained nurse. I've spent five years in a spital."

"Yes, scrubbing floors," Lund mumbled spitefully.

Nelson could not forbear a smile; but Mrs. Lund fastened such a forbidding look on her husband that he squirmed in his seat. Olga coloured dark red; and Bobby made things worse by his desperate efforts to suppress a giggle.

Supper went by under a constraint; and when it was over, the friends were glad to escape from the charged atmosphere of the house.

They got their wraps and took leave.

Olga looked after them from the door when they crossed the yard.

The air was crisp; the snow creaked under their steps; the moon stood high; the two young men stepped briskly along.

"Strange people," Niels said at last.

"Yes," Nelson agreed. "I pity the girl."

"Is he really blind?"

"I don't believe it. He is a great actor; and the laziest fellow I've ever met. The woman and the girl do all the heavy work; and the boy, too, does twice his share. The man does nothing except spend the money."

"Where does he get it?" Niels exclaimed.

"Sponges and bums and runs into debt. The homestead is his; but he hasn't proved up."

"How long has he been on the place?"

"Ten years or so. It's the third place he's had. The first was mortgaged to the hilt; and the company foreclosed on him. On the second the buildings burned down; they say he set fire to them. And here he is in debt again to the tune of some two thousand dollars. The woman and the girl run the post office and the farm. They don't want him to prove up. As soon as he gets his title, they'll lose the place; and they know it."

Success and failure! It seemed to depend on who you were, an Amundsen or a Lund . . .

"Why don't you buy?" Niels asked his friend.

Nelson laughed. "Has she put that bug into your head, too? . . . I want to be my own boss. I don't mind working out for a while each year till I get on my feet. But when I go home, I stand on my own soil; and no debts worry me. What I raise is mine. Five, six years from now I shall be independent."

"Yes," Niels said. "But the work it costs would pay for a prairie farm."

"Maybe," Nelson laughed. And after a silence he added, very seriously, "I'll tell you, I like the work. I'd pay to be allowed to do it. Land I've cleared is more my own than land I've bought."

Niels understood. That was his own thought exactly, his own unexpressed, inexpressible thought . . .

They walked on in silence, swinging along in great, vigorous strides. The last few words had filled them with the exhilaration of a confession of faith. High above, far ahead stood an ideal; towards that ideal they walked.

Suddenly, as they were entering the bush, where the moonlight filtered down through the meshes of leafless boughs overhead, a vision took hold of Niels: of himself and a woman, sitting of a mid-winter night by the light of a lamp and in front of a fire, with the pitter-patter of children's feet sounding down from above: the eternal vision that has moved the world and that was to direct his fate. He tried to see the face of the woman; but it entirely evaded him. . . .

Once more during the following week Niels and Nelson, while at work on Amundsen's yard, spoke of Lunds. "Was it true that Mrs. Lund had been a nurse?"

"I don't know," Nelson replied. "She's had more of an education than he. She works in the city after Christmas; at what nobody knows. She says she has a position as companion to a crippled lady. Most people think she hires out as domestic help. She lies, you know."

"Lies?"

"Sure," Nelson laughed. "You heard her repeat twice, the other day, that Olga and Bobby were to give the horses a good feed of oats? Well, I'll bet my bottom dollar that there isn't a grain of oats on the place."

"Is that so?" Niels exclaimed. "But why say it?"

"Pride," Nelson said. "She doesn't like to let on how poor they are. There isn't a person in the whole district, Swedish, German, or English, who doesn't take favours from that woman which she can ill afford to do. Whatever she has and anybody needs or wants she gives away and goes without herself. But it isn't merely good nature; it's part thriftlessness and part ostentation."

Amundsen, after all, did give up. The two men went deeper and deeper and found no water. Then news came that there was a well-drilling outfit in the district, working some eight, ten miles north-east. Amundsen made up his mind to try that machine, chiefly because the cribbing of a really deep well would be very expensive.

The decision came on Saturday.

Since they were not to move till the morrow, Nelson borrowed a gun and a handful of shells from Amundsen; and during the last hours of daylight the two friends went into the bush to look for game. They saw nothing but a rabbit which Nelson brought down and, on their return, contributed to the family larder.

Amundsen carefully figured out their account, prepared a receipt for them to sign, and pushed over to them the sum of forty-one dollars and twenty cents.

"I take five cents out for the cartridge," he explained.

Nelson grinned. "Well," he said, "not that it matters; but I turned the rabbit in."

"I understood," Amundsen argued without the least embarrassment, "you shot the rabbit on my place. You will remember I asked about that."

"I did," Nelson said.

"Then the rabbit was mine anyway," Amundsen decided with finality.

"All right." Nelson laughed. And even Niels could not suppress a smile.

Thus it came to pass that the two friends returned to Lund's sooner than they had expected. When they left Amundsen's place, Ellen nodded to them and said, "Good-by" as to casual strangers.

At Lund's, too, Niels saw Olga harnessing a team of big, weary brutes. She and Bobby were going into the bush after firewood.

Niels watched her as he had watched Ellen. The morning was cold; and the girl was warmly dressed. But there was a difference. None of the silks to-day; but no sheep-skin, either. She wore a multitude of ragged things, each, like those of her father, too thin for the season, but together calculated to keep the cold out, at least. And, whereas Ellen, when she donned her working clothes, had changed from a virgin, cool and distant, into a being that was almost sexless, Olga preserved her whole feminity. The nonchalance of her bearing also stood in strange contrast to the intense determination with which Ellen went after her work. About Olga's movements there was hesitation, an almost lazy deliberation very different from the competent lack of hurry in Ellen. Besides, Ellen ignored the men at their work; Olga stopped, looking on, and chatted with Nelson about his plans.

This more homely atmosphere turned Niels' thoughts back to Sweden, to his poor home where his father and mother had died . . . They, too, had worked very hard.

His mother, for instance, had to the very last, to the day when she was overtaken by her final illness, daily gone into the park owned by Baron Halson to gather dry brush for the stove. That had been allowed by way of charity. To earn her bread she had gone out scrubbing floors even when she was no longer able to do satisfactory work. The people whom she served had kept her on because they were good-hearted, after all; but they had treated her as a being from a lower social, yes, human plane.

He remembered how once, when he was about ten years old, he had stood outside of one of the mansions where she worked, for two, three hours after school, waiting for her because she had forgotten to put the key to the hut in the usual place. There he had stood in the street of the little town, looking at the brass-trimmed door with its polished brass name-plate, longing for his mother to come; for it was cold and he was scantily dressed. Yet he had not dared to touch the shining brass knocker on the well-to-do door which it was not for one like him to lift.

He also remembered how that vision of himself as a child, as a poor child, had haunted him when he grew up till fierce and impotent hatreds devastated his heart, so that at last it had become his dream to emigrate to a country where such things could not be. By some trick in his ancestry there was implanted in him the longing for the land that would be his: with a house of his own and a wife that would go through it like an inspiration: he had come to Canada, the land of the million farmsteads to be had for the asking.

Here, there were big trees which any one could fell for firewood. Nobody looked down upon him because he was poor. Money came easily: he had saved over a hundred and fifty dollars in a few months. No doubt it went easily, too. But he would hold on to it till he owned his land. . . .

Lunds? The trouble with them was that they were children one and all. . . .

In this country there was a way out for him who was young and strong. In Sweden it had seemed to him as if his and everybody's fate had been fixed from all eternity. He could not win out because he had to overcome, not only his own poverty, but that of all his ancestors to boot. . . .

Some time, during that forenoon, Mrs. Vogel came driving on to Lund's yard. She fetched her mail from the house; and then she stopped her pony for a moment at the well-site to look on. Nelson dropped his pick and straightened his back.

"No, no, Mr. Nelson," she said. "Go on; I love to watch strong men work."

Niels, too, looked up.

On her lips lay a smile; her black, beady eyes seemed to dance when they rested on his friend, and to glow with a strange warmth when they lighted on his own.

She wore a plush cap, a real fur coat, and, on the hand which held the lines, a knitted mitt of white wool.

"Oh," she said, "I don't want to keep you. Get up, Prince. Bye-bye. I wanted to see you work, not loaf."

And she drove on, not without throwing over her shoulder a glance which sent a tingling sensation along Niels' spine.

Woman had never figured as a concrete thing in Niels' thought of his future in this new country. True, he had seen in his visions a wife and children; but the wife had been a symbol merely. Now that he was in the country of his dreams and gaining a foothold, it seemed as if individual women were bent on replacing the vague, schematic figures he had had in his mind. He found this intrusion strangely disquieting.

"She seems to have taken a fancy to you," Nelson startled him by saying.

Niels scowled when he bent to his work. His friend's remark was like the violation of a confidence, like an intrusion into the arcana of holy ground; for as yet Niels was chaste to the very core of his being.

There was a distant look in his eyes when at last he brought himself to reply, "Maybe to you."

Nelson laughed. "Don't think so. She's seen me often enough. She's never stopped to flirt with me before."

This word seemed indelicate. It opened a gap between Niels and his friend; it would take time to bridge it over. . . .

A few days later, on Wednesday, Nelson had, as usual, started the digging while Niels drew up the pails and removed the earth from the pit, when a sudden shout made Niels jump back to the edge.

There, in the still shallow hole, he saw Nelson standing to over his hips in water which was still rising, though more slowly now.

"Quick, get me out of here!" Nelson shouted.

But before Niels could reach for the rope and throw it, the water had risen to Nelson's chest.

"Well," Nelson sang out as he burst through the door of the house, dripping, "you've got it!"

"You don't say so!" And Mrs. Lund who was washing the breakfast dishes, barefooted as she was, ran out over the snow.

Even Lund awoke from his contemplative lethargy and was on his feet in an incredibly short time.

"Didn't I tell you?" he triumphed. "Didn't I tell you, Mr. Linstedt?"

"Struck a pocket or a vein," Nelson called after him. "Stuck the pick in; and she bubbled up. . . ."

"Well, I declare!" Mrs. Lund said when she returned to the house. "That's the first piece of luck we've had since we moved out here. There's water enough for anybody. Thank the Lord, now the hauling and snow-melting is over at last! What'll Olga say when she gets home!"

But Olga did not say very much. Her eyes shone and rested happily on Nelson.

"Isn't it grand!" were her only words.

Bobby had all the more to say.

"And you were right in it when the water came? Was it cold?"

"You bet," Nelson replied. He was warming up by the stove, clad in Niels' summer suit which was much too small for him.

"Gee," Bobby exclaimed. "I wish I'd been there to see. She just bubbled up?"

"Like a spring," Nelson said.

The boy ran off to have another look at this world-wonder, the well.

"She's still rising," he said when he returned. "She's within three feet of the ground now."

"That makes seven feet of water," Lund admired. "Amundsen should have let me locate his well. I told him I would charge him only a bag of barley. . . ."

It was agreed that the work should be paid for out of Mrs. Lund's next "post-office-cheque" which was due in January. Niels and Nelson prepared to leave for the latter's own place, seven miles north and one mile west. . . .

Next morning, the whole family stood on the yard when they left. . . .

On the way, Nelson picked up his horses, from the place of the German settler who lived a mile south of his own place, on a homestead in the bush.

Beyond, now driving, they struck out over unbroken snow. There were drifts here, especially where a last feeler of the big slough in the south crossed their road. . . . The snow was dry and loose like powder; it sparkled and glittered as it was dusted aloft by the horses. . . . A noonday sun glared down on the landscape.

They followed a bush trail, winding from side to side over the timbered road-allowance. . . .

A last crossing: a narrow road-gap east and west: a few hundred yards to the right, and they saw Nelson's tiny yard.

A little log-shanty, twelve by fifteen feet, singularly forlorn and snow-bound; behind it, a still smaller stable, also of logs, its roof consisting of poles covered with straw which in turn supported a dome-like hood of snow. It looked like a fairy dwelling, untouched, virgin, and immeasurably lonesome . . . Bush all around . . .

"There we are," Nelson said not without a touch of pride.

"So this is it?" They had often spoken of the place. Niels was hushed with a sense of longing for his own old home, for his dead mother. . . .

They backed the wagon up to the shack and unhitched the horses. The stable was cold; but the horses stepped in: they knew it. Nelson fetched hay from a little stack which was leaning against the south side of the building.

Then they went to the house and opened the door. A small pile of wood was provided against a homecoming. In a few minutes a fire was roaring in the little tin heater which occupied the centre of the single room. Along the west wall stood a white-enamelled bed, four feet wide; against the east wall, a deal table with two chairs. A small cooking stove, back to back against the heater, and a battered trunk completed the furniture. The walls were plastered with clay but showed the raw poplar logs, peeled of their bark and glistening with tiny ice-crystals which made them look singularly cold and moist. The floor was of axe-squared poplar planks which felt soft to the booted foot.

"What did that cost you?" Niels asked.

"In money? The work I did myself, you know. Nails, door, window, furniture . . . forty dollars."

"I could put up a place for myself!" Niels thought. . . .

When they had unloaded the wagon – it held some oats and groceries brought from Hahn's, the German's, place – they pushed it out of the way and closed the door. The radiating heat from the little stove took effect; and from that moment on this little building became something like a home to Niels. . . .

Thus started Niels' first winter in the northern forest.

Henceforth his life consisted alternately of work in the bush and driving, driving. . . .

One of the two men was always on the road. Sometimes it took three, sometimes four days to make the round trip to Minor where they sold the seasoned wood of last winter's cutting. Occasionally it took a week. Niels learned to know the district. . . .

Often he dropped in on Lunds. Sometimes he saw Ellen.

Once, after a roaring blizzard, he reached Amundsen's place in the afternoon. He had seen Olga that day; and now he saw Ellen who was leaving the yard with the team of colts to go for water.

His face lighted up; he would have liked to speak to her. But she returned his greeting by a mere curt nod. It struck him that she went north-east. He looked after her as she drove swiftly along, holding her prancing and rearing horses with a firm and competent hand. She did not turn back, however. He was no more than a stranger to her, a stranger who happened to have worked on her father's place.

He crossed the bridge over Grassy Creek. On the bare Marsh, the snow was lashed into waves and crests like a boiling sea. There was no road left. He angled across the open land. It took him two hours to make the mile to a huge poplar bluff which rose like an island or a promontory jutting out from the east into the waste of snow. He intended to unhitch and to feed in its shelter.

When he rounded this bluff which, to the south, trailed off into smaller second-growth of poplar, skirting the Marsh, a great piece of good luck befell him; for around a roaring fire a crowd of men were assembled; and many teams and loads of wood were standing in the shelter of the bluff, bound no doubt for the same destination as he. Niels counted the loads; there were twenty-two. The men were a motley crowd, mostly Germans; and they greeted him with shouts and laughter as he drove into sight. They were getting ready to go but offered to wait for him. As best he could he made clear to them that he wanted to feed and to rest his team . . . The caravan set out without him.

Niels looked about as he kept the fire going. And before long it somehow was clear to him that this was his future home. One day, if the place was still open for entry, he would file on it. . . .

The next night, on his return trip, he spent at Lund's, having arrived there after midnight.

In the morning, while waiting for his horses to finish their feeding, he saw to his surprise Ellen Amundsen driving up on the yard.

In the box of her sleigh there were two tanks.

He had just looked in at the stable and was returning to the house. So he stopped in his tracks and greeted her.

Ellen, as usual, turned her eyes upon him and nodded casually. She stopped at the well and sprang to the ground. There was no pump yet; so she reached for pail and rope.

In a second Niels was by her side.

"Oh, never mind," she said. But he paid no attention to her protest and opened the well-trap. For a moment she stood undecided and then stepped back.

He lifted pail after pail and emptied them into her tanks. Not a word did the two exchange; and yet they were quite alone.

The meeting at the well seemed to call for speech; and both of them felt it. But Ellen expected some jesting remark and was on her guard not to provoke it; and Niels knew that, whenever he met her, he was on probation. Neither of them was a conversationalist.

When the barrels were filled, Niels covered them with the rags which Ellen had brought; and he even turned the horses for her.

"All right," he said almost harshly when he jumped to the ground.

Ellen got in and took the lines. For a moment it looked as if she might unbend. But she clicked her tongue, nodded, said, "Thanks," and was gone.

"That's nothing," Niels mumbled, touched his cap, and turned to the house.

The brief meeting filled him with confusion. In his heart there was a great tenderness, such as he had felt for his mother when she had been slaving away to keep her little home free of debt. But there was also a trace of resentment against the unyielding aloofness of the girl. . . .

To add to his confusion, he came at the house upon a scene which was profoundly distasteful to him at the present moment.

Mrs. Lund had picked a geranium flower from one of the potted plants which she nursed and hoarded all through the bitter winter. She stood bent over her husband where he reclined in his frayed wicker chair, and fastened the blossom in the lapel of his ragged coat.

"Don't make me too pretty, mamma," he cooed; "the girls might get gay with me."

"I wish they would, daddy," she replied and rumpled his scant grey hair with a caressing hand.

Niels stopped at the door, with the impulse to turn back. But Mrs. Lund had heard him and looked up.

"Now there's a girl, Mr. Lindstedt," she said, "that'll make a wife for some lucky fellow one day."

Niels coloured. "I don't think she ever dreams of such things."

"Still waters are deep," Mrs. Lund replied.

These long, lonesome drives were conducive to a great deal of thinking, especially on the way home when the horses could be left to themselves.

But more so still were the lonesome days in the bush. There he did a great deal of dreaming and planning; the more the wider his knowledge became of this mixed settlement. And gradually, as he worked at felling and cutting the trees; but especially in the long evenings, when he sat in that little shanty "up north," mechanically keeping his fire going; and most of all when he lay in bed, made wakeful by the mere consciousness of his utter isolation, did he build up a program and a plan for himself and his future life.

Of his material success he had no doubt. Was he not slowly and surely making headway right now? While he was hibernating as it were?

In this country, life and success did not, as they had always seemed to do in Sweden, demand some mysterious powers inherent in the individual. It was merely a question of persevering and hewing straight to the line. Life was simplified.

Yet, material success was not enough. What did it matter whether a person had a little more or less wealth? A strong, healthy body was his; with that he could make a living anywhere; he *had* made a living in Sweden.

But the accessories of life were really the essentials; they were what made that living worth while: the building up of a whole little world that revolved about him. About him? Not at all. . . .

That vision which was so familiar to him began to dominate him more and more. Already he felt, in the mental realisation of it, a note of impatience.

He himself might be forever a stranger in this country; so far he saw it against the background of Sweden. But if he had children, they would be rooted here. . . . He might become rooted himself, through them. . . .

The picture which he saw, of himself and a woman in a cosy room, with the homely light of a lamp shed over their shoulders, while the winter winds stalked and howled outside and while from above the pitter-patter of children's feet sounded down, took more and more definite form. . . .

There could be no doubt any longer: the woman in the picture was Ellen, the girl. He longed for her sight: he longed to speak to her: to show, to reveal his innermost being to her: not in words, but in deeds, in the little insignificant things of the day. . . .

But even in his dream he felt shy in her presence, bashful, unable to speak when she looked at him, with the cool, appraising expression in her eyes. He felt awkward, dumb, torn by dark passions unworthy of her serene, poised equilibrium. A good many times he saw her as he had seen her at the well, standing by as if she merely submitted to his interference: as if it were merely not quite worth the trouble it would cost to prevent it. Sometimes he caught himself in a sudden sullen anger because she would not see how he longed for her. And then again he would laugh at himself for his folly. How could she do so? What did she know of him? His whole intercourse with her had not comprised more than a few casual meetings: the sum of his conversations with her, no more than a few dozen words. . . .

How much more intimate, he sometimes thought, was his still slenderer acquaintance with Mrs. Vogel! Two or three times only had he met her; yet there was almost a secret understanding between them. . . .

But whenever he had been dreaming of her and his thought then reverted to Ellen, he felt guilty; he felt defiled as if he had given in to sin. Her appeal was to something in him which was lower, which was not worthy of the man who had seen Ellen. . . . Though he could not have told what that something in him which was lower really meant. . . .

And when he felt very self-critical, as when he had been altogether absorbed in his immediate tasks, he seemed to become conscious that in his thought of Mrs. Vogel there was nothing either of the dumb, passionate longing, nothing of the anger and resentment, nothing of the visionary glory which surrounded his thought of the other woman. He could imagine pleasant hours spent in her company; but his future life he could imagine without her. He could no longer imagine a future life without Ellen. . . .

Winter went by; the thaw-up came. Breaking and seeding, on a share of the crop. . . .

Then "working out," in the south. A year since he had come to this country . . . A winter in town, to learn English . . . Another summer. A second winter with Nelson . . .

Many things happened. Mrs. Amundsen died.

When Nelson came and joined him to put in his last season of "working out," Niels heard that the attendance at the funeral had been enormous. It was meant as a protest against Amundsen's treatment of his wife; but Amundsen, crying profusely, had taken it as a tribute to himself. . . .

Nelson had enlarged stable and house; he had built a granary; he had broken enough land to prove up; he had bought a second team. . . . He and Olga Lund were going to be married next spring. . . .

With Lunds matters were going from bad to worse . . .

Niels had over twelve hundred dollars in cash in the bank at Minor.

He filed on the north-east quarter of section seven, in the edge of the Marsh, on the Range Line, which held the big bluff.

Sigurdsen, the old Icelandic settler who had turned them back into the storm on Niels' first trip north, would be his nearest neighbour now. He had become his friend; for during the winters with Nelson he had had repeated opportunities to oblige the old man, bringing tobacco and other trifles from town. . . .

When Niels at last moved out to his claim, he took a little tent along to live in till, after threshing, late in the fall, he could get a building up. He would buy horses then; he needed hay. . . .

Amundsen acted as agent for the absentee landlords who held the hay-land. Niels had to see him.

As he had expected, he found the man on the field, a quarter of a mile north-west of the yard, embedded in the bush. Ellen was driving the team of colts while her father was picking stones off a newly brushed strip of land.

"Yes," Amundsen said in reply to Niels' enquiry. "I have two quarters left. Good quarters, too; the southern half of twenty-one, just west of Lund's. Lund has spoken for one of them; but he has no money . . . The permit is fifteen dollars a quarter . . ."

"Well," Niels said, "I'll look it over. I shall let you know by to-morrow night. Too bad, though, to let the Lunds go without hay . . ."

Amundsen shrugged his broad shoulders, looking at the ground and smiling a deprecatory smile. "That is as it is. I cannot give the hay away. Do you want it for yourself?"

"I am in partnership with old man Sigurdsen," Niels replied. "I myself have filed on the north-west quarter of seven, five miles south." He took care to speak so the girl would hear it.

"That's so? Well, it's good land. If you are steady . . ." Ellen's horses pulled. "Whoa!" he called. "I suppose we better move on." And he clicked his tongue.

For a moment Niels looked after him. He chafed at the man's complacency, at his imperturbable self-assurance, his very neatness and accuracy. . . .

His eyes fell on the girl; he saw her again as he had seen her two and a half years ago. That perfect poise, that forbidding scrutiny seemed to hold him at a distance even now. His mere thoughts of her, the fact that she had figured in his visions of the future, seemed like an intrusion, like the violation of an inviolable privacy. . . .

With a sinking heart he turned and strode off across the clearing. . . .

All around, the bush stood trembling in green. On the berries and drupes of saskatoon and plum lay the first blush of purple. . . .

Niels camped on his claim, cutting willows for fence-posts and staking off his land. . . .

He worked all the time. When he was too tired, from one kind of work, so that his muscles ached, he simply changed over to another and grubbed stones out of the ground on what he had already fixed upon as his future yard. . . .

Even on Sundays he would walk about in that big, rustling bluff of aspens, picking out the straightest trees to be cut for his buildings.

The southern part of his claim was covered with comparatively small growth; for one of the marshfires that broke out every now and then had encroached upon it, some fifteen years ago, consuming everything that would burn. For no apparent reason – perhaps in consequence of a change of wind – the fire had stopped short of that tall, majestic bluff which now stood dominant, lording it over this whole corner of the Marsh.

To the east, there was much willow; though even there, on a rising piece of ground, ten acres or so of primeval forest remained like an island.

West and north of his claim there was sand. Nothing but low, scrubby brush intervened between the claim and the cliff of the forest along the creek.

Niels lived in a continual glow of excitement. He worked passionately; he dreamed passionately; and when he lay down at night, he even slept with something like a passionate intensity. . . .

Life had been flowing placidly for a year or two. His dreams had receded as their realisation approached. But now, in the first flush of reality; now, when all that was needed seemed to be a retracing in fact of what had already been traced in vision: now that vision became an obsession.

Morning and evening he walked over to Sigurdsen's place for water, milk, or eggs – a distance of a mile and a half. These walks became something of a ritual. Always, in going, his look was fixed on that gap in the green-gold forest – gilded by rising or setting sun – where the trail led north, across the old bridge put up by the one-time fuel-hunters who had become settlers: the bush in which Ellen lived.

Everything he did he did for her. Sometimes he felt an overpowering impulse to go right over and to ask her to follow him. Once or twice, on moonlit nights, he went to the bridge and lost himself in the shadows of the road-chasm beyond. But, the nearer he came to that farmstead in the bush, the less did the girl seem approachable to him; the less distinctly did he see her as she had walked along the edge of the field, with her firm, long strides, or as she had stood by his side at the well; and the more forbiddingly did she, instead, look at him as she had done on her father's yard when he had recklessly spoken to her. Out of clear, critical, light-blue eyes she looked. . . .

He knew that he wanted her; that he desired only one thing: to melt that ice which seemed to surround her; to beat down those barriers which defended her against him; yes, finally, with a realisation that made his very body tremble and shake, that sent his blood red-hot to his brain, he became conscious of the ultimate, supreme, physical desire: he wanted to feel her head sinking on his shoulder, her body yielding to his embrace . . .

When he came home after such a paroxysm of passion and despair, he threw himself down on his hard willow-bed on the ground; and he told himself that this would not do; that no girl, no woman was ever wooed from a distance.

How was he to get near her? Her father? No father was ever an obstacle between man and girl . . .

It was she, she alone who kept him away: who kept the world away, and with the world him: for he was merely a part of that world: not a hero who came, acclaimed by the multitudes, borne high on the shoulders of his followers . . .

Haying time. In return for the help of Bobby and Mrs. Lund, Niels was putting up a stack at the post office . . .

In the midst of this work Nelson and Olga were married. Niels was one of the groom's "best men."

The wedding was no elaborate affair. It took place at the end of the regular service in the German church at Odensee. The pastor, in courtesy to the young people, merely changed into English for the ceremony. When it was over, everybody who cared to do so returned to Lund's where a supper was prepared for which Mrs. Lund had boiled a ham.

Niels had not made many friends. He was not a "mixer." Amidst the general joking and celebrating, he again stood apart, in the back of the room.

He could not help thinking of himself as he had stood in this same house three years ago, a newcomer, shy, little sure of himself, full of longings as yet undefined . . .

He looked down on his surroundings with the same critical look.

There was the bride, a bare nineteen years old; and somehow he felt that she must be glad to escape. Lunds might have had a past; Nelson was sure to have a future. For some time already the girl had been indifferent to the worries of her old home.

Niels could not help wondering at the fact that Nelson, young, strong, ambitious, industrious as he was, should have picked the mate of his life from this house. Yet, when he scanned the bride's face, he could not help feeling, either, that she would do as her husband wished; that she was sure to put forth her very best effort to make him an acceptable home . . .

Mrs. Lund, as she worked over the stove, kept softly crying to herself. No doubt she saw her own youth in her daughter . . .

Niels no longer blamed her for the state of her house. The mere fact that she felt the need of referring to better days in the certain past and the possible future showed that she was only too conscious of the fearful shortcomings of the present. Who, from morning to night, walks with bare, bleeding feet over meadow and stubble forgets about niceties, about scrubbing and polishing things . . .

Niels looked for Mr. Lund whom he discovered, as usual, reclining in the far corner of the room. There he sat, shading his eyes; and a singularly insincere smile played about his decaying teeth. It was almost visible that he hated to see his daughter go: it meant two strong arms less on the place, not of his own. When anybody spoke to him, his smile lighted up to an almost transparent artificiality which bared the gums above and below the yellow teeth, behind the straggling, grey hairs of his moustache . . .

Then, when Niels' eye returned to the groups about the table, along the north wall of the room, it passed over a face which seemed to arrest it. The smiling eyes were fixed on him, showing warm and flattering interest. They were Mrs. Vogel's. For a moment Niels looked at her absent-mindedly. Strange to say, while he did so, his thought reverted to Ellen. She and her father had been at church; he had seen her go over, after the ceremony, to speak to the bride. Of course, she had not come along with the crowd. Niels wondered how she might speak to another girl.

And then he realised that it was he at whom Mrs. Vogel was smiling, her whole face dimpled up. She was sitting close to the opposite wall, between door and window; and just as he was awaking to the summons which her eyes held, she put one hand on top of a trunk which stood between her chair and the "post-office-table."

It would have been rude not to obey the summons. Yet, as he went over and sat down by her side, he felt as if he were being entrapped: he felt what was almost a foreboding of disaster. Never in his life had he felt like that; and the memory of this feeling was to come back to him, many years later, when his terrible destiny had overtaken him. Had he obeyed a hardly articulate impulse, he would at once have got up again and gone out.

For a minute or so Mrs. Vogel did not speak but looked at him with a sidelong glance, intensely feminine, nearly coquettish, and full of smiling scrutiny. Niels had never before been looked at in that way. He had never met a woman like her.

"Is it possible," she said at last, "that you are the boy whom I saw here three years ago?" Her voice, too, was smiling, caressing, almost, triumphantly disarming.

Niels felt confused. He reddened. He wished to flee; but the strength had gone out of his limbs. His lips said, mechanically, "Have I changed?"

She laughed: a light, silvery, falsetto laugh: the laugh of a woman perfectly sure of herself and very superior to her interlocutor. "Changed?" she repeated. "I should say so. You were a boy then; now you are a man."

Niels' head was glowing. "I am older."

"Partly," she conceded. "You have learned to speak, too. When I first met you, you were dumb."

"I did not know any English."

"Where did you learn?"

"I took lessons. At night-school in Minor."

"From a lady?"

"No, a man."

"Well, your English is so good that I felt sure it had been a lady . . . You are changed altogether. You are a man with a future. Your shoulders have broadened. Your lips have become straight and firm. You have grown a moustache. I felt sure only a woman could have worked the change . . ."

Flee, Niels' genius seemed to whisper. Flee from temptation! His ears tingled; his scalp felt hot. Her laughter sounded to him as if it came from a distance. There was mockery in it.

"I wonder," she said suddenly, "whether you could smile, Mr. Lindstedt?"

This shocked him. He felt as if somebody were piling a crushing weight on him; or as if he were being stripped of his disguises. His chastity felt attacked. He wanted to get away and looked helplessly at the crowd.

But she had chosen her place well.

The sun was sinking to the west; the bright, red glow which fell through the open door stood like a screen between them and the rest. They were in the shadow of the wall. Theirs was a side-play, acted in a niche and off the stage . . .

Niels frowned . . . And the woman laughed. As if to favour her and to separate them still more from the others, somebody started the old, screeching grammophone going.

Mrs. Vogel's face became serious. She lowered her eyes as if she herself were embarrassed. When she spoke, her voice was a whisper. "I hear we are going to be neighbours?"

Niels felt relieved. This was neutral ground. "Is that so?" he asked rather readily.

Mrs. Vogel looked at him. Her demure air had dropped. The mockery in her eyes was undisguised, "Why don't you ask at least where I live. Or do you know?"

"No," he said brusquely.

"Ask then!" Look and laugh challenged him.

Niels frowned in rebellion; but he asked, though ungraciously.

"Two miles south of here," she replied, whispering, as if imparting a secret. "Of course, I don't always live there. Mostly I live in the city. But I have the place . . . Go north from your corner, across the bridge; then, instead of continuing north, along the trail which would lead you to Amundsen's, turn to the east, along the first logging trail. Three miles from the bridge you will find me. Apart from Sigurdsen who does not count I am your nearest neighbour now . . ."

There was a pause – an awkward pause, awkward for Niels. Mrs. Vogel seemed to enjoy it; she looked at him sideways with a quiet smile . . .

Chance came to his aid. Mrs. Lund had asked some of the men to arrange the tables for supper. Niels got up. "I suppose I had better lend a hand . . ."

But he found that his help was not needed. So, in order to save himself, he slipped out of the door and crossed the yard to where the children were playing about the hay-stack.

. . .

Bobby, now a fine lad of fourteen, was teasing a little girl of four or five. He stood in front of the hay-stack and shouted, "Now, May, watch out. I'm going to blow the hay-stack over. Watch." And he blew his cheeks up to perfect rotundity.

"Don't, Bobby, don't!" the little girl cried, with the tears very near the surface.

"Then I'll blow you over," he threatened, veering about.

But the little girl ran away, screaming.

And Bobby followed her, protesting that he was merely "fooling."

Niels felt as if he were waking up from a terrible dream. He passed his hand over his forehead and went to the stable.

There he met Nelson who was coming back from the gate where the teams were tied.

"Getting rather thick with the widow?" Nelson asked, grinning.

Niels coloured; and the consciousness angered him. "Nonsense," he said.

"I watched you. Better be careful. She's set her cap for you . . . What do you intend to do next?"

"Fence," Niels replied.

"Going to buy horses in the fall?"

"I think so."

"Well, you've got the hay; good hay, too; and lots of it. I'm glad you fixed the Lunds up. Better hold on to what you'll have to spare. Hay's going to be scarce. There's none in the west."

"I have no intention of selling," Niels said. "Maybe in spring . . . Going to work out this fall?"

"Hardly. I've got my hands full on my own place. Thirty-five acres to plow . . . And then . . . when a man's married . . . What am I to do with your share of the barley from the new breaking?"

"Can you hold it for me?"

"Sure. If you buy horses, better keep it. Well, I'll have to go in. So long." And he went to the house.

Somehow Niels felt that a barrier had arisen between him and his friend. So far they had had their interests in common. Nelson had stepped aside; he was going to live in a world from which Niels was excluded. Niels was left alone. He felt in need of the company of one whom he could trust, on whom he could rely, who would understand the turmoil in his heart without an explanation in so many words.

While he stood there, under the giant spruce tree, and looked across the slough at the amber glow of the sky, his thought went back, with affection, to old man Sigurdsen. His world, his workaday world of toil and worry, seemed suddenly so sane as compared with his own world of passion, desire, and longing . . .

At supper, he sat next to Hahn, the German, and his wife; but he did not take part in the general conversation . . .

Mrs. Vogel sat at the other end of the table. Niels looked at her once or twice; but she seemed to avoid his eye; and it suited him so. He was still angry at himself, for an inexplicable feeling of guilt that possessed him. She looked very lovely, he thought; but she looked like sin. She was incomprehensible to him . . .

When the grown-ups had finished their supper, they made room for the children.

While the groups thus re-arranged themselves, a sudden commotion arose. Somebody called for Nelson, somebody else, for the bride. They were not to be found.

Then a small, unobtrusive man who had gone out came running to the door.

"Come on," he shouted; "they're going."

And everybody rushed to the door.

In the confusion which followed Niels reached for his cap and caught Bobby by the shoulder.

"I'm going too," he said to the boy. "Tell your mother I'll be back in the morning to finish the hay."

"All right," said Bobby and squirmed away in the crush.

Nelson was standing in his wagon-box and backed his horses out of the row at the fence. The bride sat on the spring-seat and looked over her shoulder at the crowd which came running.

Everybody had grabbed something, a broken plate, a dish, an old shoe, a handful of rice. Niels was caught in the general onrush and ran with the rest.

A shower of things was thrown after the couple both of whom were laughing and replying to the bantering jokes flung at them from the rear.

Niels felt that part of his life was driving away with them as they swung out on the dam and away into darkness . . .

For a moment the crowd of guests lingered at the gate where Mrs. Lund stood crying unrestrainedly.

Suddenly Niels felt a hand on his arm. Mrs. Vogel stood by him.

"You are going?" She smiled up at him. "Don't forget. North across the bridge. Then east along the first logging trail. Three miles from the bridge. A white cottage. Sooner or later you'll come. Come soon. Before I return to the city. I am a lonely woman, you know . . ." And, nodding at him, she lost herself in the crowd.

What did it all mean?

Without waiting for anybody Niels dodged behind the log-shack which served as a smithy and into the thick bluff beyond.

A plank was lying across the ditch. It was almost dark. The air was strangely quiet for a summer day in the north. The atmosphere was saturated with the smell of hay from the edge of the slough . . .

Beyond, tall, ghostly, white stems of aspens loomed up, shutting out the world . . .

Already, though he had thought he could never root in this country, the pretty junipers of Sweden had been replaced in his affections by the more virile and fertile growth of the Canadian north. The short, ardent summer and the long, violent winter had captivated him: there was something heady in the quick pulse of the seasons . . .

He had been an onlooker so far. But to-night something had happened which he did not understand: he was a leaf borne along in the wind, a prey to things beyond his control, a fragment swept away by torrents.

That made him cling to the landscape as something abiding, something to steady him.

He cut across the corner of the slough; and when he had passed out of eye and earshot of the noisy, celebrating crowd, he stopped, raised his arms above his head, and stretched . . . A lassitude came over him: a desire to evade life's issues . . .

He longed to be with his mother, to feel her gnarled, calloused fingers rumpling his hair, and to hear her crooning voice droning some old tune . . .

And then he seemed to see her before him: a wrinkled, shrunk little face looking anxiously into his own.

He groaned.

That face with the watery, sky-blue eyes did not look for that which tormented him: what tormented him, he suddenly knew, had tormented her also; she had fought it down. Her eyes looked into himself, knowingly, reproachfully. There was pity in the look of the ancient mother: pity with him who was going astray: pity with him, not because of what assailed him from without; but pity with what he was in his heart . . .

It was very clear now that the torrent which swept him away, the wind that bore him whither it listed came from his innermost self. If, for what had happened to him, anybody was to blame at all, it was he . . .

As if to confirm it, there arose in him the vision again of that room where he sat with a woman, his wife. But no pitter-patter of little children's feet sounded down from above; nor were they sitting on opposite sides of a table in front of a fire-place. He was crouching on a low stool in front of the woman's seat; and he was leaning his head on her. And when he looked up into her face, that face bore the features and the smile of the woman who had spoken to him that very night . . .

CHAPTER TWO

Niels

FALL CAME. Niels "worked out."

In many ways he was changed. Every Sunday, during the summer, he had fought a savage fight with himself. He had gone across the sandy corner of the Marsh, to the bridge; and there he was torn between two desires: the desire to see Ellen and to have her quietly, critically gaze at him out of her eyes as if she were searching for something in him; and the desire to see, and to listen to, the other woman whose look and voice sent a thrill through his body and kindled his imagination.

Invariably he had at last returned to his homestead and his tent without seeing either . . .

One of these women had seemed to demand; the other, to give. Yet one was competent; the other, helpless. One was a mate; the other, a toy . . .

When, on Monday mornings, he went to work again, fencing his claim, he shook all visions off and felt a grim sort of satisfaction at having resisted both temptations. But the fight drew sharp lines into his face and made him seem older than he was. He had become reticent again as he had perforce been during his first year in the new country. He never spoke a word beyond what was exactly needed to convey his meaning . . .

He had grown tremendously strong. Among the harvest crews he enjoyed, though he never fought, the reputation of being a fighter. The men who chaffed everybody else left him alone . . .

His outlooked also had changed. Life seemed irrelevant; success seemed idle. All he did he did mechanically.

He returned to his homestead bringing a team. He began to cut the trees for his buildings, clearing a little field . . .

And he put the buildings up, a stable and a granary which, so far, was to serve as a house . . .

Then he thought of going for the grain which was his, as his share of Nelson's crop . . .

It was a cold, frosty winter morning when he set out, driving his horses.

At the bridge he saw Amundsen working on the ice of the creek.

Belated rains which, in the bush, had fallen on frozen ground had caused an abundant run-off; enough to fill the creek which usually, at the time of freeze-up, consisted merely of a string of pools at the bottom of the wide trough. The water, however, had at once frozen over; and, since the bed of the creek proceeded in a succession of terraces downward, it had run out from under the frozen bridges of ice, thus creating large, hollow vaults at the bottom of which the trickle of the stream still fell or ran from pool to pool.

Amundsen was working with the axe, breaking this ice-bridge so as to reach the water underneath.

Niels stopped and looked down. Amundsen nodded to him; and he returned the greeting.

"You never got the drill after all," Niels shouted at last.

Amundsen came somewhat closer before he replied.

"No," he said. "The beggars were at Kurtz's. Eight miles from my place. But Kelm wanted them; and

Hahn; and several others. So they asked half a dollar more to come down here, the cut-throats!"

Niels felt the same odd repulsion for the man which he had always felt.

"We get a little water from the well you dug with Nelson," Amundsen went on. "I've put the cribbing in. But it isn't enough for the stock. For a while we hauled from Lund's. But they got mad about the hay last year. There's no snow yet to speak of. So we've got to get at the creek. Going north?"

"Yes," Niels said. "I'd better be moving."

That was the last Niels ever saw of the man.

In the winding chasm of the bush road he met Ellen who was coming with her barrels in the sleigh. She was driving the run-away team.

Niels guided his horses right into the underbrush, giving her the whole of the road.

But the girl also edged over on her side, disdaining to take advantage of him.

All the while her clear, inscrutable eyes were fixed on his face as they passed each other.

In a sudden resentment he repeated a phrase which had often tingled in his ears and which the other woman had used. "I wonder," he muttered as he nodded his greeting, "whether you could smile, Miss Amundsen?"

She had not changed. She looked and acted exactly as she had done three years ago.

Then, as he drove over the virgin snow, he began, as usual, to argue with himself.

Why should he be angry with her? He had seen her, she him, a dozen times. All the words spoken between them counted up to a score or so . . . Why should she smile at him, a perfect stranger?

In due time he came out on the slough. It was near the dinner hour. Nelsons might be at Lund's. He would call there to see. But when he drove up on the dam, close to the yard, he found himself the unwilling witness of a scene which made him go on.

Lund was standing in front of the stable, pitching manure on to a sleigh-box.

Mrs. Lund, a pail in her hand, was coming from the house. Neither saw Niels.

Mrs. Lund, however, caught sight of a little calf gambolling about and sprinting off into the snow-covered clearing behind the yard.

"Who's let the calf out?" she shouted angrily and ran over to the stable. The door was open.

Lund stopped in his work, leaned on his fork, and fumbled with a shaking hand at the dark glasses protecting his eyes.

"What did you let that calf out for?" she repeated.

"I didn't, mamma," he replied.

The sleigh was gliding noiselessly over the soft, loose snow; every word sounded clearly across to Niels.

"You old thunderbuss!" she screamed. "Don't lie!"

"What?" The old man rose in arms, grasping his fork.

Mrs. Lund stopped and laughed. "Don't act silly! You can't bully me!"

But he advanced, raising the fork.

Mrs. Lund's laughter died away; and from defiance her attitude changed into one of hunted fright. "Well, I declare!" she said and dropped her pail.

The next moment they had grappled. Mrs. Lund wrested the fork from his grasp and threw it away. Then she bowled him over as if he were a child. He lay on the ground, groaning.

"Bob-beee!" Mrs. Lund's voice shrilled out, betraying undisguised alarm.

The boy came running from behind the stable.

"Quick," shouted Mrs. Lund. "Help me get daddy to bed."

The last Niels saw as he drove past the bluff shielding the yard was the picture of the two bending over the prostrate body and trying to lift it.

. . .

Niels shivered though he did not feel cold.

Could marriage lead to that? Most people would have laughed at such a scene . . .

Strange stories were current in the district about Lund. But everybody agreed in declaring Mrs. Lund to be "a mighty fine lady."

In a way Niels agreed with that verdict.

Somehow he saw Olga in her. She, too, had one day been full of love, full of hope, full of happy anticipations. No doubt her husband, then her lover, had seemed the fairy prince to her. You could still see in this wreck of him that as a young man he must have been handsome. Perhaps he, too, had promised her a carefree life and a princedom in the world's domains. But how his promises had gone to pieces!

Niels thought of himself. If he had married in Sweden, he would, like the rest, have laughed at this household. He would have accepted what is as immutable and pre-arranged.

How chance played into life!

He had emigrated; and the mere fact that he was uprooted and transplanted had given him a second sight, had awakened powers of vision and sympathy in him which were far beyond his education and upbringing. If one single thing had been different, everything might have run a different course . . .

If Lund had held on to one of the places which he was said to have owned in his life, instead of giving in to adverse circumstances; or if his boy had not been drowned, success might have been his instead of failure . . .

What, then, was in store for him, Niels?

He could not defend himself just now against a feeling of fear: the fear of life . . .

As, late in the day, he neared his last turn, he shook the lines over the horses' backs; and a few minutes later he was within sight of Nelson's yard.

The house looked very different as compared with a few years ago. There were three rooms now, the kitchen being the old log-shanty to which the main building had been added. The walls were of logs; but the roof was shingled.

The stable, too, had been much enlarged; and there was a granary. The yard was neatly fenced with woven wire: the gate was a real farm-gate, of bent pipe.

But nothing struck Niels so much as the pleasant look of the white-curtained windows in the house.

He alighted, went to the door, and knocked. It was a minute or so before it was opened.

"Well, I declare!" Olga greeted him. "If it isn't Mr. Lindstedt! Come in."

Niels hardly recognised in this young woman the girl he had seen slaving behind the plow, barefooted, dishevelled, clad in rags.

She wore a loose-fitting dress of dark print, a white dusting cap, and shoes which were almost high-heeled.

Under his look she blushed.

"I have the horses to look after," Niels said. "Nelson in?"

"No, Lars is out in the bush. That way, I believe. Cutting logs for a smoke-house. Put your horses in the stable, Mr. Lindstedt, and come in and get warm."

"Thanks," Niels replied. "I'm not cold. I think I'll walk out to Nelson. Everything all right?"

"Everything is just grand!" Olga said emphatically. "Have you had your dinner?"

"No, I haven't. But I'd like to see Nelson first. He'll knock off, I suppose. We'll come in for a bite if it isn't inconvenient."

"All right," Olga said.

Nelson greeted Niels in a very cordial, though not the old way. "Hello, Lindstedt," he sang out and shook him by the hand. Formerly he had called him Niels though Niels had never called him Lars. "Coming for your grain?" Nelson had always spoken Swedish to Niels; he was using English now.

"Well, yes," Niels said.

"It's waiting for you. You're in no hurry, I hope? Stay overnight?"

"If it isn't too much trouble?"

"Well, I guess the wife'll fix you up. Seen her?"

"I went to the house," Niels replied, somehow embarrassed by Nelson's way of referring to Olga.

"Find things much changed?"

"Yes. As I expected."

"Dropped in at the old folks'?"

"No. Fact is, things don't seem to run smoothly there."

Nelson laughed. "Guess not. They miss their slavey. We haven't seen them for several months."

"That so?"

"Old man thinks we should both work for him now and pull him out of his hole. Well, I suppose I better knock off and call it a day."

But Niels had seized one of the logs that lay ready to be loaded; and so they worked on for another half hour.

Then they drove back to the yard. Nelson talked.

"Tell you," he said. "When I got my supplies from Minor, along in the fall, I came back with a wagon load of groceries, flour, etc. I put in at Lund's for the night. In the morning I hitch up. But the load seems somehow small. I start to check things over and find that I'm two bags of flour short. I in and asks the old man, Do you know anything about that flour of mine? – Flour? He says. I? What should I know about it? – Well, I says, I'm two bags short. – Must have lost them on the way, he says. – Lost them on the way, nothing! I says. I checked them over last night. – Where did you leave your wagon? he asks. – Well, you know, I says. By the hay-stack. – Maybe some Indians sneaked in and stole them, he says, lying there in his wicker chair as you know. – Indians? I says. I'll find them Indians. – And out I go and back to the load; for I had an idea. There I begin to stoke about in the hay; and sure enough, before long I pull them flour-bags out of the stack. I back to the house. Well, I says; and the old lady looks at me kind of funny. I've found the Indians. They were in the hay. – The old lady screams. Daddy, she cries, you're a disgrace to the fambly!" And Nelson laughed uproariously at the recital.

Niels looked out on the road, his eyes fixed on vacancy. Was this man his friend? He was glad that at least Olga had not been present.

When they entered the house, Nelson sang out, "Hello, girlie! Got a bite for your men?" And he stepped up to his wife, kissed her, and pinched her cheek.

Olga reddened; but she seemed pleased.

The conversation turned to Niels. What had he been doing?

Niels was glad, after supper, to return outside where Nelson helped him to load his grain. It made a heavy load.

Meanwhile they spoke of common acquaintances, of their problems . . .

"I've got my patent," Nelson said. "I'm getting a loan on the place. A thousand dollars. I want to buy stock and a pure-bred bull."

"Clearing new land?"

"Don't know yet. Hope so. But a man doesn't seem to get any time when he's married. Need a lot of frills you never thought of before . . ."

Next morning, just before breakfast, Hahn came over on horseback. He was the German neighbour of Nelson's, a giant in stature and strength. The two friends were harnessing their horses in the stable.

"Heard the news?" Hahn shouted over to them as they came to the door.

"No. What?"

"Amundsen's dead."

"What?" Niels fairly jumped. "I saw him well and alive only yesterday morning."

"Yes," the giant said, dismounting. "Chunk of ice fell on him in the creek. Crushed him right up, they say. Bobby Lund was over to tell me this morning. The girl didn't know what to do. He lived till noon. She rode over to Lund's to ask them to drive for a doctor. When the doctor came, after dark, Amundsen was dead; and the girl asked Bobby to let the people know. So he up and rode about, from midnight till daylight. I promised to tell you."

Niels was white.

Nelson said thoughtfully. "There'll be a pretty good farm for sale . . ."

Olga stood in the door of the house, her apron thrown over shoulders and bare arms.

"Well, come in," Nelson said. "Breakfast's ready."

And they all went into the house.

"My God," Olga said. "How did it happen, Mr. Hahn?"

And Hahn repeated as much as he knew.

"Poor Ellen!" Olga cried. "She mustn't be left alone. Couldn't we go down, Lars?"

Nelson frowned. "What could we do?"

And Olga subsided at once.

"There'll be lots of people about," Nelson went on. "They'll do all that's needed. If I thought she'd be left alone, I'd go myself. But Lindstedt's going . . . No doubt your mother's gone . . . And all the others."

Niels rose. "I'll hitch up," he said.

Niels was reclining on the bags that were piled on the grain while the horses slowly plodded along.

A sense of oppression was weighing on him . . . The apparent futility of all endeavour was almost more than he could bear. Amundsen's impeccability in life, his trivial vanity, his slow deliberation and accuracy: where had all these taken him? To our common goal, the grave . . .

Niels thought of the girl, almost critically, without any personal bias: of her unquestioning obedience to him who was dead; of her youthful strength; of her inscrutable look which, in the light of yesterday's disaster, seemed to peer out into life and to reject it: where would her life take her?

He thought of himself and his great strength which had become a marvel to him; of his work on the homestead which he carried on without fathoming any longer the why and the wherefore. Inside of himself, in his mental make-up, he carried a spring which was tightly wound and which would keep the works of his life revolving till it had either unwound itself or spent its strength. Was it really best not to question and just to live on? But living on – what was the use of it if it led him . . . There? Where?

That was the circle of his thought . . .

When at last he stopped at the gate where several other teams were tied, he felt vacant; his gloomy pessimism had exhausted itself; he was apathetic.

Slowly he crossed the yard. Ellen came out of the house. She wore sheep-skin and tam; apparently she was about to do her chores.

Niels looked at her, dully, incomprehendingly. How could she be doing chores? . . . Except for a slight pallour and a touch of weariness about her eyes she seemed perfectly composed.

She nodded briefly. "The body is inside," she said. "There are others there." And she proceeded, pulling on her mitts as she went.

At that moment the sound of singing struck Niel's ear. A hymn was being sung inside.

Not knowing what to do, he entered the house. The door to the room beyond the kitchen was open; and Niels caught a glimpse of a body which lay on a bed, rigid and still, covered with a sheet which revealed its form . . .

The German pastor from Odensee was standing in the centre of the kitchen. A dozen men and women were standing about him, singing. Among them Niels recognised Mrs. Lund and old man Sigurdsen. Their faces were solemn, as if cast in an unyielding mould.

Somehow their sight as well as that of the big, fat pastor was distasteful to him. He slipped out again before the singing was finished.

He crossed to the stable where he found Ellen feeding a strange team of horses, presumably those that had brought the pastor.

For a moment he looked on. Then he asked, "Anything I can do?"

"Thanks," said Ellen without turning, though she had stopped in her work.

"I'm sorry," he faltered. "I went to Nelson's yesterday. I did not hear about it till this morning."

"I saw you going," she replied, calm and indifferent.

"I wish . . ." he began and hesitated.

"I know," she nodded. "There is nothing . . . The crowd has been here all day. They look after everything . . ."

"I'll be back in the morning . . ."

"Don't bother. They'll be sitting up with the body. I'll go to Lund's."

A feeling of utter uselessness invaded Niels; and he resented it. For a moment longer he lingered; then he turned and went away.

Between him and the girl an abyss seemed to yawn which nothing could bridge . . . He untied his horses, turned back to the road, and drove on.

When he got home, he went to work on the clearing of his yard as if he had to give vent to some pent-up powers within him in order to avoid an explosion . . .

. . .

Niels did not go to the funeral. He saw the teams file out from the gap of the bridge and turn west, along the road at the edge of the bush, past Sigurdsen's. He came near succumbing to an impulse to run and to get his horses ready. But he caught himself and, swinging his axe high through the air, he gathered all the tremendous strength of his body into one single blow and brought it down with a vicious bite into the butt of a giant tree . . .

Henceforth Niels thought of his former dreams with nothing but silent scorn. And yet there was only one excuse for his life in the present; and that excuse lay in the possible future. He had, in the past, planned a homestead with that future in view; and the plan persisted.

His only intercourse was with Sigurdsen now. The old man was slowly decaying. At best he had only a few years to live.

All through the winter Niels worked at clearing yard and field, at squaring and fitting timbers . . .

In the beginning of March he began to dig a well. He intended to get help as soon as he reached a depth of seven or eight feet. But when he reached that level, wild blizzards began to blow, wiping out all traces of the roads and throwing up trenches and bulwarks all about the entrance to his yard. Niels went on digging by himself.

On the fourth day the temperature fell to one of its lowest levels; and all through the night, while lying in his improvised house, the granary, Niels heard the frost booming in the big bluff . . .

Again he went at his well alone. He made a sort of ladder of poles and put it into the hole; and that way he carried the clay and marl out in pails. Then he struck gravel and sand; and before laying off for dinner he noticed a slight trickle of water from the upper edge of the sandy layer. Under ordinary circumstances this sight would have filled him with exultation. As it was, he heaved a sigh and worked on before eating till he had the proper depth below the spring. Next morning there were six feet of water in the well. He got the lumber for the cribbing ready.

In the evening, it being a clear, frosty night, he walked across to Sigurdsen's to bespeak the old man's help.

On the north side of Niel's yard, in the lee of the big bluff, lay the squared timbers, thirty-two feet long.

"What that?" Sigurdsen asked when he came in the forenoon of the following day.

"For the house," Niels said briefly.

The old man whistled. "How big?"

"What?"

"The house."

"Four rooms and kitchen."

"Big rooms."

"Fifteen by eighteen," Niels said.

Again the old man whistled. "You going get married?" he asked while they crossed the yard.

"No," Niels said; "don't think so."

. . .

Spring came. The breaking began; Niels had lumber to haul besides, for the house.

While breaking in daytime, he dug the basement of the house at night . . .

May went; June opened up. Blossoms broke out all around: plums, pincherry, chokecherry, saskatoon, cranberry: the brief saturnalian summer of the north . . .

White mists crept over the Marsh at night, filling the hollows with snow-white pools.

A sort of intoxication came over Niels; work developed into an orgy . . .

One night Sigurdsen came over, driving.

"You done anything about hay?" he asked.

"No."

"Hm . . . tya," the old man ruminated. "Go together?"

"Like last year? If you want to. Who sells the permits?"

"The girl."

"She staying on the farm?"

"The Amundsen girl? Tya. They all want buy. She say no. Get married, I say. She say, No; I can do the work."

"All right," said Niels. "You see about the hay."

The old man looked at him, his toothless mouth tightly shut; his chin seemed to touch his nose.

"You come along," he said at last. "Go now."

"I don't mind," Niels replied casually; but his heart was pounding.

The seemingly common-place phrases had been charged with electricity. A struggle was concealed in them. The old man carried the victory. Niels was like a son to him . . .

It was just before dark when they crossed the bridge.

Ahead of their own team they saw another wagon disappearing around a bend in the winding trail. Since there were barrels in the wagon-box, Niels had no doubt but that it was Ellen . . .

But when, on a straighter stretch of the road, they came once more within sight of the team, he saw somebody climbing over the front barrels into the back of the box. This somebody looked like a lad, not like a young woman.

"That Bobby?" Niels asked.

"Hi . . . tya!'" the old man laughed. "Naw. The girl. Wear overalls for work."

Niels coloured; his heart beat faster again . . .

When, in a little less than an hour, they drew up at the gate, Niels saw the wagon with the barrels still standing on the yard. While Sigurdsen tied his horses, he saw a slim figure flitting into the house.

He felt strangely moved. Had it not been for his companion, he would have turned back . . .

From the barn across the yard the sullen, slow bark of an aged dog rang across . . .

Sigurdsen knocked at the door. For a moment no answer. Then the girl's voice rang out from within.

"That you, Mr. Sigurdsen?"

"Yea."

"Go into the kitchen. I'll be out in a minute."

The two men entered. It was very dark inside. But a line of light showed where the door led to the other room.

"There's a lamp on the table. Just light it," Ellen's voice rang out for the third time. "You'll find matches on the shelf by the stove."

The old man had matches in his pocket . . .

Niels stood by the door, in a dull and incomprehensible excitement. He had known, of course, that Ellen was living alone on the place; but for the first time he became aware of what that meant. Loneliness had weighed upon him at times; now it assailed him like a savage beast. He was a man!

The door to the next room opened. Ellen came out, carrying a second lamp.

Niels fastened his eyes upon her.

She had changed to a light print dress. She seemed taller, slenderer than she had looked; more girlish, younger even; above all, less impersonal.

There was still the same poise; the same level, critical look in her eyes. But something happened which destroyed the distancing effect of that look. For, as she caught sight of Niels by the door and recognised him, a scarlet flood suffused her face. Her lips parted as if about to smile . . .

Niels felt that his own head glowed.

She turned to the table and put her lamp upon it.

"Sit down, Mr. Sigurdsen," she said with a steady voice; and, turning to Niels, she nodded and repeated, "Sit down."

She avoided his name.

"We come about hay," Sigurdsen said.

"Yes?"

"The south-west quarter of twenty-one, in the slough."

"You can have it," the girl said quickly, with a voice that was almost ingratiating.

"How much?"

"Thirteen fifty," the girl replied, still speaking fast. "It's fifteen dollars with my commission. I am not going to let you pay for that."

"But the stamps?"

The girl laughed lightly. "Oh, never mind . . ."

"We go together," Sigurdsen explained. "Lindstedt and I."

"Oh?" – with a questioning inflection. "All right. Drop in when you want to start. I'll have the permits ready."

"Hm . . ." the old man mused. "Got your seed in?"

"Yes," the girl answered. "I have it all done."

The two men rose. In vain Niels searched for something to say.

Sigurdsen held out his hand. Then he suddenly bethought himself and drew his pocket-book.

"Never mind," Ellen said. "Pay when you get the permit."

"All right."

And a moment later they were outside in the dark.

As they crossed the yard, the girl, too, came out, carrying a lighted lantern and two pails which she deposited at the door of the house. Then she turned back and, just as Sigurdsen was untying his horses, she followed the men to the gate. The darkness made her move more freely, more gracefully still . . .

She came and stepped to the side of the wagon.

"I baked to-day," she said to the old man. "I brought you a loaf of fresh bread."

"Tya . . ." Sigurdsen said. "You mighty good to me . . ."

She laughed as she slipped back through the gate. "Good-night."

The two men remained silent while they drove the four miles through the bush. Even at parting neither spoke a word.

The last mile Niels walked.

Why had the old man insisted on his coming along? Apparently he was on the most friendly terms with the girl . . .

Why had she blushed when she saw him, Niels? Did she know what his thoughts had been with regard to her? For the first time she had smiled and even laughed. She had stepped down from a pedestal and walked among humans . . .

Did she even suspect what his thoughts had been with regard to her? Had been? . . .

The blood sang in his veins as he stepped briskly along the familiar Marsh trail.

The darkness was peopled with blushing faces and strange, soft voices . . .

There, in front of him, behind that dimly looming bluff, he suddenly saw his house erected: a palace in the wilderness; and behind it stretched the farm, a secluded kingdom . . . The farm and the house . . . His farm and his house! The work of his hands, dreamt of, planned, and built to harbour her!

When he reached his yard, he could not think of going in to sleep . . .

The song of the softly rustling leaves, just sprouted on the poplars overhead, held a new and perturbing note. The stars in the heavens were eyes and smiled at him. The sound of his horses, champing in the stable, munching their hay, had a strangely home-like, sheltered, protected ring. A whip-poor-will whistled his clarion call in the bluff . . .

Niels lighted a lantern and walked about on the yard: his yard, as for months it had no longer seemed to be. He went to the stable, patted the horses on the rump, and gave the newly bought cow an extra feed of hay.

He went over to the site of his house where the logs lay ready, squared and notched to be fitted together; and the lumber for floors, partitions, ceilings, rafters, roof, and stairs, neatly piled; doors and windows were stored in the granary. Stones were gathered in a huge pile for the foundation; the cellar was dug . . .

He went to the clearing where his first breaking lay, seeded to barley. Soon he would add to it . . . Already he had started to cut the brush . . .

At last he returned to the granary, his provisional house. It was not lonely now; it was peopled with dreams. He lay awake till dawn; and then he looked out into the eastern gates of heaven, aflame with glory . . .

That very day he went north to bespeak help in building the house . . .

Soon it grew up, a mansion, holding four rooms, with a lean-to kitchen . . .

But then, here he was sitting on the Marsh; five miles north, she was sitting in the bush. How were they to get together?

He went to Lund's. She was not there. Instead, there was the usual crowd.

Kelm, the German, and his cronies were playing at cards . . . Lund, as ever, was reclining in his wicker chair . . . Bobby greeted Niels, blushing with pleasure, for Niels and Nelson were still his idols: he was a big boy of fifteen now, with the angular movements of adolescence.

Niels drifted about, anxious to make his escape.

But so as not to be lacking in common civility, he turned to Mr. Lund and sat down.

"Got any hay this year?" he asked.

"No," the man replied, groping about with uncertain hands and smiling his overdone smile. "Oh, it's Mr. Lindstedt, is it? . . . No. The south-west quarter of twenty-one is still open . . . But we don't know . . ."

Mrs. Lund, having heard a word or so of the conversation, came over and spoke in a lowered voice. "The truth of the matter is, Mr. Lindstedt, we have to wait till the seventeenth. Then the post-office-cheque will come in. But you know, that cheque cannot pay for everything . . ."

"Oh, mamma," her husband broke in, "how you talk!"

"Well," she flashed back. "It's true, ain't it?"

"We'll get a loan . . ."

"There you go again. Who is going to give you a loan? You haven't even got your patent."

"I can prove up any time," Lund said, darkening with displeasure. "I have forty acres broken . . ."

"Yes," she snapped, "and the Jew takes it all . . . Mr. Lindstedt," she added in desperation, tears almost in her eyes, "there isn't enough flour in the house to make breakfast with to-morrow morning. Whatever we get the Jew puts his hand on. We've three acres of potatoes in; and the crop is sold already for twenty cents a bushel. Other people get fifty cents and sixty cents; but we get twenty because we've got to sell in advance . . . That's the way it goes with this man . . ."

Niels felt immensely embarrassed. "Mrs. Lund," he said, "will you let me help you out? I've got ten dollars in my pocket which I don't need just now. Take it and pay me back when your cheque comes in."

"Well," she said, "thanks, Mr. Lindstedt. I'll take it. But be sure to come over on Sunday the eighteenth . . ."

As he drove home, Niels thought, Where is Nelson? Where Olga?

. . .

It was the middle of July before haying began. Rains had delayed it.

Three days after, it was Sunday, the eighteenth.

Niels returned to Lund's. Mrs. Lund had his money ready.

Niels was untying his horses from the fence in order to leave again when he saw Mr. Lund coming blindly across the yard. The old man was in a hurry; he stumbled forward, feeling his way, nearly running into the wall of the smithy, but swerving back the very last moment.

Niels waited for him.

"Mr. Lindstedt," Lund called. "Ah, there you are . . . Say, Mr. Lindstedt, will you give me a ride down to Sigurdsen's?"

"Certainly," Niels replied, not a little astonished at the man's air of mystery and abject apology.

He helped him on to the seat and drove out on the dam in a brisk trot.

The two sat in silence. Niels was thinking, thinking . . .

Suddenly the man by his side began to speak.

"Mr. Lindstedt," he said after clearing his throat repeatedly, his voice grating with artificial cordiality, "You have helped me out before . . . Can you loan me thirty-five dollars?"

Niels betrayed his surprise by his silence.

At once Lund tried to forestall the implied refusal.

"You see," he said, "I have a brother living in Minnesota who is very well off. I want to go and see him. I am sure he would help me. If I can get a loan of two or three thousand dollars, I can prove up and straighten things out . . ."

"Well," Niels said without harshness – the man was a visionary after all – "I haven't the cash . . ."

"You could give me a cheque . . . I'd pay you good interest . . . I'd pay . . . I'd pay you ten percent a month."

That decided Niels. This man could not be trusted with money. "As far as the interest goes," he said, "I don't care about that. But I can't."

"You think it over," Lund pleaded. "Think it over, Mr. Lindstedt. I shall see you again . . ."

When Sigurdsen saw whom Niels had with him, he glared with suspicion. Apparently he wanted to speak to Niels alone. "Go to the house, Lund," he said.

And when Lund had gone, he turned to Niels. "The girl . . . She come this morning see me. She want help in haying."

"Well," Niels pondered. "How would it be if we did our work in the morning and then went and helped her together?"

"Fine, tya. You go tell her."

"Now?"

"Yea. She be waiting for me. You go."

"All right," Niels consented though he felt a sudden panic running through his body; and he turned his horses and drove back the way he had come.

He tied his horses at Ellen's gate, hardly knowing what to do next. But the difficulty solved itself: the girl stepped out of the house and came to meet him.

"Hello," Niels said, his head aglow.

"Hello," she replied, her voice strangely steady.

"Sigurdsen was speaking to me . . ."

"Well," she asked, "may he come?" It sounded as if she were faintly amused.

"We'll both come to-morrow. Right after noon. Where is your hay?"

The girl nodded backwards. "Beyond the field. Have your dinner here. We'll use my teams."

Niels assented.

"Won't you come in?" she invited casually, opening the little gate.

Niels followed mechanically as she led the way.

She did not go to the house but to a spot in the bush, north of it, where a little table and a folding chair stood in a sort of bower formed by hazelbrush and plum trees. A tin box with smouldering grass inside spread a smoky haze to keep the mosquitoes away.

"I'll get a chair," she said.

"Never mind. I'll sit on the grass . . ."

They sat down, Ellen resuming a crochet-hook and some wool with which she had beguiled the time.

"You've been building?" she asked after a while. She was quite at ease.

"Yes," he said. "I've built a house."

"A large house? A regular mansion, Sigurdsen says."

Niels coloured. "Four rooms; besides the kitchen which is a lean-to."

"Four rooms?" Ellen exclaimed, dropping her hands to her knees. "What do you want four rooms for?"

"And there is space for two small attic rooms besides," Niels went on with sudden recklessness.

Ellen stared at him. Then both laughed; and Niels, too, felt at ease.

"Well," he said, "people here think more of their

machinery than of their houses; more of their farms than of their lives. The house is merely a piece of the farm, a place to sleep in while you are not at work. I want a house of which the farm is a part, the place where what is needed in the house is grown. These people here, when they get anywhere, are rich at best. Their life has slipped by; they have never lived. Especially the women."

The girl looked at him. Her eyes had lost their critical, distancing look; they were frankly questioning.

Niels looked back at her, without speaking. He noticed that her abundant, straw-yellow hair was no longer so severely brushed down. It had little waves and ripples in it; a looser way of doing it up had given it freedom to follow its natural bend. He remembered how, as a girl, she had seemed to him singularly mature; now that in age she was a woman, she seemed almost girlish . . .

"I've looked about a good deal," he said at last. "I've seen Lund's place; Hahn's; and a few others. Of course, I believe the men do work hard . . ."

"Lund doesn't," Ellen interrupted.

"No," Niels agreed quite seriously. "Not Lund. But Hahn. He's strong. If he does work hard, he can stand it. His wife works just as hard . . ."

"Harder," Ellen interrupted again.

"Yes," Niels went on. "She has the house and the children; the cows to milk; the sheep to feed. In summer she stacks the grain and the hay; and when threshing time comes . . ."

"Help is hard to get," Ellen objected.

"Perhaps . . . Then why not do a little less?"

"Well," Ellen pondered, "I'll tell you. During the first few years it is really the woman that makes the living on a pioneer farm. She keeps chickens, cows, and pigs. The man makes the land."

"But when it is made?"

"That's where the trouble comes in. Then there are children; and the house takes a fearful amount of time. Nobody thinks of relieving her of any work. She has always done it. Why can she not do it now?"

"I passed Kelm's place last year," Niels said. "He was breaking with his new tractor. He sat on his engine. But she walked behind the plows, bare-footed, and picked out the stones and dragged the roots into piles. Kelm passes as a well-to-do man."

Ellen laughed. A low, self-possessed laugh. "I've done it myself," she said. "I am still doing it, though on a smaller scale."

"You shouldn't," he answered boldly.

"I'm independent," she objected and resumed her work. But after a silence of a few minutes she dropped it again. "Isn't it strange that we should have been neighbours for over a year and have never spoken?"

"I did not dare," Niels said.

"Dare?"

"You looked so forbidding. As if you would resent it if I spoke."

She mused for a while. "Do you remember," she said at last, "how you first came here to dig the well and spoke only Swedish?"

Niels blushed. "I do."

"Do you know what I thought? One morning you did speak. 'A penny for your thoughts, miss,' you called."

Niels felt uncomfortable under the remembrance.

"And I probably frowned. Another one of those silly youngsters, I thought. When they see a girl, they think they must act up in order to please her. I knew the kind . . ."

"I was silly enough," Niels admitted ruefully.

"I suppose. But you kept silent after that."

And silent they kept for another half hour.

Then Niels stirred. "Hadn't I better go?"

"If you wish."

He did not wish; but he got up nevertheless.

"Well, good-by," he said and hesitated.

Ellen held out her hand; and he touched it.

"Till to-morrow," she said. "I shall have dinner ready at twelve."

The hand he had touched was small and shapely; but it was hard and calloused from work.

What a fool I have been! What a fool I have been! Niels said to himself as he drove home . . .

Next morning, Sigurdsen joined Niels in the meadow west of Lund's place only after he had taken Lund home. It was easily seen that he was out of sorts.

"Anything wrong?" Niels asked.

Sigurdsen grunted. "That man! He keep me awake till two in the morning."

"Talking?"

"Yea," Sigurdsen grumbled. "Begging."

"He didn't ask you for money, I hope."

"No? He ask you?"

"Yes," Niels said. "He asked me for thirty-five dollars."

"Get it?"

"No. I hope he got nothing from you."

"Every cent. Twenty-two dollars."

"What a shame!" Niels exclaimed.

He was angry with himself for having taken Lund over to the old man's . . .

The morning went by; they stacked a few loads in the field; by eleven o'clock they were ready to go; both had their racks filled again.

When they reached Ellen's yard, the girl stepped out of the house. "Dinner will be ready in a few minutes. Come in and rest." Her manner was that of a man to two friends.

A thought struck Niels. He spoke to Sigurdsen.

"Ellen!" He was surprised at the ease with which her name came from his lips. "How if we pitched these loads off? We'd have three racks. To-night we could each take a load of your hay home."

"Why," Ellen said. "I hadn't thought of that. It would save time, wouldn't it?"

"Sure," Niels said. "Where do you want it?"

"In the loft," Ellen called from the door.

In the meadow, a quarter of a mile north-west of the yard, Niels proposed that Ellen and the old man should stay on the rack while he pitched to them.

Ellen objected.

"Get up there," Niels laughed. "I'll keep you busy."

And when she obeyed, he pitched as he had never pitched before. The load was up in record time.

Niels stood leaning on his fork and shook the sweat from his head, laughing.

Ellen, too, laughed. She was flushed with exertion. It was very hot.

"You take the load home and pitch it off on the yard," she said. "So you have a rest."

"Rest, nothing!" he replied. "We want to get five or six loads in at least. You take it home. Meanwhile we'll get the next load up."

The third load Sigurdsen drove. Niels pitched again.

"You are as good as a man," he praised the girl.

"I can load," she said. "I'm no good at pitching."

"You shouldn't do it. That is a man's work."

"But you said I was as good as a man."

Both laughed. The hay was in cocks. With every forkful Niels lifted such a load as left only gleanings where the pile had been.

The girl's eyes widened in admiration of his strength. He, feeling it, was childishly happy in his exertions.

Sigurdsen returned; and again Niels was urged to take a load home. Again he declined. But this time he proposed to fill the three racks and to take them home in a body so they would be able to stack properly and to round off the top in case it should rain. Again it was done as he suggested.

The sun was sinking. The old man began to show signs of wear.

"Now we'll fill up for the last time," Niels said. "To-morrow we'll be back. You'll have nine loads to-night. As many to-morrow and once again, and your hay will be in."

When they returned, Ellen invited them for supper. But the old man declined. "Unload and feed . . . soon dark."

"Well," she said when they were ready to go, "I am sure I am grateful. How much do I owe you folks?"

"Hm . . ." Sigurdsen began, much embarrassed.

Niels laughed. "I haven't been working for wages. I've been working for the fun of it . . ."

Ellen frowned. "But that isn't right . . ."

"Oh, let a man do something for you once in a while," Niels said lightly. "Come and help us to-morrow. We'll get a load more."

Laughingly Ellen consented.

Next day, however, when Ellen appeared in their meadow, Niels absolutely refused to let her work. 'I'll pitch three loads," he said. "And then we'll stack. The next three loads go to your place. You take the first one home and get dinner. Then there's an odd load at night; you haul it; to Amundsen's to-day; to my place to-morrow."

This was a deeply laid scheme of his to get her to look at his house . . .

The sun was touching the horizon when they emerged from the bridge on the Marsh, next day, and parted from Sigurdsen who turned to the west.

Niels slipped off his load; his horses knew the road and needed no guiding.

Before them stood the bluff that sheltered his yard: a softly glistening dome. From the east beyond, dark shadows rose; overhead, the sky was still shot with polished beams.

"Look at that," he called to the girl as he strode along beside her load and waved his arm aloft.

She nodded in silence.

Satisfaction with what he had, longing for what he had not were strangely mixed in him as he stepped out, his head erect, by the side of her wearily plodding horses.

Again the blood sang in his veins. He felt like an adventurer coming home with booty; he longed to shout to his house which lay hidden behind the trees. This girl that was reclining on her load should be there, should be waiting for him and look out as he rounded the bluff . . .

A moment later the vista opened on his yard.

The girl gave a little cry of surprise. Niels swelled with pride.

"Well," she exclaimed as they turned. "I don't wonder that everybody talks of your house. It is a mansion."

He opened the gate, and they drove in. Niels took her horses by the bridle and led them up to the stack.

"Come down," he called. "I'll pitch the load off."

She obeyed.

"Go in," he said. "I want you to look at the house."

She blushed. "I'd like to. But . . ."

"But nonsense," he ruled. "Go in. There's a lamp on the table in the kitchen. The house isn't furnished yet. I use only one room. By the time you've looked it over I'll be through with your load."

He watched her as she walked across the yard and opened the door and disappeared in the house. For a moment his old, familiar vision became so strong that it amounted to an illusion. Yes, such was his home; this was what he had wished and longed and worked for; and children running out to the gate to meet and greet him . . .

In thought he followed her through the house: now she was standing in the front room, a sort of hall: a wide, hardwood staircase, without banisters so far, led up into the upper story. Behind the front room lay the dining room from which a door led into the lean-to kitchen to the east. Would she go upstairs? To see the two rooms there, half joined, half parted by a little landing?

Ellen came out again. And when Niels had finished pitching her hay off, he sprang down from the rack.

"The house is lovely," she said, her cheeks aglow. "But so large . . ."

"Did you go upstairs?"

"Yes, and even into the cellar."

He longed to cry out, "I built it for you!" But his tongue was tied . . . He reached for the lines and turned her horses.

A moment later they stood by the gate in the dusk: the sun had sunk. She held out her hand.

"I don't know how to thank you . . ."

"May I come?" he asked. "To call? . . ."

"Of course," she laughed as if his shyness put her at ease. "Come on Sundays. I am always sitting behind the house in the afternoon . . . Get up, Pete."

And he found himself holding the gate for her to pass out . . .

That night Niels did not sleep. A thousand times he repeated to himself, "What would she have said if I had asked her to-night?" . . . And then he answered himself, "No; not yet; I must have thirty acres cleared and broken before I can ask her."

Next morning he went to work again with a will . . .

On Sunday, in order to have the pretext for calling on Ellen that he was passing her yard, he went to Lund's to ask for his mail . . .

It was early; there were no guests yet.

For the first time he thought he detected a certain coolness of manner in Mrs. Lund. He attributed it to the fact that he had refused her husband the loan.

"What we are going to do for hay this year," Mrs. Lund said at last in the course of a desultory conversation, "is beyond my guessing . . ."

"Mrs. Lund," Niels said, "if you'd like me to loan you the money for the permit, I'd be glad to do so. That I refused the loan to your husband is an entirely different manner . . ."

"My husband? Did daddy ask you for a loan?"

"Did you not know?" Niels asked. He realised that he had blundered; he hesitated. But, after a moment's thought, he went on, determined not to shield the man; surely his wife had a right to know . . . "He asked me for thirty-five dollars to pay his fare to Minnesota so he could see his brother about that loan . . ."

"He did, eh?" Mrs. Lund said, stopping in her work of washing the dishes and fixing a cold eye on Niels. "Well, let me tell you, daddy has no brother in Minnesota; nor anywhere else; and don't you let him have any money."

"Well," Niels went on, "if that's the case, I suppose I'd better tell you that he borrowed twenty-two dollars from old man Sigurdsen; and it was all the money the old man had."

Mrs. Lund laughed: a bitter, hollow laugh.

Niels understood that her coolness sprang merely from her exasperation with life.

"You going already?" she said as he reached for his mail. "Just as well, Mr. Lindstedt; just as well. This is no place for you any longer. I suppose daddy must be thinking of skipping the country. But where he'd go if he left us here, I don't know. Don't worry," she went on. "Old Sigurdsen shall get his money back. Don't you worry."

Niels hesitated. "I'm sorry, Mrs. Lund," he stammered, feeling that he had touched on things beyond the remedy of words. "I didn't mean to give you pain . . . As for the hay . . ."

"Don't worry about the hay either," she said. "Soon there will be no need for hay here any longer. You helped us last year, Mr. Lindstedt. It isn't forgotten."

Niels left the house. On the yard, Lund was tinkering about at a mower, sitting on the seat of the rickety machine.

When he heard a football, he looked up and smiled his most artificial smile. "That you, Mr. Lindstedt?"

"Yes," Niels replied.

"About that loan," Lund went on, getting to his feet and whispering. "I'll pay you ten percent a month; and I need the money only for a week. I'll send it back as soon as I get to my brother's . . ."

"I'm sorry," Niels interrupted him curtly. "I can't do a thing in the matter."

And with that he went quickly to the gate to untie his horses.

Lund looked vacantly after him. Then he dropped back to the seat of the mower.

When Niels swung up on the dam, he heard Mrs. Lund's piercing call, "Dad-deee!"

It was half past two when he reached Ellen's place in the bush. For a moment he hesitated. Then he saw the girl in the little clearing north of the house. She, too, had seen him and came to the gate.

"Come in," she said, smiling. "Put your horses to the hay. You'll stay for a while, won't you?"

"If I may," Niels said.

Instead of an answer she opened the gate . . .

Soon after, Niels went south, with his team this time, as foreman of the threshing gang . . .

"It has been pleasant this summer," Ellen said when he took leave. "I shall miss our Sundays."

Niels had arranged with Sigurdsen to look after the harvesting and threshing of his own little crop.

It was a different man who joined the threshers this year. He was as quiet as ever; but he no longer treated his fellow workers with that silent contempt which had galled them . . .

Then, with the snow-up, he returned to his claim, carrying in his wagon things galore for his house . . .

Once more the old life began: work from dawn to dark: he was clearing the land that was to bear his crops . . . Was he making progress? He was. Last year his little store of grain had come from Nelson's place; this year he had twice as much; and it came from his own . . . Had Sigurdsen faithfully looked after cutting and threshing? He had. There were three hundred odd bushels of barley in his granary; and a hundred of them he took to Kelm's to get crushed. He thought of chickens and pigs for the following year: for then he would have a crop to sell, a crop of wheat . . .

He worked at the house again: the walls were to be finished with plaster-board inside . . .

On Sundays, he resumed his trips to Ellen's place. He told her, of course, how things were going: well indeed, but much, much too slow . . . They could not sit outside any longer; so they sat by the fire in the kitchen . . .

Though Bobby was a strong lad now, things went badly with Lunds. Not even the crops of forty acres and the hard work of a woman and a boy can keep things going on a pioneer farm when it staggers along under debt . . .

"When Olga was still here," Mrs. Lund said to Niels one day, "I could go to the city in winter. Daddy was still able to get along by himself . . . But daddy is getting to be like a child, Mr. Lindstedt. He cannot be trusted any longer alone. He cannot be trusted . . ."

"Oh mamma," said Lund, "how you talk!"

But he sat in his wicker chair which was fraying more and more and which would soon break and fall in a heap. Even his meals were now served to him there: pancakes and molasses three times a day . . .

"But Nelson . . ." Niels said.

"Don't mention Nelson," Mrs. Lund exclaimed. "The least said, the best . . ."

Niels cleared his land . . .

Spring came.

He enlarged his stable and built a chicken house. He sold hay . . .

Then breaking and seeding, with propitious weather towards the end of April. He had eighteen acres in crop, six of wheat, four of oats, and the rest in barley.

This spring, one day, Lund disappeared. No one knew where he had gone. For a few days the excitement was great. Everybody helped in the search . . .

Then . . . Well . . . Mrs. Lund went to Odensee and opened a little store. Bobby went to Nelson's. He was cheap help; you don't pay a brother-in-law the regular wages; you give him a little pocket-money, that is all . . .

The summer went by. Sunday afternoons in the open, north of the house in the bush . . .

Working out in the threshing crews . . . Niels bought a team of pure-bred Percherons, an enormous gelding, a mare for breeding, with filly and in foal . . .

And winter again . . .

Between Niels and Ellen a friendship had sprung up; an intimate friendship . . . And yet . . .

Niels was not quite sure of his impression; but he thought he noticed a change, an ever so slight change in her of late . . .

She was almost gay when, apart from himself, the old man was present. But when he saw her alone, there seemed to be something of restraint in their intercourse. Sometimes he thought this restraint arose from him: from his efforts to hold back the all-important question. At other times he was fully convinced that, on the contrary, there was something she wished to say and held back . . .

When a silence fell . . . Always their intercourse had been full of silences; but they had been more friendly even, more companionable than their conversations . . . When a silence fell, they seemed to drift apart. Ellen was apt to muse along lines of her own . . . An expression as of sadness and pity came over her . . .

Yet, since more and more he persuaded himself that she knew, that she must know, he also became convinced that she accepted his courtship; that silently all things were agreed upon . . .

The strange thing was that, whenever he felt surest of himself, the next moment there came over him a realisation as if what he longed for had somehow become quite impossible of fulfilment . . .

Then he sought for a pretext to leave – which Ellen did not contradict . . .

After Christmas the true western winter came: with winds that roared through the bush and leapt careering over the edge of the Marsh to hit the bluff with sounds of cannonading. Snow-sheets were whirled and flung; forts were thrown up, and trenches dug; and the world seemed to reel and to dance madly about the big house which he had painted white by now: the house which Niels had built for Ellen . . .

On such days, when work in the open became impossible, Niels went about in those large rooms that were like a coat too loose about his shoulders.

Every now and then he would go out, over his sheltered yard, and look in on the horses and the cow; and then he would stroll over to the gate which remained open now. There, the wind would strike him, whistling or moaning around the corner of the bluff, and throw the snow into his face in a fine, prickling, pelting dust . . .

He would go back to the house and open boxes and bundles and take out stuffs for curtains: plain, white scrims, and others with coloured borders; and he would hold them up against the bare windows and fold them again and put them away . . .

Or he would take a book and read for a while: books he almost knew by heart: the English Bible, old magazines, some volumes of reports of the Department of Agriculture . . .

When night fell, at five, he would go once more and feed his horses and milk his cow . . .

And sometimes, on such days, he would then go to bed and lie and dream wakeful dreams and perhaps get up again: perhaps to put wood in the stove; and perhaps merely to walk about once more . . .

At other times he would put on sheep-skin and leggings and fight his way blindly across the ribbon of the Marsh that intervened between his and Sigurdsen's places . . .

The old man was getting to be stranger and stranger. Sometimes he would talk to himself for a long while, taking no notice of Niels' presence.

"Hi . . . tya," he would say. "Listen to the wind. That's the rigging howling! How she keels over! Mind, George, that girl in Copenhagen? Hi . . . tya! She laugh . . ."

He had been a sailor in his day.

Niels would nod. He understood that the old man was talking to the phantoms of his youth. Strange, disquieting things he would sometimes say, trailing off into Icelandic which Niels understood only half: things that seemed to withdraw a veil from wild visions, imcomprehensible in one so old . . .

"Tya . . . Yo, she laugh . . . and she turn her hips. And her breasts . . . Hi . . . tya. And she bite! Sharp teeth she had, the hussy . . ."

And this decay of the human faculties, the reappearance of the animal in a man whom he loved, aroused in Niels strange enthusiasms: as if he could have got up and howled and whistled, vying with the wind . . .

Thus half the night would pass. And perhaps the wind would cease; and morning dawned bright and clear, with the temperature down to its lowest levels . . .

Then Niels would set out with a load of wheat, or perhaps of barley or hay . . .

That winter Niels became naturalised . . .

And soon after, when he heard that Bobby had left Nelson's because he wanted to earn real wages, he went and saw him, in the livery stable of Minor, and proposed to him to come to his, Niels', place, at regular wages, the year around . . .

And Bobby came . . .

Thirty-four acres under crop . . .

Spring again. Breaking and seeding . . .

Niels proved up.

Sigurdsen was unable to do his work: Niels and Bobby did it for him.

More changes: an American moved into the district, having bought Kelm's farm. Kelm received nine thousand dollars in cash. He bought a half section of Hudson's Bay land, just across the creek, north of the bridge . . .

There was much discussion about this between Niels and Ellen. They would not sell. They were on their land because they loved it: to them it was home.

Yet, since Niels had proved up, there was no obstacle any longer . . . Why did he wait? . . .

There had re-entered into their relationship something of the distancing effect of the first few years . . . Niels began almost to dread the coming of the decisive moment . . .

There was some unsounded depth in him or the girl . . .

Something dreadful was coming, coming . . .

CHAPTER THREE

Ellen

A CHANCE happening disturbed Niels still more profoundly.

He had gone to town, driving his Percheron team. The mare was in foal. Last year's filly still ran with her. So he stayed overnight. The next day was hot; he made up his mind to attend to some business he had long postponed and to wait for the evening coolness before he started out for home . . .

Some time before dinner the train from the south was due. To put in time, he went to the station.

As is usual in small towns, half the population of the place crowded on to the platform as if in greeting or reception of the arrivals. A few – elderly or middle-aged men in shirt-sleeves – were there on business; less – ladies, these – to receive visitors or members of their households; most – young boys and girls in "citified" clothes – because the arrival of the train furnished a pretext for joining a crowd or for meeting those of the opposite sex.

To Niels it always seemed that for town-people the most important problem was what to do with their time.

Niels stood silent and alone, frowning, as the train, this "link with a wider world," lumbered to a stop with screeching brakes and hissing steamvalves. He stood opposite the coupling of two cars. With absent-minded curiosity he scanned the passengers as they alighted.

The first to appear was a bulky, powerful man – from the studied and conscious "magnetism" of his bearing a travelling salesman. Next came two Slavic-looking men, each carrying on his back a gunny-sack full of tools; self-effacing men who slipped through the crowd as if anxious to hide. Then, a girl who was at once taken to the ample bosom of a lady and kissed. Fourthly, another young man, in glaringly polished, pointed shoes, grey-checked trousers, short enough to reveal a fascinating piece of blue silk socks, a loud, striped shirt with flowing necktie, and a tight-fitting coat of the same grey check as his trousers: his line – "ladies' ready-to-wear" – written all over him . . .

Last, after a short wait, there came a lady dressed in the height of fashion, a long, narrow skirt enforcing a short, tripping step; a mannish summer coat of "tango" colour; and a wide lace hat – bergère style – under which a peculiarly engaging, smiling, and dimpled face looked out as if it were used to the attention she attracted.

Niels stared; and then he froze into a statue of almost indignant aloofness: that lady was Mrs. Vogel.

She, too, stared at him as she alighted.

And then, as she came straight up to him, her face broke into that smile which had once thrilled him.

"Why," she said as she held out her hand, "this is the nicest of all surprises. Coming back as I do, almost a stranger in these parts, to be greeted by the face of a friend!"

Niels was at a loss what to say. The consciousness of old thoughts, dreams, and thrills sent a flush into his face. Awkwardly he doffed his cap when he accepted her hand which was encased in a grey suède glove. But Mrs. Vogel relieved him of the necessity of speaking.

"I'm on my way to the place in the bush," she said; and the old expression of feminine helplessness came over her. She had looked tall and commanding on the steps of the car; now she seemed to dwindle till she was no more than a bit of humanity which needed protection. "I am selling the place and have to attend to all kinds of things. I am quite at a loss, not being a business woman. I was going to hire a livery rig. But perhaps I could get a ride with you?"

"I can give you the ride," Niels said; "but I'm not going out till late. My Percherons must not sweat . . ."

Niels was aware that they formed the centre of a watching group. Mrs. Vogel's appearance had become the object of the local young ladies' absorbed attention; he himself was being scanned by the travelling salesmen . . .

A commotion arose. The conductor's "All-aboard" rang out; and with a jerk and a great puffing of steam the train began to glide out to the north.

"That would suit me just right," Mrs. Vogel said. "I shall have to see Mr. Thorpe, the lawyer; and I shall have to change before we start. I am just in time for dinner at the hotel, I believe."

Shortly after, they sat in the dining room of the hotel.

When the rouged and powdered waitress came, Niels gave his order in a curt, gruff tone which was almost insulting.

Mrs. Vogel smiled; she seemed to be making fun of him: her voice, in addressing the waitress, was so pointedly sweet and measured.

"How strange," Mrs. Vogel said after a while, "that you should be the first man I meet. Of all men you. Do you know, Niels, how often I have thought of you during these years in the city?"

Niels felt as he had felt years ago, at Nelson's wedding, in the house that was falling to ruins in the bush: Lund's house, ages ago . . . He almost trembled when she used his first name.

Mrs. Vogel inquired after Mrs. Lund, after others . . .

"I still have that pony and buggy," she said. "I hope Bert Rowdle is going to buy them . . ."

"Is he the one who is taking your place?"

"Yes," she replied. "Bert Rowdle has been farming his brother's and my places together. His brother left a few years ago, playing hide-and-seek with his creditors, I believe. He is coming back. So Bert wants to buy . . . And you are on the old place still?"

"Yes."

"Doing well?"

"Not too badly. I have proved up."

"You have? That's splendid." It sounded like mockery. "Too bad you should still be unmarried . . ."

Niels kept silent. At last, by chance, he looked up.

Her eyes were resting on his, not mockingly now, but with a serious, glowing interest that seemed to deprive him of his speech. For the first time he noticed her hair: it was parted in the centre, rolling out in big puffs to both sides, and twisted into curly roll after roll behind. Strange that it should never have struck him before that it was coppery-red . . .

Her complexion was still that almost transparent white; her lips, full and red; her cheeks, covered with a roseate bloom. A faint, heady perfume exhaled from her . . .

When this scrutiny became embarrassing, Niels tried to recall what she had said. "How do you know?" he asked.

"I can tell." She smiled again.

And in sudden exasperation he said, "How?"

For a moment she looked at him in silence. Then she said very slowly, "You are a conqueror, Niels; but you do not know it. With women you are a child. A woman wants to be taken, not adored. But if you are ever to marry, the woman will have to take you . . ."

Niels reddened and frowned.

"Well," said Mrs. Vogel when the meal was finished, "when do you go?"

"I'll come for you at six," he said. "I'll put plenty of hay in the box." And it struck him as absurd to offer this lady of the city a place in the hay.

But she nodded. "So long then."

Niels had really nothing to do. But he strolled over to the bank to inquire about his balance which he knew as well as the banker.

The manager, a slim and exceedingly polite young man by name of Regan, asked him into his private office when he saw him.

"How's the farm?" he enquired. "You're in a good location there, Mr. Lindstedt. They've never had a failure yet in that district . . . And it seems you have the right idea; always keeping a comfortable balance on the right side of the ledger . . . However, I have been wanting to say this to you. Should you at any time wish to do something for which your cash resources are insufficient, come in and talk it over with us. The chances are that we should be glad to back you."

"I believe in going without when I cannot pay cash."

"A good principle, very good," Mr. Regan said. "However, if we had no credit, there would be few binders or sewing machines on our farms . . ."

"I have my binder," Niels objected.

"No doubt. In fact, I know. You might want a tractor one day . . ."

"Not till I can grow gasoline on my fields . . . I am raising colts . . ."

"Good stock, too. They'll make money for you. Well," and the banker rose, chiefly in order to uphold the fiction that he was a very busy man . . . "should the occasion arise . . . Good-day, Mr. Lindstedt . . ."

Niels went to the stable to feed his horses.

Then he left town, following the road to the east, along the Muddy River, walking.

A feeling of general dissatisfaction possessed him. This was the first time he had spent more than a few hours in town. He had often had the same feeling before.

On his land he was master; he knew just how to act. Here in town, people did with him as they pleased. Store-keepers tried to sell him what he did not want; at the hotel they fed him with things he did not like. The banker with whom he had sought no interview dismissed him at his own imperious pleasure . . .

And the attitude of superiority everybody assumed . . . They were quicker at repartee – silly, stupid repartee: and they were quick at it because they did not do much else but practise it . . .

Women want to be taken, not adored . . .

Mrs. Vogel perhaps, had he wanted her, might be taken . . . Had he wanted her . . . But he had wanted her!

Yet, she had been in the city: and he had not even known it! She had simply disappeared from his horizon . . .

Would such a thing have been possible with Ellen? It would not . . .

He was impatient to get back to the farm . . . Yet he waited where he had crouched down on the bank of the little river . . .

In front of the hotel he sat in his wagon for half an hour before Mrs. Vogel appeared.

"Why, Niels," she exclaimed, "what a team! . . . I'll be out in a minute."

Shortly after, she appeared again. She wore a plain skirt and a waist, carrying her coat over her arm.

When Niels reached for her suitcase, he noticed that several faces had crowded together behind the glass of the door to the lobby. She climbed over the wheel to the seat by his side.

He had never been quite so close to her before; he had never, since he had been a man, been so close to any woman on earth. And this was an artful woman. She enveloped him in a cloud of delicate scents; she smiled at him from her black, beady eyes when the horses bent into their collars and stretched the traces.

They left the town.

He felt as if he were thrown back into chaos . . .

He had thought that he had fought all this down years ago. His conquest had been a specious one. He had conquered by the aid of a fickle ally; circumstance . . . Something was still stirred in him by this woman, something low, disgraceful . . .

In spite of his twenty-nine years he was not experienced enough to know that this something would have been stirred in him by any woman . . . And this was an artful woman: artful enough not to speak . . .

The sun had set. They passed the point where the trail branched off to the east, angling over the sand-flats. This was wild land, overgrown with low brush which was washed by the almost palpable bluish light of the high half moon. Every now and then a patch of silvery-grey wolf-willow glistened softly in the dark-green cushions of symphoricarpus.

Niels slipped off the wagon. "I'll walk for a while," he said.

And he did so, the filly that followed her mother whisked her furry tail and shot ahead.

He took his supper out and munched away while he walked, the lines idly slung over his shoulders.

Soberly, now, the filly trotted ahead of him.

Hours went by . . . At last Niels spoke.

"I am going to stop," he said. "I want to feed. I suppose you had better lie down;" – vaguely addressing the woman on the seat.

She nodded, almost overcome with sleep.

He pulled out on the side of the trail, in the lee of a copse of willows . . .

Slowly he stripped the harness off his horses, tied their halter-shanks to the wheels, poured oats on a piece of canvas, and spread the hay.

The woman climbed into the box of the wagon. She smiled and nearly stumbled with sleepiness.

"Won't you lie down yourself?" she asked.

"No," he answered. "It isn't worth while . . ."

She smiled up at him, half asleep already, as he stood between the horses by the wagon-box; and just as she was on the point of closing her eyes, she reached languidly up with one hand, pushed his cap off, and rumpled his hair.

It was as if a stream of liquid fire had run through his veins. Completely bewildered he stepped back . . .

Grey dawn crept over the eastern world . . .

Niels who had lain down after all, on the ground, got up and stretched. Then he yawned and reached for the harness which was hanging over the tongue of the wagon.

He glanced at the woman. She was sound asleep. Somehow her artificiality was half stripped away; she looked like a relic of ancient temptations . . .

A few minutes later the wagon was jolting along; the filly nickered, prancing about on her stilt-like, heavy-jointed legs . . .

In front of him, by-and-by, rose the sun, lifting himself out of glowing vapours. All about stretched the sandy margin of the Marsh, level as a prairie field, for the hollows were filled with snow-white mists. It was chilly.

Thus Niels was nearing his homestead with unexpected freight . . .

The woman behind him stirred, awoke, sat up. Niels did not turn. Several minutes passed.

Then her voice, shot with mocking notes, "Don't look back now. I am going to fix myself up a little." But it sounded more like a summons to look than like anything else.

Niels chose to disobey the implication rather than the explicit words . . .

Higher and higher rose the bluff in front. The woman claimed his help in climbing forward to the seat.

"I'm going to change horses," Niels said. "I can trot the Clydes . . ."

They reached his gate; the view on the yard widened out. In front of the stable Bobby was harnessing the other team. Beyond, in the horse-lot, the older filly set up a piercing call . . .

No sooner did Bobby see his employer than he came running to open the gate. At sight of Mrs. Vogel he stared. Then, with his high-pitched, boyish voice, he said "Hello!"

"Hello, Bobby," Mrs. Vogel answered. "My, but you've grown!"

"What were you going to do?" Niels asked.

"Haul hay for the loft."

"No, wait. I want the Clydes. Turn Jock and Nellie out. I'm taking Mrs. Vogel to her place."

In a few minutes the change of horses was completed.

Mrs. Vogel sat on her seat and looked about, half mockingly, half in admiration.

Niels did not ask her to enter the house. He climbed back to his seat, turned, and drove off the yard. To the south, before they reached the gate, a little vista opened on to a newly built shack.

"What is that?" Mrs. Vogel asked.

"I'm going to take Sigurdsen over," Niels answered. "We've built that shack for him."

"You've surely made progress," the woman said.

Silence again . . .

In a little less than an hour, following the winding bush trails, they emerged on a clearing. There were two groups of buildings: the near ones those of a pioneer homestead, log-cabin, stable, shed; the far ones a little cottage, frame-built, painted white, with a diminutive stable behind.

"This is Bert's place," Mrs. Vogel said. "We'll stop here, please. In the cottage I used to live before I moved altogether into the city."

Niels wondered why a strong man like Rowdle did not homestead rather than buy.

"Bert is lazy," Mrs. Vogel explained. "He's a bachelor. There were thirty acres broken on this place. He'll never break any more . . . No, don't drive in. Just go to the house and call Bert, please."

Niels noticed a pig coming out through the tattered screen-door of the house, grunting. In the one-roomed cabin chickens were picking up crumbs; a second pig was contentedly lying behind a dirty couch. On a sheetless bed, covered with grey blankets that lay in a heap, there reposed the enormous girth of the man. He was just opening his eyes and jumped up.

"Hello, Lindstedt," he said, fumbling under the bed for his shoes. "How are you?"

"I brought Mrs. Vogel over. She's waiting outside."

"The deuce she is," Rowdle grumbled. "Don't let her in. Tell her to wait till I get my pants on."

Niels returned to the gate and reported.

Mrs. Vogel alighted. "Won't you wait for breakfast?" she asked, smiling enigmatically.

"Seems to me," Niels said, "I should have offered you breakfast at my place. I didn't know what this was like."

"No," Mrs. Vogel smiled. "Since you never came three years ago . . . However, it's only a hundred yards to my cottage."

"I am anxious to get back to work."

"Well," said Mrs. Vogel, "don't worry about me. Thanks for the ride. I have enjoyed it." And she held out her hand.

August came; and harvest drew near.

Sigurdsen had moved into the shack on Niels' farm. Niels had bought his stock . . .

Niels was working, brushing more land . . .

Yes, there could be no doubt. His farm was a success. In a material sense he was prosperous beyond his boldest expectations . . . He had made his land; it was his . . . If only . . . But that, too, had to come to a decision. It had to be decided at once; else there would be chaos . . .

On Sunday afternoon he went to see Ellen.

Ellen was waiting for him. She stood at the gate, looking down the winding trail to the south.

Was there something in his face which betrayed him?

Somehow she was different. In her face, too, there was a new expression: something of expectancy, emotion, inner struggle which had disturbed her usual balance.

He was aware of it as soon as he looked into her eye.

He knew more clearly, more convincingly that the moment was at hand. Whether he brought it or not, it was there. In the smile with which she greeted him there was something hunted . . . For the first time in their intercourse this girl awakened in him the protective instincts. More than ever before she was the only woman in the world for him . . .

In silence they went to the accustomed place, that natural bower in the fringe of the bush . . .

As they crossed the yard, imponderable things, incomprehensible waves of feeling passed to and fro between them: things too delicate for words; things somehow full of pain and anxious, disquieting anticipation: like silent discharges between summer clouds that distantly wink at each other in lightning.

The air, too, was charged; its sultriness foreboded a storm. Yet, there was not a cloud in the upper reaches of the atmosphere; only at the horizon there lay, in the far north-west, a white bank which, above the dark cliff of forest, showed a rounded, convoluted outline, its edge blushing with a golden iridescence.

The slightest breeze ambled into the clearing from the east, scarcely perceptible, yet refreshing where it could be felt.

Between the two, as the silence lengthened – between man and woman, boy and girl – the consciousness arose that the other knew of the decision which was at hand: it was almost oppressive. Some step was to be taken, had to be taken at last: it was a tragic necessity no longer to be evaded . . .

Yet neither spoke; each waited for the other. They stood by the chairs which the girl had provided.

Furtive glances stole across, to be averted forthwith. Colour came and went in two faces, imperceptible almost, yet divined.

Then the girl spoke. Her words came hurriedly, precipitately, as if to forestall the arrival of the moment; as if to postpone what was unavoidably coming; as if to plead for a term of grace.

"Shall we sit here?" she said. "Let us have a walk rather, shall we?"

Niels nodded. The appeal in her voice could not be denied.

"Sometimes," the girl went on, still hurriedly, "the bush frightens me. I cannot find the horizon. I want to see wide, open, level spaces. Let's go to the slough."

Again Niels nodded. He did not trust himself to speak. There was no barrier between them: they looked at each other, as it were, stripped of all conventions, all disguises . . .

The moment was coming. It had prepared itself. It was rushing along the lane of time where neither he nor she could escape it. Yes, it was already here. It stood in front of them; and its face was not smiling; it was grimly tragical . . .

"Wait," said the girl. "I'll get my hat." And she slipped past him, into the house.

Half conscious only of his movements he idled back to the yard and stood there, eyes fixed on vacancy.

Dark, green, gloomy, the bush reared all about. Aspen-leaves shivered, revealing their silvery undersides.

"I believe a storm is coming," said the girl, somewhat steadied as she rejoined him, her hat slung by its ribbons over her arm. "I wish it would come while we are out. I like to watch a storm."

They turned and passed into the bush road, side by side.

The tension between them grew less. The moment was coming. It did not depend upon them. Why tremble?

On and on they went; between them peace arose. Both seemed to feel that it was for the very last time: drain what you can to the dregs . . .

The storm, too, was coming. But all the clearer, all the more brilliant was the sky overhead.

First they followed the bush road; then they left it, threading a cattle path which branched off to the left. Birds fluttered up as they touched the bushes: shy birds and bold birds: waxwings, catbirds, tow-hees – these merely flitted away; blackbirds, kingbirds, and jays – these scolded at them, resenting their intrusion into the home of their young. Bush rabbits sprang up and scampered away in a panic: and both of them laughed: laughter released the tension completely.

The cattle path forked: the girl followed one, the boy another; they flitted and ran; whoever was first to arrive at the rejunction of the trails stood and waited for the other, smiling or laughing . . .

They came to the clearing of the little school.

The yard was densely overgrown with raspberry canes which held a profusion of heavy, overripe berries. They picked them, eating as they went or offering handfuls to each other. Not a word did they say, except that now and then the one or the other exclaimed, "Here!" or "Look at that!"

True enough, the moment was coming. But between them had arisen something like a silent compact not to hasten it along; to delay it, rather. That moment was fraught with pain!

They went to the building and peered in through broken window-lights; they laughed at the sight of benches and blackboards; thoughtlessly, happily, as children laugh.

They crossed the road that led north, past the school house, winding through the virgin bush. And just as they were in its centre, they caught a glimpse of a democrat coming from the south. As if in play, fleeing from pursuit, they plunged into the bush beyond. Behind a thicket of hazel-brush they crouched down, laughing, their movements as simultaneous and nearly instinctive as those of a flock of birds.

The democrat rattled up, along the trail, the horses snorting; horses are scary in the bush.

A man's voice sang out, "Hi, you there!"

Silence.

They heard, though they could not see, that the man climbed down from his seat. They looked at each other in mock fright. Evidently the man wished to enquire about the road . . .

In a common, instinctive impulse they rose, flitted deeper into the thicket, to hide, not to be found . . .

Heavy steps crashed through the underbrush, wending this way and that.

The man's voice again. "Well, I'll be doggonned . . ."

Silence.

A woman's voice, "You were mistaken, Jack."

"I saw them as plain as daylight. They're hidding, that's all."

"Well . . ."

The man's steps crashed as he turned to the road. He climbed back to his seat and clicked his tongue. The horses pulled; the vehicle rolled on . . .

Breathlessly two human beings listened, their faces flushed: a boy and a girl . . .

Bent forward, shape of an arrow, a bird peered at them around a screen of foliage.

The girl sprang to her feet and laughed: a loud, mocking laugh, irresistible, so that the boy had to join her: both were flushed with guilt . . .

At the laugh, however, the horses stopped out there on the road.

Boy and girl caught their breath, listened, and once more broke cover and ran, away from the road, flitting this way and that, around thickets and tree trunks . . .

Again the girl stopped, breathless, flushed, but laughing. "Oh Niels!" she sang out, exuberantly, exultantly.

In an instant he was by her side, reaching out for her hand. "Ellen!" His voice is hoarse, intensely serious of a sudden.

"No," she begs. "Not now. Let's be happy!"

But she leaves him her hand.

On they go, following a wider path; sun-spots filter through the leaf-mosiac of the trees, dancing and flitting over their heads. There is hardly room for the two side by side; their shoulders touch.

The slough opens up: a wide expanse, first of meadow, recently cropped; then of sedge, interlaced with low-growing bands of willow.

Far on the other side, a cliff of forest, black, mysterious, threatening . . .

A few hundred yards in front of them rise the haystacks which they had piled a few weeks ago.

Slough and forest are steeped in sweltering sunlight and heat. Higher now looms a dark-grey mass of cloud in the north, edged with enormous, whitish scallops.

They stand and look.

Then the girl heaves a sigh.

"There's the storm," she says. "Let's stay and watch. Let's go to the hay-stacks. We can crawl in when the rain comes. Shall we?"

"Yes," says the boy.

And they cross the edge of the slough, hand in hand.

When they reach the first stack, he scoops out huge armfuls of hay, making a hollow on the south-east side, where the rain will not strike them, a cave, overhung by a roof twenty feet thick.

"Let's get on top," she says.

Without a word he takes hold of one of the ropes weighted with stones which are thrown across the hay to hold it down in a wind. Bracing his feet against the flank of the stack he climbs upward, making steps as he goes by tramping; and then he reaches down with one hand and lifts the girl clear off her feet and pulls her up.

"Now wait," he said when she has a firm foothold; and he repeats the manoeuvre, two, three times.

Then they stand on the top and laugh, looking at each other's flushed faces and beady brows.

The girl puts her hat on, a wide-rimmed hat, the rim bent down at the sides and fastened with ribbons under her chin: her face looks out as from a cavern.

The air is breathless: even the slight, wafting flow from the east has ceased. Nature lies prostrate in expectation of the scourge that is coming, coming. The wall of cloud has differentiated: there are two, three waves of almost black; in front, a circling festoon of loose, white, flocculent manes, seething, whirling . . . A winking of light runs through the first wave of black. A distant rumbling heralds the storm . . .

The two have squatted down in the hay, forgetting themselves. They sit and look. Then a noise as of distant breakers in the surf; the roar of the sea, approaching nearer, nearer.

The bush in front through which they have come stands motionless, breathless, blackening, as the sun is obscured. Birds flit to and fro, seeking shelter, silent . . .

Then a huge suction soughs through the stems. But already the lash of the wind comes down: like the sea in a storm tree tops rise and fall, the stems bending over and down and whipping back again, tossed by enormous pressures. They dance and roll, tumble and rear, and mutely cry out as in pain. And the very next moment the wind hits the stack, snatching the breath from the lips of the two who sit there crouching. A misty veil rushes over the landscape, illumined by a bluish flash which is followed by nearer and nearer growlings and barkings.

Up rises the girl in the storm, holding on to her bonnet with both her hands, leaning back into the wind, her skirt crackling and snapping and pulling at her strong limbs. Once more she laughs, laughs into the storm and sweeps her arm over the landscape, pointing.

The first rain drops, heavy, large, but few, strike against her body. She looks at the man, the boy still crouching at her feet and calls, "Now down!"

They run to the edge of the stack, squat, slide, and make for the shelter which the boy has prepared.

Down comes the rain in a cloud-burst, forming a wall in front of them where they sit in the sheltering cove in which all the fragrance of the meadow is concentrated. Flashes of lightning break on the slough like bombshells; rattling thunder dances and springs.

On sweeps the storm; less and less rain falls; the drops begin to sparkle and glitter; the sun bursts forth. Over the bush huge clouds are lifting their wings; and a playful breeze strikes into the cave where Niels and Ellen still crouch silent . . .

Ellen is looking out, straight ahead, her eyes fixed on she knows not what.

Niels is looking at her, from close by, his face almost touching her shoulder. The longing actually to touch her, to take her in both his arms, grows so strong that his joints ache with it . . . A moment ago he still could have yielded to this longing . . .

But already something has stepped in between them: as if a distance had stepped between them, a great, infinite remoteness not to be bridged . . . As he sits there and looks, it is as if her face were receding and fading from view. And suddenly he is aware that in her eyes there are tears which are quivering on her lashes, white, sun-bleached lashes, before they fall.

The realisation of a bottomless abyss shakes him.

"Ellen," he calls with an almost breaking voice.

The girl slowly rises. "I know," she says. "Don't speak. The moment has come. I know what you want to say. Oh Niels, I am going to hurt you deeply. Let it be as it is, Niels. Why can't you?" She sobs and turns, touching his cheek with her hand. Then almost impatiently, almost angrily, "Oh God, I can't understand it! Why has it got to be like this? I've seen it coming, Niels. Ever since I first saw you, years ago. I knew it would have to come to this! I knew it! I knew it! I did what I could to keep it away; but it did not help. Oh God!" she cries out once more, "I've had only one single friend in my life! And now I must lose him!" And her tears run freely at last; and she makes no longer any attempt to check her sobs.

Niels has risen. He is shaken to his very depths. He does not know what to do, what to say. He stands helpless, sobs pressing from within to be let out.

"Ellen . . ." he stammers at last.

At that the girl sinks down before him. "Niels," she implores, "it is hard, oh so hard! I cannot! . . . Niels, promise . . . promise that you will let things remain as they are. Come, come . . ." She reaches for his hand and strokes it. "I shall be all alone again, Niels. Promise that you will not say another word!"

Niels stands ghastly white. His knees shake under him. Once more he stammers, "Ellen . . ."

"At least to-day, Niels," she begs; "promise that at least to-day you will not say another word . . ."

"I won't," he breathes.

"Thanks," she says, "thanks." And she feels for her handkerchief to dry her eyes.

"Let's go," she says as she rises to her feet and smiles at him. "The rain's over. It is beautiful now. Let us take the road."

So they went home through the bush where the drops showered down upon them as the breeze ran through the leafy tops of trees.

They went in silence: Niels as through a vacant dream devoid of feeling. It was Ellen who reached for his hand as if begging forgiveness.

At Ellen's gate they stopped.

"Niels," Ellen said, "will you believe me when I tell you that I know? What you wish can never be. When I can, I shall tell you. If it's any comfort to you, you may know I shall never marry. You've been my only friend. I've suffered, Niels, when sometimes you did not come. I know why you have stayed away when you did. Because you, too, felt that at last something like this would be coming. I've dreaded it; I've dreaded it more than I can tell. Let things remain as they are. Don't leave me alone. You will come again? Promise me, Niels, promise that you will come again!"

Niels nodded and went on his way . . .

Niels sat in the granary on his farm. The house was distasteful to him . . . Bobby had gone away in the morning, on horseback, as he often did. Sigurdsen looked after the stock on such days . . .

Not only the house was distasteful to him: his yard, his stable, his farm . . . He wished it were winter and he were out, fighting the old, savage fight against the elements . . .

He did not understand what had happened to him. He did not enquire into it. It was final . . .

He was hiding like a wounded beast. Bobby might soon be back. Sigurdsen would come, hobbling about, bent on his stick . . . Niels wanted to be left alone.

The hours went by; it grew dark. What awakened him from his lethargy was the impatient lowing of his cows at the gate.

There, he thought, I have two men on the place; one I pay, the other I feed; and neither feels called upon to open the gate and to water my cattle . . .

He went and attended to them; for half an hour he pumped water into the trough. The horses had drunk it dry.

Two of the cows had to be milked. Let it go? He drove them into the cow-lot, and with an angry feeling against Bobby he went and fetched the pails . . .

Then he looked into the stable. The mangers were empty; at the noise he made the horses came pressing in through the door from the horse-lot.

He lighted a lantern and reached for a fork.

As he did so, he heard Bobby's merry whistling from the corner of the Marsh. He had half finished his task when the boy joined him, grinning sheepishly.

"I'm late," said Bobby. "I thought Sigurdsen would look after things. I asked him to."

"Sigurdsen hasn't been around," Niels said curtly. But he felt ashamed of the slur on the old man this implied. "Better go and see whether there's anything wrong."

He was closing the door of the stable when Bobby returned, running. "I believe the old man's dying," he said.

Sigurdsen lay in his clothes, not on the bed, but on the floor, his head reversed, his legs curved back, sprawling; his body bent hollow so it did not touch the floor;

his thick, swollen tongue lolling out of his mouth. A rattling noise came from his throat.

Niels and Bobby undressed him and lifted him up on his bed.

Bobby was frightened. "Is he going to die?"

"I think so. Better go to bed. I shall watch."

Niels pulled the one chair to the side of the bed and sat down for the long night.

Why did it have to be to-day? When life was hard to bear as it was . . .

What was life anyway? A dumb shifting of forces. Grass grew and was trodden down; and it knew not why. He himself – this very afternoon there had been in him the joy of grass growing, twigs budding, blossoms opening to the air of spring. The grass had been stepped on; the twig had been broken; the blossoms nipped by frost . . .

He, Niels, a workman in God's garden? Who was God anyway? . . .

Here lay a lump of flesh, being transformed in its agony from flesh in which dwelt thought, feeling, a soul, into flesh that would rot and feed worms till it became clay . . .

Once a woman had been, his mother. She had been young, pretty, pulsating, vibrating in every fibre with life: at best she was a heap of brittle bones . . .

Did she live on? In him, Niels? . . .

Yes, that was it! The highest we can aspire to in this life is that we feel we leave a gap behind in the lives of others when we go. To inflict pain on others in undergoing the supreme pain ourselves: that is the sum and substance of our achievement . . . If that is denied, we shiver in an utter void . . . Thus would he shiver . . .

Niels laughed in the presence of death . . .

This man had loved him. Yes, after all it was good that he could die . . . Could die without seeing the horrors that were sure to come . . .

Niels sat and watched. The body relaxed. The heart was still beating . . . And then it stopped . . .

Quietly he got up and drew a blanket over it that had been he.

An hour or so later he went to the house, wakened Bobby, and sent him to town to see the doctor and get the death certificate . . .

He held the gate open when Bobby drove out.

Then he turned his face north, to the farm where Ellen lived. He had, in a flash, made up his mind to plead once more the cause of life . . .

He found her at the house, preparing breakfast.

"Come in," she said when she saw him at the door.

"Sigurdsen is dead," Niels said slowly.

She looked at him with wide, haggard eyes.

He straightened. "He's dead. Let that go. I am alive. I want to speak about myself."

"Niels," Ellen pleaded, "I sent you away last night. I am not going to put you off again if you insist. But had we not better wait?"

"No. I have got to know. I have to get this clear. I am quiet. There is no use in waiting."

"Very well," she acquiesced. "Sit down. I shall listen."

"Ellen," he broke out, "there's a house on my place, the best-built, roomiest house for many miles around. In it there are things that I've bought through these years and which I've never used. There's a sewing machine; there's a washing machine; there are curtains, packed away; there are parcels with towels, bed-linen, table-cloths, and what not. Do you know for whom that house was built, for whom those things were bought?"

"I know," she said, smiling sadly. "I have feared it ever . . . ever since I saw the house."

"Feared it?" he repeated . . . "Ellen, when I filed on that homestead, I did so because it was near to you. When I fenced it, I drove your name into the ground as the future owner with every post. When I cleared my field, I did it for you. When I dug the cellar of the house, I laid it out so it would save you work. When I planned the kitchen and the dining room, I thought of nothing but saving you steps. When I bought the lumber, I felt I was taking home presents for you. Whenever I came driving over the Marsh, I saw you standing at the gate to welcome me. When I laid out the kitchen garden, I thought of you bringing in the greens. Ellen, no matter what I have done during these years, it was done with you in mind."

An infinitely soft expression had come into the face of the girl; slowly she reached out with her hand and laid it on his where it was resting on the table that stood between them.

"Yes," she said. "All that I know, Niels. At least I often thought so. I could not help it. What was I to do? I always feared that one day I was going to give you pain. Yet I hoped you would understand . . ."

"Understand?" he repeated. "Understand what?"

"That between me and any man there can be but friendship."

"Friendship?" he echoed dully.

"Yes. You know I was lonesome. You know how lonesome I was. There were plenty who were willing to make me feel less lonesome. They wanted marriage. Long ago there were plenty of them. Your very friend Nelson had been among them. I turned all of them away, harshly, so that a few weeks after my father's death I was the most lonesome woman in the district. You came. I did not turn you away. I liked you. I had liked you from the day when I first met you. I was fond of you. I am fond of you. As of a brother. I would not do anything that might hurt you if I could help myself. You must feel that. Don't you, Niels?" – Her voice was as full of passionate pleading as his had been.

"Yes, but . . ." And in helpless non-comprehension he shrugged his shoulders.

"Oh, it is so hard to explain," Ellen exclaimed. "Niels, I do not want to lose you. I am fighting for you with all my strength. I know a farmer needs a woman on the place. Take me as a sister. Marry another woman. But let us remain what we are!"

"Another woman . . ."

"Yes, Niels, you are thirty. You cannot but have seen other women. Surely you have sometimes thought of others but myself! Surely there are plenty of girls in the world; there are some in this settlement that will gladly be your handmaiden, that will jump at the chance of becoming the wife of a man like you."

Niels sat and brooded. He tried to follow her thought. He even tried to visualise a fulfilment of what she suggested. His vision was a blank. He shook his head.

"Ellen," he said, "before your father died, before I had filed on my claim, when I was living with Nelson, up in the bush, in winter, in the little shack he had; when I was fresh from the squalour and poverty of the old country – then I used to dream of a place of my own, with a comfortable house, with a living room and a roaring fire in the stove, and a good, bright lamp burning overhead, of an evening. I was sitting with a woman, my wife, in the light of that lamp, when the nightly chores were done; and we were listening to the children's feet on the floor above as they went to bed; and we were looking and smiling at each other. Ellen, always then, in that dream, the woman was you . . . At other times, when I was thinking of my mother . . . How, even when my father was still living, she had to slave away, all day, getting wood, getting water, and taking in washing to pay for the children's clothes – for my father was just a labourer, hiring out from sun to sun; his wages were low, not more than ten, twelve dollars a month the year around; and there were six children to feed . . . And when my father died, she had to go herself, for little wages; and some of her employers were mean to her; but others gave her a pot of beans, or the bones of a roast in addition to her wages – a Krone, a quarter, a day – to take home . . . I still fumed and raged at it in retrospection . . . And I vowed to myself that no wife of mine should ever have to work as she had done. That was why I had come to this country. And when I thought of how I would rather slave and work my fingers to the bone than let my wife, the mother of my children, do one single thing beyond what it would be a pleasure for her to do – then, for six years now, I have always thought of you as that wife. Why was that? What do you think?"

"Oh Niels . . ."

"I will tell you. It was because I loved you, loved you from the very first day that I had seen you. Do you remember? . . . There I sat, at the breakfast table; and you were busy over the stove. I kept watching you; and your father did not like it. I did not know, of course, then; but I knew later on that already I had seen in you the mate of my life . . ."

Ellen smiled a reminiscent smile and nodded. "Yes," she said. "And then . . . Will you listen, Niels? It's a long story; and I don't know whether I can tell it. I don't know whether you will understand. I have to strip myself before you. I have to show you leprous scars in my memory. I will try . . .

"What I must tell you is the story of my mother. Much of it I did not understand at the time. I was a child when these things happened. But I must speak to you as a woman . . .

"You speak of your mother . . . How she used to work and to slave. Probably you know only the least of what she had to go through. You know the outside. You were a boy. Only a girl or a woman can understand another woman. I was a very observant child, old and experienced before my time. I saw and understood many things which even my mother did not know, did not suspect I could understand. She often said, you will understand that one day, when I understood it right then. But some things I did not understand at the time. I saw them, and they lived in my memory; and I came to understand them later . . .

"Niels, if I am to make this thing clear to you, I shall have to speak to you, not as to a man, especially not a man who had hoped to be more to me than a brother. I shall have to forget that I am a young woman. There are things which even between older people are skipped in silence. If you are to understand, I must strip my soul of its secrets . . . I could not bear to have you look at me, Niels, while I tell them. But I know – I think I know what this means to you. I will do it if you wish . . ."

Niels rose and walked up and down through the room. Then he took his chair, turned it, and sat down, facing the window that looked out on the yard.

"Thanks," she said.

"I was nine years old when we came from Sweden. My father's people had been day labourers in the rye-districts of Soedermanland. They were prosperous in their small way. They had a little house of two rooms and a piece of land, half an acre maybe. They fattened a pig every year and kept a cow and a few hens. On the land they grew garden truck for the city.

"My father was also a farm hand as you say in this country; but he had to pay rent for the house in which we lived. There were three children, all girls; and my mother was weakly. Her illness had involved him in debt.

"Slowly, through years of discussion, against my mother's wish, the plan to emigrate took shape. My grandfather proposed to keep mother and children while father went out to explore the land. My father declined.

"But one day he proposed to leave the children and to take only mother. At that my mother revolted. But in another year he wore her resistence down till she consented to leave the two younger girls and to take only me. I was her first-born; she would not listen to leaving me behind. She always spoke of letting the others follow as soon as possible.

"But my grandparents were very fond of children. They were not old yet. They had never had but the one child of their own. And when they agreed to take my two sisters, they made their bargain, made it with my father: they were to be in the place of father and mother to them; and my parents were not to have any rights whatever over them any more. He did not tell my mother, thinking that she would give in later when she had got used to having one child only. She never did, of course. The separation remained to her a lifelong sorrow. But as you will see, that was the least she had to bear . . .

"We came away. My father had no difficulty in finding work in this country. He was strong and healthy. I don't know by what chance he came to Odensee. He had been working on a German estate in Sweden. He understood German well and spoke it a little; probably that was the reason. At Odensee he rented a one-roomed shack with three acres of land where he grew potatoes and raised pigs. He worked on the big farms in summer; and in winter he went to town, till he took up his homestead three years later.

"The place he rented in Odensee was part of a quarter section of almost wild land, south of the village. It belonged to an old man who had moved to town. The rest of the land was rented to a man by name of Campbell who had married a Swedish girl. He is now living north of here, on a place of his own; you may know him.

"As if it were yesterday I remember the first meeting between my mother and Mrs. Campbell. We had moved into the place a day or so before. The Campbells' house stood a quarter of a mile east of ours, a large, unpainted frame building half gone to ruin. The man was in the cattle business; but he was not yet making money. There were three acres of land broken near the house; and he had planted them to potatoes. There were four children. The woman had to look after the little crop, for the man used his business as a pretext to be hardly ever at home. So, from the first, I got used to seeing the woman work in the potato-patch.

"Since my mother knew neihter English nor German, she was lost in the settlement. She had heard that Mrs. Campbell was Swedish. And, being in a strange country the ways of which she did not know, she was anxious to become acquainted with somebody she could talk to.

"It was in the afternoon of a summer day when we crawled through the fence of our yard and crossed over through the brush to the potato-patch.

"As I said, there were four children on the place. The oldest one was a girl of seven or eight: and she was watching the smaller ones – two were twins – while she picked weeds from the rows of the plants.

"The mother, a big, bony woman, was hoeing between the rows. She did not show any pleasure at meeting my mother.

"You have four children! my mother said.

"Yes, the woman replied with an exaggerated groan of disgust; and if another were coming, I'd walk off into the bush . . .

"My mother probably betrayed surprise; for the woman laughed and added, when a woman has got to work like a man, children are just a plague . . .

"When we came home, mother cried. She was thinking of the two little ones she had left behind; I knew; and I went to her and patted her hand, begging her not to cry.

"I knew and understood more, in a childish way, than the grown-ups thought. When you change your country, at that age, it somehow gives you an insight into things and a curiosity beyond your years.

"I asked her, Mother, where do children come from?

"I had often asked her that question before, and she had always answered, God sends them! – But this time she said, When men and women live together, children come. That is nature.

"Soon after, I was sent to school and began to learn English. I also began to see many things. Soon we had a cow; and then two or three; and half a dozen pigs. And my mother was working as hard or harder than Mrs. Campbell.

"My parents spoke in my presence as if I did not exist. You have noticed that that is the rule in these settlements where houses are mere cabins in which grown-ups and children are crowded together.

"So, from many things that were said and from some that I saw I inferred that mother expected shortly to have another child and that that greatly worried her; but even more did it worry my father. He began to speak still more curtly to my mother; and he treated her as if she were at fault and had committed a crime. He prayed even more than before, both more frequently and longer. Gradually my mother began to get into a panic about her condition.

"So, one day, taking me along, she went over to see that woman in the potato-patch once more.

"A number of things were said back and forth which I remember with great distinctness but which have nothing to do with my story.

"At last Mrs. Campbell laughed out loud. Of course, she said, it's plain to see by now. It's a curse. But I can tell you I wouldn't be caught that way. Not I! I'm wise.

"But what can you do? my mother exclaimed. He comes and begs and says that's what God made them male and female for. And if you want to hold your man . . .

"Again the woman laughed. I see her now, standing

there in the potato-patch, straight up, with her red face to the sun and her hair blowing in the wind as she put her hands on her hips and held her sides with laughing . . .

"I was only ten years old. But I tell you, I knew exactly what they were talking about. And right then I vowed I should never marry. I was furious at the woman and afraid of her.

"You're innocent all right, she said at last contemptuously. I don't mean it that way, child. But when I'm just about as far gone as you are now, then I go and lift heavy things; or I take the plow and walk behind it for a day. In less than a week's time the child comes; and it's dead. In a day or two I go to work again. Just try it. It won't hurt you. Lots of women around here do the same.

"So, when we came home, my mother took some heavy logs, dragged them to the saw-buck, and sawed them. I begged her not to do it; but even I could see that she was desperate.

"Next day she was very sick. I was sent to the house of the German preacher in the village. And when I was allowed to come back, my mother was at work again on the land. She looked the picture of death; but she was cheerful. My father prayed more than ever.

"Once again the thing happened while we were still at Odensee. The Campbells had moved away to where they are living now; and mother had absolutely no intercourse any longer with anybody. Mother dreaded my father's visits at home by this time.

"Then, early in the spring of the third year, we moved out here. There were no buildings. We camped. Our few things stood under the trees. There was no tent even. Nothing but the sky.

"My father began to clear the yard and to pile logs for building. Mother worked with axe and brute force, helping him. Even I had to help, lifting and pulling when the logs were too heavy for them.

"Then haying time came. My father bought a team of oxen and a mower. He had no wagon yet. The hay was carried over in huge bundles slung with ropes. Mother and I did just as much, together, as my father.

"But don't think for a moment that I am complaining about the work. I liked it. I was strong. Already I dreamt of one day having a farm all by myself, with mother to keep me company.

"Then the stable was built; just as it stands to-day. My father hated make-shifts. When it was up, we moved into one end of it, the other being occupied by the cows and oxen. Late in the fall, when my father had bought a wagon, he hauled some cheap lumber and built the implement shed, just as it stands to-day. We can make out where we are, he said; but oxen and machinery cost money.

"In winter he went to town again; and we were left alone in the bush. Not a soul knew we were there. The school had not been built.

"Mother cried a good deal; more and more she confided in me, treating me as an equal. Oh, he is hard, she would say of father; as hard as God! And to think that I shall never see my little ones again!

"And she began to speak of me. You are big and strong, she said. You are as good as a boy. Don't ever marry. Marriage makes weak . . .

"And in my childish understanding I promised fervently.

"I remember how I used to sit on the bare, frozen ground and to press my head against her knees where she sat, close to the little stove, on the only chair in the place. At night I sprang up every hour or so and replenished the stove, or we should have frozen . . .

"Towards the end of winter my father came home and began to clear land. From then on we worked with him in the bush, piling the wood and the brush, often wading through snow knee-deep. The work was much too hard for my mother; but I thrived on it. My father often praised me; but already his praise had become distasteful. There was a note of reproach in it for mother. I tried to hide how much of the work I did, how little mother.

"In spring he broke a patch of ground; and we picked the stones and piled the roots.

"That year the school was built. A teacher came out and boarded with Sterners, straight north from it . . .

"As soon as my father had seeded his patch, mother began to beg that I should be sent to school. But my father would not let me go; he wanted to build a house. Not that he thought the house so necessary; but he intended to buy a team of horses – the two old mares that I still have; it's only ten years ago, you know – so he could haul cordwood in winter and make more money.

"The house, a one-roomed shack – it is the granary now – was not quite finished when harvest time came; there was no roof on it, no floor in it yet. My father went away; and mother and I cut the barley with the mower and tied it by hand. The cattle and oxen could still stay outside; so we carried the bundles into the stable, to be threshed by hand when my father came home.

"Still, mother insisted on my going to school now. I went. The teacher was a young girl, not more than eighteen years old; but she let me come whenever I could. She treated me as a grown-up, as indeed I was. When I was at school – for an hour a day at most – she gave me all her time. And one day she came to see mother and told her she would put me through my entrance if I could attend for one full year; I should become a teacher myself because I was so gifted.

"But I had already made up my mind to become a farmer, though not a farmer's wife. I liked horses and cows and pigs and chickens and could handle them. I was strong; and I was not afraid of work . . .

"When my father came home, I stopped school, of course. He brought horses along.

"It's no use to detail to you any further the growth of the farm; you know as much of that as I do . . .

"I remember one day in the spring of the following year. Mother had been very ill for several days. She had again been lifting things; and my father had taken a little box into the bush to bury. But she had got up and made breakfast, in spite of my protest. You go and help father, she had said; and I had gone out. And when I returned to the house, my father followed me.

"This shack looks a disgrace to the place, he said in a matter-of-face tone when he entered. You better go at white-washing it to-day.

"Mother looked a protest, appealingly.

"But he shrugged his shoulders. Poor people have to work, he said. We'll spare you from the field. Ellen and I will attend to the seeding. I'll mix the white-wash for you before we go.

"We had breakfast; and when my father had left the room, I lingered behind and whispered, Don't you do it! You go to bed!

"Oh, mother moaned, I hate him! I hate him!

"But the worst is to come. The thing that makes marriage for me an impossibility; that makes the very thought of it a disgust which fills me with nausea.

"I know, Niels, if I tell it, it will ever after stand between us. I hope it will change your feelings towards me into those of a brother. I feel sure that no man can still be the lover of a woman who has spoken so plainly to him about such things.

"This house had been built meanwhile. I had grown. I was seventeen years old by that time. Mother had become a mere ghost of herself. She was dragging herself about; she could not get up for weeks at a stretch. Always she suffered from terrible backaches.

"One night when I had gone to bed in that room there I could not sleep. I was so worried that I was almost sick myself.

"Mother came in and dragged herself to the bed. It took her half an hour to undress; she lay down with a moan.

"My father followed her. I acted as if I were asleep; not in order to spy on my parents; but to save mother worry about me. My father got ready to go to bed himself. As a last thing before blowing the lamp he bent over me to see whether I was asleep. Then he knelt by his bed and prayed, loud and fervently and long.

"Suddenly I heard mother's voice, mixed with groans, Oh John, don't.

"I will not repeat the things my father said. An abyss opened as I lay there. The vile, jesting, jocular urgency of it; the words he used to that skeleton and ghost of a woman . . . In order to save mother, I was tempted to betray that I heard. Shame held me back . . .

"Once she said, still defending herself, You know, John, it means a child again. You know how often I have been a murderess already. John, Please! Please!

"God has been good to us, he replied; he took them . . .

"And the struggle began again, to end with the defeat of the woman . . . That night I vowed to myself: No man, whether I liked him or loathed him, was ever to have power over me!

"A few months later haying time came again. Mother went on the stack. Soon after she went to bed, never to rise again . . .

"And now, Niels, if you still can, ask me once more to be your wife. But if you do, it will cut our friendship even."

Niels stood up.

"When death came," Ellen went on, "as a great relief to her, you may believe it came as a relief even to me."

"Three or four days before the last my mother – to me she had become a tender, sweet, and helpless creature; to him a living indictment, I hope – mother, I say, called me and whispered, Ellen, whatever you do, never let a man come near you. You are strong and big, thank God. Make your own life, Ellen, and let nobody make it for you!

"I sank down by the side of her bed; and I lifted this hand up to God and said, mother, there is one man who is different from the others. I hope he will be my friend and brother. But I swear to God and to you he shall never be more!

"Her head sank back on the pillow; and her thin, transparent hand lay on my head."

Niels turned and went to the door. For a moment he held the knob; then he shrugged his shoulders convulsively and went out.

Ellen sprang up and ran to the door. "Niels!"

He stopped without looking back.

"Niels," she repeated, "promise that you will come back. Not now. Not within a day or a week. I know you can't. But I shall be so lonesome. You must fight this down. Don't leave me alone for the rest of my days. Promise that you will come back . . ."

"I shall try," he stammered and left the yard.

He did not see that over that farmyard there followed him a girl, her hand pressed to her bosom, tears in her eyes; nor that, at the gate, she sank to the ground and sobbed . . .

CHAPTER FOUR

Mrs. Lindstedt

ONE NIGHT, late in the fall, Nelson came with Hahn, his German neighbour. Both were on horseback, driving a big bunch of steers which Nelson had sold and which he had to deliver at Minor.

"Hello, Lindstedt,' he sang out while he was circling his drove, spurring his horse in wild-west style. "For God's sake, open your gate. Let us drive these creatures in on your yard. They're wild as can be. We've got to rest our horses. We haven't had dinner yet. They take to the bush every chance they get. We can't stop while they're out in the open . . ."

Niels did as requested.

And as the two riders put their heels into the flanks of their frenzied mounts and once more circled the drove, the steers tore into the enclosure of the yard, racing around it, along the fence, their heads lowered, bellowing with excitement. There were over thirty of them: round, fat animals that had all their spirit left after seventeen miles of road.

As soon as Bobby caught sight of the men, he busied himself preparing a second supper: he was frying eggs and cutting bread of which by chance there was a supply in the house. Every few minutes he came to the door to look admiringly out into the turmoil on the yard.

"Thank the Lord!" Nelson's voice boomed when the gate swung shut. "That was a piece of work, I can tell you, Lindstedt. Thank the Lord, there's no more bush for a while. All day long we've sighed for this corner. Out on the Marsh you can see the beggars. Hi! What's that? Your own cattle coming?"

From the south-west, Niels' little herd came slowly home, a cow stopping and lowing for water through the dusk that rose over the Marsh.

"Where's your cow-lot?" Nelson asked.

"In the bluff."

"You don't mean to say they've got to go over the yard?"

"I don't see what else we can do . . ."

"Man alive, they'll tear them to pieces."

"Take the fence down outside," Hahn advised.

So the three men ran to pull each a fence-post out of the ground. The herd was driven through the gap, and the posts replaced as best it could be done.

"Well, you scamp," Nelson called at sight of Bobby when they went to the house. "So this is where you keep yourself instead of helping your brother-in-law?"

Bobby grinned. "I get real wages here."

"Sure, sure," Nelson agreed noisily. "Lindstedt's a rich man. What's that I hear?" – Turning to Niels. – "You've got full-blooded Percherons they say?"

"Yes, four."

"Let's see." And he, Hahn, and Niels went out again.

The steers were quieting down. But the horses were all the more excited by the unusual noise. With flashing eyes the gelding looked at the intruders; the fillies were racing about, their heads raised, and nickering in their babyish voices.

"Isn't he a beauty?" Nelson said as he looked at Jock by the light of a lantern.

"Yea," Hahn drawled. "That's the kind to have."

"What's the matter with you?" Nelson asked as they sat at the supper table. "Why don't you ask how Olga is and what we're doing in our backwoods country?"

"Well," said Niels, "what are you doing?"

"Increasing the population." Nelson laughed boisterously. "Doing our dooty by the country. Hahn here's got twins. I've got a boy. You know about the girl that was born before old man Lund disappeared. That's doing better than you are doing."

"Any new breaking?" Niels asked wearily.

"You bet," Nelson replied. "A little every year. But cattle, that's my real business. To-morrow I'll have twelve hundred dollars in my pocket. Then I'll pay off the loan. And there'll still be sixty head of them left in the bush. Any crop's profit."

"Yea," Hahn drawled, "there's money in cattle if you can put them in the bush. But it's too much work in winter. When summer's over, I want to rest . . ."

"Say," Nelson asked after a while, "how about the gay widow? Ever seen her again?"

"Once," Niels replied monosyllabically.

"Well, I'm astonished she hasn't netted you yet . . ."

They stayed till ten o'clock. At night the road would be free of traffic.

The gate was opened; the two men waited on horseback, outside; and the bellowing herd charged away into the moon-lit Marsh . . .

Settlers were moving into the district, Canadians, Americans, chiefly Germans . . .

Kelm was going to clear an enormous tract north of the creek; to provide work for himself and Bobby during the winter, Niels contracted for a piece of it: he was to get no wages, but the wood instead: he longed to be driving, driving . . .

Heirs had turned up and claimed old man Sigurdsen's property. Niels had harvested the crop on shares . . .

Life was useless; there was no meaning in it . . . no justification . . .

Niels became more and more prosperous. But the

farm owned him; not he the farm . . . It grew according to laws of its own . . .

Niels hauled his wheat . . .

On the second trip out he had a revelation . . .

The very first farm to which he came in the Minor belt was owned by a German of fifteen years' standing.

It was a mild, spring-like day in November, with snow on the ground . . .

As he neared that farm, a strong, full-bosomed girl came from the house and walked across the yard to the pump which stood close to the road, in the corner between barn and fence. With an absent-minded look he noticed that she was peering out for him as he approached.

She was rocking herself on quivering hips as she went. With a few quick strokes of the handle she filled the wooden bucket and then stood, looking at Niels.

In a perverse impulse he stopped his horses right in front of the gate to rest them.

The girl wore shoes; but her legs were bare.

As he stopped, she turned, picked her bucket up, and laughed at him. With her free hand she reached around and raised her skirt, so that her bare legs showed behind to above her knees; and then she walked off, rocking herself on her hips and throwing provocative glances over her shoulder at him where he stood by the side of his load.

A trifle. What troubled him in retrospection was that his first impulse had been to call to her or to run after her. Worse: whenever he pictured that scene to himself – and in spite of all endeavours he did so, often – a wave of hot blood ran through him: he wished for a recurrence of the incident . . .

Then he took himself in hand, started his horses, and muttered, "I am going to the dogs . . ."

Once he fell in with Hahn. Hahn, too, was hauling wheat to Minor, in spite of the fact that he had an elevator closer by. "I've got a friend in Minor," he said in explanation.

He came up with Niels when the latter was resting his horses. He tied his own team behind and climbed on to Niels' load . . .

Niels sat in silence; Hahn talked.

"There's one thing about you, Lindstedt," he said after a while, "which I can't understand. You're getting to be pretty prosperous. Nelson and you are the two most successful fellows among the new settlers. Nelson's married. You haven't even got a woman on the place . . ."

Niels' laugh was bitter; but he said nothing.

"Doesn't it bother you?" Hahn asked.

Niels looked his non-comprehension. "What?"

Hahn laughed, embarrassed. "Well . . . a man needs a woman, doesn't he?"

"Perhaps he does."

"Look here," Hahn exclaimed, "I'm butting into things that are none of my business. But I'd like to know. Do you go to the town or the city?"

"I've never been to the city," Niels said. "I go to town when I've got business there . . ."

"You mean to say you never see a woman . . .?"

"I *see* them . . ."

"But you don't . . . you don't . . ."

Niels frowned. "I don't see what you mean . . ."

Hahn laughed and slapped his thigh. "Say," he exclaimed, "you're a corker! I like you for that . . . Do you mean to say you've never touched a woman? . . ."

"You know," Niels said after a while, "I'm unmarried."

Hahn laughed as if in expostulation to the sky . . .

In town, Hahn stayed with Niels. It was evening. Dusk was rising fast.

A short distance beyond the hotel they met three ladies who were still more conspicuously powdered and painted than the ordinary young ladies of western towns. They were dressed in aggressively fashionable style; and they smiled at the two men as they passed them.

"By gosh," Hahn whispered. "Let's hook in, Lindstedt."

"What do you mean?" Niels asked, reddening.

"Let's turn and go after them."

"What for?"

"By jingo," Hahn laughed. "You're as innocent as a new-born babe. They're from the city; they're . . . I don't know enough English to find a word that's decent enough for your tender ears . . . One of them'll be your wife . . . for an hour or so . . ."

"Do you mean," Niels hesitated, "they're whores?"

"Yes," Hahn said, greatly relieved, "that's it."

"I don't intend to marry a whore."

"Man alive!" Hahn fairly shouted. "Ock! What's the use!" And he turned on his heels and left him.

On the way home, during the night, Niels brought the topic up. "Hahn," he said, "is the friend you have in town a woman?"

Hahn laughed. "Of course," he said.

"But you're married . . ."

"Well," Hahn explained, "I'm young and strong. I need something younger and fresher . . . So long as the wife doesn't know, it doesn't hurt her. That's why I go to town and not to the Hefter woman . . ."

"Who's that?" Niels asked brusquely.

"Don't you know? Two and a half miles west of my corner . . . Plenty of customers, nothing to worry about. Amundsen used to go there. Baker. Smith. The boys from the English settlement. That's where Bobby spends most of his Sundays . . ."

Niels sat up as if stung by a needle. "Bobby?"

"What I don't understand," Hahn went on, "is that you should have lived here for years and never seen anything of it. There's one like that Hefter woman in every district. If there weren't, the boys wouldn't leave the girls alone. There's one in yours . . ."

Bobby! Niels felt responsible for the boy.

The next time Bobby asked for the loan of a horse Niels refused it. "Not if you want to go to bad places," he said. "Whenever you want to see your mother, you can have it."

Bobby was as red as blood. "I'll stay at home," he said, slinking off.

From that day on Niels owned the boy body and soul.

Again blizzards blew; snow enveloped the world; blinding winter suns threw an ineffectual glare, over Marsh and bush; a new year ticked off its hours, days, and weeks.

Bobby and Niels worked in the bush, clearing land for Kelm.

Driving, driving . . .

Niels had come to think without bitterness of Ellen; but he felt he could never see her again . . .

When he glimpsed at his old dream, a lump rose in his throat. His muscles tightened when he turned his thoughts away . . .

This gradual negation of his old dream had a curious effect on others: it gave him such an air of superiority over his environment that the few words which he still had to speak were listened to almost with deference. They seemed to come out of vast hidden caverns of meaning. His face, scored and lined so that it sometimes seemed outright ugly, held all in awe, some in terror. Once he heard a man say to Bobby, "I shouldn't care to work for that fellow. I'd be scared of him."

The truth was, lightning flashes of pain sometimes went through his look, giving him the appearance of one insane; or of one who communed with different worlds . . .

A new dream rose: a longing to leave and to go to the very margin of civilisation, there to clear a new place; and when it was cleared and people began to settle about it, to move on once more, again to the very edge of pioneerdom, and to start it all over anew . . . That way his enormous strength would still have a meaning. Woman would have no place in his life.

He looked upon himself as belonging to a special race – a race not comprised in any limited nation, but one that crossed-sectioned all nations: a race doomed to everlasting extinction and yet recruited out of the wastage of all other nations . . .

But, of course, it was only the dream of the slave who dreams of freedom . . .

Once more the thaw-up came. The roads were a morass, the fields a mire . . .

Niels had to go to town for repairs to some of his implements. A blind chance happening, a breakage on his wagon, forced him to stay in town overnight.

He walked the streets. It was warm, almost summer-like: a night that made you feel tired; a night to relax in; a night to stretch, to saunter and linger about . . ."

From the hotel he went east, in the direction of the little park in the bend of the river . . .

One store-window still showed light: that of the drugstore. Aimlessly Niels stopped in front of it, looking at the display of soaps, face-powders, and similar toilet goods . . .

Something within him stirred, something hidden, shameful . . . He turned.

That very moment the door opened, and out stepped a lady. She was on the point of passing him by with a casual glance; but she stood arrested.

Out of a dream, a dismal dream, almost forgotten, sunk in the past, a voice accosted him as he touched his cap.

"Well," the voice said, "if it isn't Niels, of all people! Why, this is nice. I came in from the city to-day, on business regarding my place. I am waiting for the midnight train. Were you out for a walk?"

"Oh, I don't know . . ." There was nothing of his ancient hostility against the woman in his voice.

"Well," she smiled up at him, "let's have that walk anyway. Or are you going out again to-night?"

"No . . . I am staying at the boarding house . . ."

"Good," she exclaimed; and without hesitation she put her hand in his arm and led him along. "How are things?"

"Pretty much as ever . . ."

She laughed: that old, light, silvery laugh of hers; she had not changed.

At the touch of her hand a warm, exciting and yet benumbing current seemed to flow from his arm through his body: a current which slowly wore down resistance . . .

They came to the end of the street.

"How about the park?" she asked. "Is it dry enough to go in?"

"It's dry enough, I think . . ."

So she led him on, crossed the road and entered a foot-path.

There, in the darkness, it seemed that the touch of the hand became a touch of a body. Her head brushed his shoulder . . .

The path wound about, hardly visible in the moonless night. To the left the trees opened up where the river flowed, starlight dimly reflected from its surface; slight, gurgling sounds came up from the margin where there was still a ledge of snow-covered ice . . .

The hold on his arm relaxed; the woman stood in front of him, her head bent back, her face raised to his.

Intensely whispered came the words, "Kiss me!"

Not knowing what he did, he bent down and kissed her; and then, in a paroxysm of passion, he crushed her against his body, released her, and ran off into the night . . .

Two, three hours later, when he had walked the road for many miles, till his joints began to ache, he returned to the boarding house. He had no intention of going to bed. He wanted to sit down for a while and then to leave town, letting his business go . . .

He had done what he had never done before: he had touched a woman: the touch had set his blood aflame. He almost hated the woman for what she had done to him. He wanted oblivion: he wanted death-in-life; and she had kindled in him that which he had hardly known to exist: she had given a meaning and a direction to stirrings within him, to strange, incomprehensible impulses. His instinct urged him to flight: it was impossible that he should see her again. All this was dimly felt, not distinctly told off in thought.

In the lobby of the hotel there were still some loungers. One or two he knew: the doctor, a merchant. They would speak to him . . .

He stood undecided. Should he go to the stable instead? No; he had paid for his room; there he would be alone . . .

The loungers got up from their chairs. It was a minute or so till midnight . . . At midnight the lights would be turned off; he would not be able to see the number of the door to his room . . .

He ran up the stairs; into the uncarpeted corridor where his steps resounded loudly.

He was too late; that very moment the lights went out. He was just aware, before he stood in utter darkness, that somewhere along the corridor a door had opened.

The very next moment he felt two warm, bare arms about his neck; and a warm, soft, fragrant body seemed to envelop his. A hand closed his mouth; he was drawn forward; he yielded . . .

. . .

It was late on the evening of the third day, on Saturday night, that Niels returned to his farm. Bobby had already milked the cows and fed the horses. When he heard Niels calling at the gate, he ran to meet him.

"Hello," he sang out, "I . . ." And he went silent, for he saw the woman on the seat, by the side of his employer.

He swung the gate open and greeted her, smiling in his embarrassed way. "Hello, Mrs. Vogel."

She laughed; and then she corrected him. "I am afraid you'll have to say Mrs. Lindstedt after this."

Bobby's eyes widened till they stared.

Niels sat stiffly and looked straight ahead, without smiling. He was not a tall man; but his breadth of shoulder made him look almost colossal in the darkness, by the side of her.

"Well," said the woman, laughing again, as the horses pulled, "why don't you say something? . . . Congratulate me and . . . him?"

But Bobby said nothing. He was very red as, at the stable, he bent over the traces to unhook them.

Niels sprang to the ground, went heavily to the other side of the wagon, and helped his wife to alight. Then he reached for the two suitcases and led the way to the house. The woman followed.

"So this is the famous White Range Line House?" she said as they entered.

And for the first time Niels spoke. "You will have to put up with things," he said. "This is a bachelor's establishment. We shall get order into it shortly." His speech was brief but not unkind.

In the north room a lamp was burning; its glass was smoky. The four chairs were plain, straight-backed kitchen chairs; it held two beds and a deal table. Overalls and other workingman's apparel were strewn on floor and furniture.

The woman looked about. "That is the kitchen?"

Niels went in, struck a match, and lighted a lamp.

The kitchen held a stove, two chairs, another deal table, and a small array of enamelled pots and dishes, most of them unwashed. A colander contained some eggs, a bag some potatoes, a large baking tin some soggy biscuits, a box by the stove some wood, and a pail on the bench by the door fresh water in which a dipper floated about . . .

She smiled at it all and nodded.

"How about Bobby?" she asked.

"I'll see," Niels said and left her alone.

He went out and stood a moment in the darkness, musing. Then he crossed the yard to the stable.

Bobby had watered the horses and was stripping the harness off their backs, by the light of a lantern. Jock, the Percheron gelding, nickered at sight of his master. Niels stepped in by his side and patted his breast. He seemed lost in thought . . .

Bobby poured oats for the Clydes. Niels took a fork to go for hay.

"How about the sloughs?" he asked of Bobby when they had finished. "Dry enough to plow?"

"I think so."

"All right. By the way, you will have to move to the shack."

"To-night?"

"Just as well. And you'll have to help me in the house for an hour or so. You'll get your meals there, of course . . . I'll raise you five dollars . . ."

"Well," Bobby said . . . "Thanks."

In the house, they carried one of the beds upstairs; another bed which was stored there they put together. The things that littered rooms and landing they removed into the west room which Niels locked.

When they had finished, the east room bore some resemblance to a civilised bed-room though it still looked bare. His own bed Niels had placed on the landing, in front of the door which was locked.

They were looking at their work and finding it good when the woman's voice rang out, "Will you men be ready for supper in about fifteen minutes?"

"I think so," Niels replied.

"I've had my supper," Bobby called.

"Well, have another," the voice said, laughing.

They went down and loaded up with Bobby's things. "You'll have to use a lantern," Niels said, "till there's time to send to town for a lamp. I forgot."

"That's all right." And Bobby shouldered his mattress.

. . .

At supper, which had been set on the oil-cloth-covered table in the large, bare north room, Bobby kept casting furtive glances at the woman presiding.

She had changed into a silky sort of dressing gown the like of which he had never seen in his life. When she reached for anything on the table, she gathered the wide, flowing sleeve with the other hand to prevent its brushing over the dishes. The lapping panel of the gown that covered her breast fell back as she did so and revealed a white, round shoulder with a pink silk ribbon over it and the lace-trimmed edge of some undergarment below her throat. When she saw Bobby's stare, she smiled and folded the panel back into place.

Bobby looked at Niels who sat there sternly, looking straight ahead and chewing absent-mindedly a freshly baked biscuit. When Bobby pushed his chair back and rose, his eye fell on a suitcase standing open by the wall – the contents of which, the appurtenances of modern feminity, made him blush to the roots of his hair.

Awkwardly he stumbled out and mumbled, "Good-night."

On Sunday many things were done in the house, Bobby being banished to stable and shack.

Niels looked forbidding; Mrs. Lindstedt went about the rooms, busy with curtains and things.

Bobby felt lost and went at last to call on the new neighbours to the south . . .

In the afternoon, Niels strolled all over his farm; his wife had lain down for a nap.

When Bobby returned, late at night, after supper, Niels gave him his directions for the morning. He did so in a softer, almost indulgent voice; with few words, but words which sounded as if he wished to conciliate an ally in a struggle to come . . .

Moday morning Bobby walked behind the drag-harrow; Niels rode the seeder.

They had worked for some hours when along the edge of the field a female figure appeared, dressed in a light, washable frock, with a "tango" coat over her shoulders, her chestnut-red hair flaming in the morning sun. Her eyes smiled at Bobby; and when Niels came by, she picked her way over the soft, brown seed-bed.

He stopped and looked at her.

"Well," she asked, her whole face dimpling up, "how does it feel?" And she went around the machine, to his side, resting her elbows on the seedbox, leaning against him.

For a moment silence. Then, as with an effort, "How does what feel?"

"Everything . . . Being married . . ."

He looked ahead and did not reply.

She cast a quick glance at Bobby; and, since his back was still turned, she reached up with her hand, rumpled Niels' hair, raised herself on her toes, kissed his ear, and whispered, "Oh, I love you; you're so big and strong! How I love you! I love you so much it hurts!"

An embarrassed look flitted over his face. "Don't . . . the boy . . ."

"Oh," she cried, "go, you big bear!" She pushed his shoulder and laughingly picked her way to the edge of the field and sat down on a boulder.

Never once did Niels look at her; but she followed him with her eyes. When Bobby passed her, she smiled.

Niels was a prey to a whirl of thoughts and feelings . . . Already his marriage seemed to him almost an indecency . . .

He looked back at the thing that had happened, as if it had happened to another man.

Many points he did not understand . . . The astonished look of the woman, for instance, when, the morning after the night, he had asked her about the arrangements for their marriage. At first she had laughed. "Marry?" she had asked with widening eyes. As if there could be any question about the marriage! And, after some time, as if a re-adjustment of a preconceived idea had taken place, she, too, had treated that point as settled, as a matter of course. Then she had suddenly fallen about his neck, half laughing, half crying. "Oh," she had whispered, "how I have wanted this! I have wanted it for years; for seven years, I believe. Ever since I first met you. But Niels, listen! Promise me that you will never leave me. Never, never! Not for a single day! It would be terrible if you did, Niels. Terrible for you and me. Promise, Niels."

He had not understood then; he did not understand now . . .

She loved him; had loved him for seven years: so what was there to fear? Everything was plain and simple. He, it is true, could no longer respond with any great passion. But he, too, had wanted her once, would want her again. He would do his duty . . .

The other woman had sent him away . . . The other woman? . . . The world went black before his eyes . . .

He put the thought aside with an effort. His look assumed a steely expression; his mouth was set in rigid lines. He looked old.

"Come on, there, Nellie," he shouted and swung his whip, the first time he had ever done so, over the Percherons. Jock jumped as he heard its swish . . .

From the neighbours where Bobby had carried the news, it had flown abroad. The settlement was astir with it: Lindstedt, the powerful Swede, had married the Vogel woman!

"Well, I'll be jiggered!" Mrs. Lund had exclaimed at Odensee.

"Yooh-hooh!" Kelm had yodled across the creek.

The timid young settlers south-east of Niels' had looked at each other, almost frightened . . .

Not a person called at the White Range Line House . . . Nor did the pair call on any one . . .

Just now, of course, everybody was busy seeding; but even after seeding was over . . .

Niels broadcasted a mixture of grasses in his slough. Perhaps, if he seeded grass, he could get along without additional hay . . .The other woman held the permits . . .

But the meeting had to come, of course.

One evening, still in the early summer, he went to see Kelm on business; and as he drove over the bridge, into the road-chasm, where the bush still stood in its primeval thickness, he saw her team coming, water-barrels in the wagon-box . . .

His heart stood still. There was no way of turning. He had to go to the side to give her the road. His horses stopped, and he sat, his head bowed low.

Slowly her team approached, came up, and stood . . . For a moment silence.

Then her voice, a mere whisper, full of anguish, "Niels, how could you! . . ."

Without answering he drove past . . .

Summer went on its way.

More and more Niels realised that the woman who had become his wife was a stranger to him . . .

It had not taken above three days before he knew that, if ever there had been in him the true fire that welds two lives together, it had died down. He had made an effort to conquer something like aversion . . . It was his duty to make the best of a bad bargain . . .

Distasteful though they were, he satisfied her strange, ardent, erratic desires. Often she awakened him in the middle of the night, in the early morning hours, just before daylight; often she robbed him of his sleep in the evening, keeping him up till midnight and later. She herself slept much in daytime. He bore up under the additional fatigue . . .

Whenever she came, she overwhelmed him with caresses and protestations of love which were strangely in contrast to her usual, almost ironical coolness.

She read much, restricting her work in the house to the least that would do. Yet, during the early part of the summer, meals were always prepared, the house in order when he came home at the regular hours.

Once a week Mrs. Shultze came over, the frail little wife of the German neighbour, to do the heavy washing, the scrubbing, the baking, the churning . . . as Niels' mother had done . . . Her own wearing apparel Mrs. Lindstedt washed by hand, upstairs, in her basin . . .

Twice, when Niels had entered the house at an unusual hour, once at eleven, once at four o'clock, he had found it exactly as he had left it, with the breakfast and dinner dishes still on the table, the beds unmade: she did her work the last minute . . . Niels tried not to see it.

The interior of the house was much changed.

Mrs. Lindstedt had had a flat in the city and owned furniture of her own. She had had it shipped out to Minor; and Niels had made two trips with the hay-rack to haul it from there.

It had converted her bed-room into somehing which he did not understand: upholstered chairs, rugs, heavy curtains, and a monstrously wide, luxurious bed with box mattress and satin covers; a mahogany dressing table covered with brushes, combs, flasks, jars, and provided with three large mirrors two of which were hinged to the central one; a chiffonier filled with a multitudinous arrangement of incomprehensible, silky and fluffy garments, so light and thin that you could crush them in the hollow of your hand; a set of sectional bookcases filled with many volumes; a couch upholstered in large-flowered damask; cushions without number; and above all mirrors, mirrors. The whole room was pervaded with sweetish scents.

The only other room which received any of this furniture was the dining room. There, a round extension table of fumed oak occupied the centre, surrounded by six chairs. Along the wall stood a large buffet; in the corner, a china cabinet filled with dishes too delicate for Niels' calloused and clumsy hands . . .

In both these rooms there had, at first, appeared many framed pictures; a few of them landscapes; most of them human figures, photographs, so she had explained, of famous paintings . . . naked figures . . .

Famous or not, Niels had – timidly, with a reference to Bobby – objected to them; so they had gone upstairs, into the bed-room.

The former furniture of the dining room stood in the front room now which was being used as a hall.

Niels himself slept in his iron bedstead where he used grey blankets and coarse linen: only when he had seen her things, had he realised their coarseness; he would have been uncomfortable with anything else.

In Bobby's presence Niels felt ashamed even of the elegance of the dining room. For himself and the boy he insisted – timidly – on using the coarse, heavy dishes of his bachelor times.

Mrs. Lindstedt received letters and parcels through the post – the post office was again on Lund's former place where a Ruthenian settler had squatted down. The parcels contained mostly books inscribed with the names of the givers: invariably names of men. Niels never asked for the contents or after the writers of these letters. He knew she burned them . . .

What she had told him of her former life, was this.

Before she was married for the first time, she had been a sales-girl in the city, first in the book, then in the "art" department of a large store. There, Mr. Vogel, floorwalker, had fallen in love with her; and they had married. Mr. Vogel had been sickly, but possessed of some money, the savings of a lifetime. His trouble being "nerves," the doctor had advised him to live in the country. So, as a speculation, he had bought the place where Rowdle now lived and had built the cottage, renting the land to Rowdle from the start. There, they had lived for two years, till Mr. Vogel had died from heart failure. He had left some money behind but not enough for the widow to live on. So, before Rowdle bought the place, for two thousand dollars, on crop payments, she had been forced to live on it for long periods at a time, in order to save, though she had been exceedingly lonesome . . .

Niels easily surmised that this was not all. There was a vast background of things not ordinarily touched upon. Yet, in hours of effusion, she sometimes cried, Niels sitting helplessly by; and then she would hint at dark, incomprehensible things.

"Oh, Niels," she would say, "if you knew what terrible things I have had to put up with: brutal things!"

He wanted to know; but he did not press for confidences. Oddly, while he wished for them, he feared them. He felt that there were things which, revealed, would break what there was left of his life: things which would lead to disasters unthinkable. And he forbore.

This feeling was strengthened – sometimes into an almost uncanny dread – by the attitude of others: nobody spoke to him about his marriage. Occasionally, when he had business with others – and he had more and more such business: the farm grew, the country became settled – he would enter a house where two or three were assembled. At sight of him all would go silent. And yet he was the oldest settler in the Marsh, the one from whom help was expected, encouragement, employment even.

Not a congratulation, not an invitation for neighbourly intercourse: nothing . . .

Niels could not but be aware of enveloping reticences; he felt as if he were surrounded by a huge vacuum in which the air was too thin for human relationships to flourish . . .

Bobby even! . . . Niels could not help reverting again and again, in thought, to that first evening of his wife's arrival on the place: Bobby had blushed and hung his head, speechless at her announcement that she was Mrs. Lindstedt now.

Already, during two short months, a conviction had grown in him that there were things which all about him knew: he alone was ignorant of them . . .

He shrugged his shoulders: they were broad: they could carry much . . .

Of the work on the farm she no longer took any notice, not since the first novelty had worn off.

Once, timidly, Niels had mentioned the garden, the cows. She had smiled.

"Niels," she had said, conciliatingly, but almost condescendingly, "I hope you didn't marry me in order to make me work. I *will* try to keep house for you. But that is all I can undertake. I am not the kind of woman that works."

Niels had felt it coming that the next moment she would mention the "other woman"; and so he had quickly said, "No, no; of course; that's all right."

He had gone on milking the cows; and whenever, at night, it was not too dark, he hoed in the garden. That he always took water and wood into the house went without saying. In the morning, work in the field or at haying started with daylight.

Thus matters drifted along to the end of July.

Then, one day, a little tussle arose. Niels carried his point; but he did so by a compromise. Unlike her, he had not prepared for the occasion.

"Niels," she said one evening when he came in after the chores were done and while he was washing in the kitchen. "Just how did Bobby and you divide the housework when you were alone?"

Niels looked up, stopping in the vigorous rubbing and splashing of face, neck, and head in which he indulged. He divined what was coming. "We worked together, as in everything else. You know we did nothing but what was absolutely necessary."

"Well," she continued, "I have been thinking, since he gets the shack and lives there by himself, why should he not look after his meals as well. You might give him a small raise . . ."

Niels answered somewhat hotly, "I gave him a raise when I sent him to live there. He's a mere boy. He can't be expected to look out for himself. He misses the company he had before you came."

"Yes," she said, "probably he does. But I'm sure he'd do anything for money . . ."

"He would not . . . But let me finish washing."

So he gained a little time to think.

"I don't see why you should wish this," he said at last, entering the dining room. "You can't complain about too much work?"

She began to cry. "Oh," she said, "you're hard! . . ."

Somehow this word struck him with such force that, for a moment, a lump rose in his throat. Somewhere, some time, he had heard it before. He could not at once trust himself to speak.

"Look here, Clara," he said at last – it was very rare that he used her first name; and as he pronounced it, she smiled up at him, brilliantly, gratefully, as if expanding under a caress; and that smile disarmed him once more. There was in it something which abashed, which confused, but which also antagonised him. It was meant to sweep his sensual being off its balance . . . Then he rallied. "Surely," he said, "there is very little difference whether you fry eggs for two or for three."

"It isn't that," she said, her voice tearful.

"Well, what is it?"

"Oh, I can't express it. You wouldn't understand." Then, with a helpless gesture, "You can't know how terribly hard life is for me; oh, everything . . . I sometimes don't know what to do. I am so unhappy . . ."

Niels looked at her. Then he shook his head.

"No. I don't understand. I thought you wanted this."

"I did, Niels," she protested. "I did. I thought things would be different with you. You are a man. You are more of a man than any one I have ever known. I only wish you didn't have to work!"

"Not have to work!" – in amazement.

"Yes," she said. "So you wouldn't have to leave me, not for an hour, not for a minute!"

Niels laughed good-naturedly. "You are taking things too hard . . . You exaggerate them . . ."

Hopefully she reached for his neck to draw him down and kiss him. "Niels," she whispered, "help me, help me."

He was embarrassed. He wished to help her. "If I only knew what it is . . ."

"Oh," she said with a vain effort to explain, "I am so tired all the time. And then I lie down. And such thoughts come. This cannot last. Niels, one day something terrible is going to happen to me . . ."

Niels remained silent for a minute or so. Then, hesitatingly, "I even believe you should do more than you do. Take your thoughts off yourself . . ."

"I can't," she exclaimed. "If only I could! But even dressing is too much. I don't stay for breakfast any longer. I shouldn't mind Bobby if only I didn't need to come down for dinner and supper."

"Well," Niels gave in on the minor detail, "if that's the case, suit yourself. As for the boy, I cannot send him away from the house altogether. I am responsible for him. If I leave him to himself, he'll either quit or go wrong . . ."

Thus things rested, not to the enhancement of Niels' prestige in his own eyes.

The farm was a law unto itself. It demanded his work. Nellie and her oldest filly were both in foal. Two big hay-stacks in the yard, one, monstrously large, in a slough east of the place. While the field-work rested, a new stable was erected, a huge structure with drain channels, built inside of three-inch lumber. Cutting started. The wheat was heavy, sixty acres of it. Before threshing the granary would have to be doubled in capacity . . . Work galore . . .

At this time something happened which was irritating in the extreme.

Niels had just stabled the horses; Bobby was washing in the basin at the pump which was run by an engine now.

Niels was in a hurry. Rain threatened. It had been misty for a day or so in the early morning.

When he entered the house, he saw, in passing through the dining room, that the breakfast dishes were still on the table: the stove in the kitchen was dead and cold. On the table lay a ham which he had brought in from the granary – there was no smoke-house yet; and the ham was uncut.

He had hardly entered the kitchen and was pouring water into the basin – well water; the house was still without eave-troughing: work, work everywhere – when he heard his wife's voice from the staircase.

"Oh," she called, "I'm so sorry. Surely it isn't twelve yet!" But she held her watch in her hand and was staring at it in dismay.

"Quarter past," Niels sang back, his eye on the clock, "We're in a hurry, too. It's going to rain."

"But Niels," she cried, "I can't come. I have my hair all bundled up."

Niels went into the front room and looked up the stairs – they had no balustrade yet: work waiting everywhere – and there she stood, in white kimono, her head bandaged in a turban of Turkish towels.

"What's wrong?"

"Henna," she said.

"What's that?"

"Henna leaves," she repeated. "I'm dying my hair."

Niels stood speechless.

"We're in a hurry," he said once more, impatiently. "It's going to rain. There are just three acres of wheat left. He spoke grimly and hurried back into the kitchen.

"Oh Niels, wait!" she called. "I simply can't come. I never thought it was so late. I'm sorry, Niels. It isn't going to happen again."

That moment Bobby knocked. She fled upstairs.

"Come in," Niels called from the door of the kitchen. "Quick, Bobby, get a move on you. We've got to get dinner ourselves. Get a fire started. Put the kettle on. And the frying pan . . ."

They ate in the kitchen. But it was past one before they were back in the field.

In the evening Mrs. Lindstedt had a great cry over it as soon as they were left alone . . .

Dying her hair! Yes, the lower edge had looked different of late, brown, with a little grey mixed in . . .

The incident was not repeated during the fall. Niels allowed it to pass in silence. What else could he do? . . .

Other things gave food for thought: not always, these days, was thought as charitable as it should have been.

One day – observation was sharpened by the knowledge that her hair was dyed – a new suspicion ripened into certainty. Not only the colour of her hair was artificial, but the colour of the face as well. Niels knew, of course, that she used powder: even that he did not understand nor approve of. Always, in the morning, her lips had looked pallid; now he noticed a greyish, yellowish complexion in her face.

One morning early – he intended to see Kelm about his threshing before he went at the work of stacking his sheaves – he entered her room to waken her so she would prepare breakfast while he attended to his chores.

There, as he looked at her in the pale light of a windtorn dawn, he stood arrested.

From behind the mask which still half concealed her face, another face looked out at him, like a death's-head: the coarse, aged face of a coarse, aged woman, aged before her time: very like that of Mrs. Philiptyuk, the Ruthenian woman at the post office: strangely, strikingly, terrifyingly like it: but aged, not from work but from . . . what?

For a moment Niels stared. Something like aversion and disgust came over him. Then, carefully, almost fastidiously, he lifted a corner of the satin coverlet, baring the shoulder and part of the breast which were still half hidden under the filmy veil of a lacy nightgown. There, the flesh was still smooth and firm: but the face was the face of decay . . .

For another minute he looked; then, without waking her, he turned and left the room on tiptoe.

But he had wakened her. "Niels," she called a moment later. "I'm coming. I must have slept in. I read late last night. I did not hear the alarm . . ."

Ten minutes after - Niels had just started the fire as he always did and was washing - she came down, in dressing gown and slippers, to mix the dough; for his bachelor life had made him partial to hot biscuits for breakfast.

He scanned her face: he reproached himself for doing so: but there was an irresistible fascination about it. The mask was repaired; but it was an imperfect piece of work, betraying hurry. Since he knew it was there, he could detect the true face under the mask.

She felt his scrutiny and asked peevishly, "What are you looking at me that way for?"

Niels came near saying a harsh word and betraying himself. But he laughed and said, with an almost grim jest, "I suppose I can look at my wife if I want to, can't I?"

. . .

Shortly before the threshers were expected, she began to sit often in absent-minded musing.

One night she said, with a sigh, "I'm suffering from the tooth-ache."

"I'm sorry," said Niels, though he did not know what a tooth-ache was. "I've heard they've got a good dentist at Balfour. How if I took you over as soon as threshing is done? I want to buy a democrat anyway. Might just as well get it there. I could take a few steers. Bobby might come along on horseback."

"Oh no," she replied. "Never mind."

But three , four days later she introduced the subject again. "I'll tell you, Niels," she said. "I'd like to go to the city for a week. I need a few things in the line of wardrobe; and I could get my teeth attended to at the same time."

"Wardrobe?" he asked, much surprised. "Surely you've got much more as it is than you can ever use here in the country."

"You don't understand," she replied, after a pause which had the effect of a reproach. "Most of my things are out of style. I want them made over."

"But your teeth . . . They say the dentist at Balfour is equal to any man in the city."

"He wouldn't be at Balfour," she said distantly. "It always pays to get the best."

"It'll cost a mint of money," Niels said musingly. He had never been in the city himself except when he had passed through as an immigrant.

"I've got my own money," she said. "Rowdle is supposed to pay up after threshing."

"That so?" he said absent-mindedly. Then, rousing himself, "Well, I expect to pay my wife's way." And, after another few minutes of silence, "I've half a mind to come along. I've never seen the city . . . The crop is good . . ."

She did not answer right away. At last, "I'm afraid you'd find it very tedious."

He looked up. A question hovered on his lips: How about you, then? But he did not utter it.

A day or so later she reverted once more to the topic. "I ought to look after my money, too. It's in the bank, drawing three percent. I could do better than that by investing it."

"Sure," Niels replied with a sigh. "By all means do."

Niels threshed. Mrs. Lund – whose store in Odensee had been closed by the creditors – came to do the cooking, with Mrs. Schultze to help her. Mrs. Lund was going to take a position at Judge Cameron's in Poplar Grove, as house-keeper at good wages.

Mrs. Lindstedt sat in a corner of the kitchen, in a silk dressing gown, relieved of all responsibility, gossiping, smiling, ironical. Niels had no time to notice her. She was outside of things, an onlooker pure and simple.

Wheat yielded forty bushels to the acre. The granary proved much too small to hold the wealth. The last of it had to be bagged and carried up into the loft of the new stable. Niels took it there, carrying two bags at a time, to the huge admiration of Bobby and others. The threshers made a jest of it, shouting and blowing the whistle for him to hurry up. Even Niels could not help laughing, a thing he rarely did these days.

On the third day the threshers departed, wending their way across the corner of the Marsh. The White Range Line House sank back into quiet and night.

A week or so later Niels took his wife to Minor, drew a few hundred dollars from the bank, and saw her off.

Plowing started.

No matter what his worries, his thoughts, his suspicions might be, the farm demanded his work, and he gave it.

While the work was done, thoughts came and went . . .

He thought of concrete things, of his Sunday evenings, for instance.

He and his wife were sitting in that dining room on the lower floor . . . Perhaps in the gathering dusk, accentuated by the shadows of the trees in the big, rustling bluff that overtowered the house; perhaps by the light of the tall floor-lamp with its huge, silken shade. Each of them was dreaming, musing: each along his own, peculiar lines: smiling perhaps; or perhaps a prey to some hidden anguish. Sometimes she was reading; and when he, too, got up to fetch book or magazine, she would raise her head and follow him with her eyes through the room and smile at what he reached for. He would have liked to fathom that smile, to probe its significance; but somehow he never did. Still, once or twice he had tried her kind of reading: some of her books, perhaps most of them, were translations from the French: one of them she had given him to read: Madame Bovary. She had given it to him with a peculiar look in her eyes . . . After the first hundred pages or so he sat aghast. He had not read on. The story of this little doctor's wife amazed and terrified him. What might it be written for? . . . He tried an American novel. He laid it aside because it seemed silly. In vain he searched for something that might enlighten him as to his mentality, that dealt with problems which were his . . .

On week-day evenings it was different. He tried to sit up with her, lounging in one of the chairs: her life seemed to begin at night. She often became gay, sometimes reckless when the day was gone. "I wish there were a show around the corner," she said once; another time, "If only there were a street nearby, with electric lights and a crowd of people rolling along; with faces to watch and clothes to criticise . . ."

Then he would be overcome by the sleepiness of him who all day long has given of his strength without stinting: he spared neither himself nor others. He would stretch and yawn. She would drop her book and look up, with a curious smile. He would try to hold out; but in vain. Perhaps he would say, after a while, "Well, how about hitting the hay?" And she would nod, perhaps. Then he would bolt both doors – before he was married, he had never troubled about that – turn the light out, and go up, she following. Five minutes later he would be asleep. But should he wake up, at midnight or later, he would still see the light from her room which cast a yellow gleam on the partition between the landing where he slept and that mysterious second room about which she had never evinced curiosity.

Or he would not say anything at all. He would simply sit and stare and yawn till drowsiness overcame him: then his head would fall back, and he would go to sleep, snoring. As soon, however, as he heard himself snore, an uncomfortable feeling would come over him: for he seemed to feel her eye, critical, condemning. He would rouse himself; but if he succeeded, it was not for long.

And finally, when he was sinking away into the very depths of sleep, he would suddenly feel her touch on his shoulder: a summons to go to bed . . .

In the mornings he had been getting up very early, at half past three or four o'clock: she had risen half an hour later to prepare breakfast and to go to bed again. He had milked the two cows and put the milk in pans in the cellar for the cream to rise; the cream from the previous milking he had dipped off and taken to the kitchen in a pitcher; and the skimmed milk he had fed to the pigs. The rest of the cows were not milked: the calves were left with them. Then he had lighted the kitchen fire, put the kettle on, and gone to the stable to feed and harness the horses. There, Bobby would join him; and the plans for the day would be outlined briefly. The morning had rolled off like clockwork. Nearly always he had heard his wife's alarm bell ringing when he crossed the yard on his way to the stable.

Yes, the daily routine looked peaceful enough as he reviewed it, ruminatingly, while riding the plow.

But ! Was there anything in it that bound man and wife together? . . . Nothing.

They lived side by side: without common memories in the past, without common interests in the present, without common aims in the future. Why were they married?

The worst of it was that there were decades upon decades of exactly the same thing ahead . . .

He saw himself sitting on his yard, an old man, a man of eighty: and by his side sat an old woman, eighty-six years old: and both followed separate lines of thought: each followed his own memories back over half a century: not a pulse-beat in common . . .

Each was facing eternity alone! . . .

They were strangers; strangers they would remain . . .

What had led them together? Niels thought of the thrills which this woman had had power to send through him in years gone by. He thought of the night of their union: their pulses had beaten together: they had beaten together in lust. For how long? Still, there had been hope. That hope was gone.

He wanted children. Did she?

Something that had been puzzling him very much arose again before his mind.

In certain moments there was a peculiar look in her eyes. He had seen that look before: alluring, seductive, appealing to something in him of which he was ashamed.

And as he rode the plow, in those days of the Indian summer: those days that before all others are reminiscent and chaste: when the light of the sun seems to be floating in the air like millions of bronzed little powdery particles – one day that memory crystallised.

He had been going with Hahn through the street in Minor; they had met three ladies, painted and powdered and dressed conspicuously, so as to make their appearance, in the light of Hahn's revelation, an advertisement of their trade: and from under their heavy eye-lids the same look had shot forth . . .

What was it that had led them together?

Lust was the defiling of an instinct of nature: it was sin.

When he shuddered at this realisation, the memory of the feeling came back to him which had assailed him on that evening of Olga's wedding in Lund's house: the feeling of disaster, of a shameful bondage that was inescapable. His doom had overtaken him, irrevocably, irremediably: he was bond-slave to a moment in his life, to a moment in the past, for all future times . . .

And as he reached this conclusion, in those halcyon October days, he at last faced once more his ancient dreams. Quite impersonally, with a melancholy kind of regret, with almost that kind of homesickness which overcomes us when we look back at the destinies, fixed and unchangeable, as unrolled in a very beloved book. He thought of that vision which had once guided him, goaded him on when he had first started out to conquer the wilderness: the vision of a wife and children.

The Wages of Sin is Death! I shall visit the Sins of the Father . . .

What?

Children?

His eye went dim; his head turned with him as he realised it. No . . . Children would be a perpetuation of the sin of a moment . . .

He did not want children out of this woman!

Mrs. Lindstedt did not return after a week. Instead, a letter came, asking for more money. Friends had taken much of her time. The various matters of business of which he knew were only half attended to . . . She would need another week . . . So, with her love . . .

Niels left Bobby alone for a day, went to town, sent the money . . .

During her absence a marsh-fire broke out, threatening the whole settlement which had been growing, growing . . . .

All the settlers turned out during the night, to draw a fire-break across the Marsh, four, five miles south of Niels' place.

In the lurid light of the approaching flames, half choked with smoke, Niels and Bobby strode along behind their plows . . .

A tall, slim figure passed them, plowing along on the other side of the strip of breaking.

Niels peered across; he could not make out who it was. The head was turned as if on purpose.

"Who was that?" he asked of the boy behind him.

"Ellen Amundsen, I believe," the answer came.

For a moment Niels' heart stood still. Of her he had not thought. It had come to this that they passed each other silently in the night . . .

When the time came, Niels went to town to get his wife. Snow had fallen prematurely.

Mrs. Lindstedt seemed pleased to be back. She had had everything she had gone for attended to. She made an attempt to be friendly, conciliating: as if she wished to make up for her absence. And yet, there was something subtly new about her: something almost as if she were disappointed; something also which was disappointing to Niels.

Niels went to town once more. He thought his wife might wish to be taken out, to see the country, perhaps to visit . . . He bought, at a sale, democrat, drivers, and cutter . . .

Then it came home to him. Yes, in the White Range Line House an indefinable change was taking place between husband and wife.

From the beginning there had been about their moments of union something artificial, perhaps because their importance was so hugely exaggerated, they being the only bond between them . . .

It would be wrong to say that Niels did not see or at least try to see her side of the matter. Sometimes he thought of her not without sympathy; but only since, in those fall musings, he had accepted his own life as irretrievably ruined – at least as far as a life is the gradual approach, through an infinite number of compromises, to a preconceived goal, to an ideal, a dream or a vision which may never be completely realised.

What was her side of it?

She, a city woman, with the tastes and inclinations of such an one, was banished to the farm. It was her fault, granted. Yet her life was a life in exile. She had lived it before; she knew what it meant; if she had blindly gone into it, she had no excuse; all that was true. The fact remained that it was so.

He realised the dreariness, the utter emptiness of her life. She got up in the morning to prepare breakfast and went to bed again. She rose to prepare dinner and to get some semblance of order into the house and went to bed again. She rose to get supper . . .

The work she did was hateful to her; yet she did it. Was not that an attempt to do what was expected of her? With almost any other woman it would have been a matter of course. Was it with her? He had, so far, blamed her in his heart because his meals were as monotonous now as they had been in his bachelor days. He was suddenly inclined to give her credit for the fact that they were not more so than formerly.

What her city life has consisted in, of that he had no very clear idea. No matter; it had been different. To please him, she made an attempt to adapt herself. He would show a little more sympathy, a little more appreciation.

But somehow, right from the beginning, he felt himself thwarted . . .

He had, for instance, expected that she would open her suitcases and show him where his money had gone. It might have been spent on cold creams, perfumes, silks, gewgaws: things he did not approve of. No matter what it had been spent on, he had expected to see it; he was prepared to express approval of what he condemned, simply for the sake of even a fictitious companionship.

She gave him no chance to do so; she showed him nothing . . .

He came to the conclusion that perhaps it was expected of him to betray curiosity. He would ask her; he would seize the very next opportunity . . . The trouble was that no opportunity offered. His wife seemed to wear an armour since her return. . . .

He had also expected that, after an absence of almost three weeks, there would be, on her part, a re-awaking of physical desires. Even he, having tasted of the forbidden fruit, was conscious of them.

His expectation was disappointed.

This puzzled him greatly.

But there was still something else . . .

Of an evening, of a Sunday afternoon, when he felt her scrutiny, he became aware of a new quality in her look: she was no longer merely amused at his ways, at his choice of reading matter.

With an uncomfortable realisation of possible shortcomings, unsuspected by himself, he became convinced that he was being weighed, compared . . . with whom?

Her eyes showed a new expression: there was a dreamy quality in them . . .

Once or twice, when crossing his yard, he caught himself dreading that look in her face: he turned back and went to the granary, instead of the house. He sat down in its door, looking across at that big dwelling of his which contained a mystery . . .

But he must make the best of a bad bargain! . . .

He offered to take her out for drives.

"Oh no," she said curtly. "I don't care for it."

Yet she, too, was restless. When they had been sitting, she would suddenly get up and begin to pace the room. Sometimes she hummed a tune, smiling to herself; her step became almost a dance. Then, with a sigh, the look in her eyes seemed to come back from an infinite distance and to refocus reality: it became serious, then, almost hostile, as if she wished to erase reality.

Early in December more snow fell. Hauling began. Niels hired a second man; and they went with three teams, starting out in the morning at three, getting home again next morning about the same time.

In the most natural way, thus, another change came about.

Niels got up about two o'clock at night and prepared breakfast for himself and Bobby. When they returned, at uncertain hours, he made breakfast again.

Thus the first few trips were made.

Then, one morning, when they came home, after a particularly hard trip, against a sharp north-east wind and drifting snow, exhausted, cold, almost desperate, Niels found in the kitchen the dishes his wife had used the day before, and even his own breakfast dishes unwashed. They were simply piled together.

In an impulse of anger he went to the staircase and called. But, receiving no answer, he did not call again. He went to the kitchen, heated water, and washed the dishes himself.

This happened once; then, after a week, it became the regular routine. Niels did not comment on it at all.

In this manner, what with his absences and reticences, an almost complete separation of husband and wife came before he realised it. It was a demoralisation of all human relationships . . .

And yet, as if to perpetuate this state of affairs, he took out a timber lease on government land, so as to provide work in the bush for the rest of the winter . . .

What was the woman in the White Range Line House doing meanwhile?

He hardly knew.

He did know that she spent hours and hours in front of her dressing table, combing her hair in ever new ways. To her, too, life seemed to be a burden.

When she was aware of being watched, she moved about with extreme slowness.

She made the impression of being always absent-minded. She would take up a brush and lay it down again; a comb, and drop it back into place; and finally she would reach for a shell hair-pin and put it slowly, tentatively, into a dozen places in her hair before she left it where it was . . .

To his occasional shame, Niels got into the habit of spying on her . . .

Sometimes, when he was at home, there would pass between them no more than half a dozen words.

But Saturdays, mail-days, she would invariably ask, "Can you send Bobby to the post office?"

And Bobby would go on horseback and bring back a bundle of letters, circulars, papers, sometimes a parcel . . . The letters were all for her; the parcels, too. Niels had never asked from whom they came; she had never volunteered any information. Without glancing at them, she thrust them into her waist or the pocket of her dressing gown.

For a long time Niels was not aware of the fact that he himself looked at the addresses on the envelopes; but one day he realised that he knew every single hand-writing on them and noticed when this or that one was missing.

Christmas came.

On the eve Niels had seen one of his neighbours, a settler on the sand-flats, returning from the bush with two little Christmas-trees.

Children!

Early on Christmas Day Bobby went on horseback to call on his foster mother at Poplar Grove . . .

The White Range Line House lay dead and cold . . .

Restlessly Niels went here and there, back and forth on the yard, clad in his sheep-skin, a fur cap on his head, big, roomy boots on his feet, leggings rolled about his legs: he was a burden to himself.

On a silken bed upstairs in the house, there lay a woman, it is true . . .

Horses, cows, and pigs were a semblance of company. Niels went ever back to the stables.

He was there when, shortly before noon, the merry jingle of sleigh bells caught his ear. The sound came from the north, from the bridge trail over the corner of the Marsh. Niels stepped to the door of the stable to listen . . . Nearer and nearer came the sound. It reached the bluff and rounded the corner . . .

Callers for some one; not for him . . .

And yet, there they stopped in front of his gate! Niels went past the cow-shed and crossed his yard.

Strangers belike who wished to enquire about the road: it was a big cutter filled with furs: three children on the front seat, two grown-ups behind.

And then a voice, loud, boisterous, laughing.

"Hello! Step lively there, you hulking muskrat!"

Nelson's voice!

A titter sounded an echo to it; behind Nelson's shoulder a woman's face peered out: Olga's!

Niels opened the gate. "Hello," he said, forcing a smile of welcome.

"Haven't seen you for ages," Nelson said, shaking hands. "Thought we'd do the right thing and call, seeing that you're married at last. Well, she nibbed you, didn't she, old hoss? The gay widow? Well, well!"

Olga laughed. But she reproved her husband. "Here, Lars, behave."

Nelson drove in; and they alighted. Niels helped to unhitch the drivers: great, strong-limbed beasts.

"So you've built a stable?" Nelson said.

"And such a big one!" Olga admired.

She looked the same as years ago when Niels had first met her as Mrs. Nelson. The crisp winter air had driven a flush into her face.

"Made it in a little over two hours," Nelson boasted. "How's that for drivers?"

"Bought them this year?" Niels asked.

"After threshing. Had to have something to offset your Percherons."

They entered the stable.

"Gosh," Nelson exclaimed. "Look at that, Olga. "If this dormouse hasn't got ten head of horses! He beats me on that. Six's all I have. But I've got cattle. No end of cattle. Herefords. Say, Lindstedt, I've got a little bull, a two-year-old that's a beauty. Just the thing for a small herd like yours. Sell him to you for two hundred, for old sake's sake. Make you a present of him for two hundred . . . Well, how does it feel to be married?"

Niels was white. "Come to the house," he said.

They went.

"What a beautiful yard!" Olga exclaimed. "So sheltered!"

"How much have you broken?" Nelson asked.

"A hundred acres."

"Whoo-pee!" Nelson shouted in his booming bass. "You sure beat me on that! I'm sticking around fifty. But grain's a side issue with me. I'm the cattle man. I prefer a crop that'll walk to town on its own feet."

Niels held the door. Olga pushed two of her children ahead; the youngest one Nelson picked up as he entered.

Niels led them through to the dining room.

"Make yourselves at home," he said, taking their wraps.

Olga and Nelson wore black-dog coats. Nelson, as he peeled himself out of his, stood in black "store-clothes," with stiff white collar and blue satin tie, patent-leather shoes on his enormous feet. Olga was dressed in shiny black silk, very pretty, and plainly with child. The two boys were encased in brand-new suits, with knickers and Norfolk jackets; the little girl, the oldest, in fluffy white muslin.

"Excuse me a moment," Niels said as he ponderously stepped back into the almost bare front room.

There he hesitated; then, with an expression of set determination on his deeply lined face, he went slowly upstairs.

As he entered his wife's room, for the first time in months, the woman, in a sky-blue dressing gown, reclining on her bed, looked up at him, dropping the hand which held her book. There was a curious expression on her face, half a smile, full of irony, challenge, hostile provocation . . .

For just a second Niels was tempted to yell at her, Get up and dress and come down!

The strange thing was that he felt instinctively that that would have been the right thing to do; yes, that it would have pleased her. He did not know why. He did not fathom this woman's psychology. Later, much later, he understood that such a course might have righted much that was wrong between him and his wife . . .

Clear and sharp, perfectly self-possessed, as if she were not concerned, her voice rang out, calmly enough, but to him like the bell of doom. "Well?"

Niels took himself in hand. As he mastered his almost unconquerable impulse of violence, he felt humiliated, almost humble, and said very quietly, "The Nelsons are here. They came to call."

"Well?" the voice repeated.

Niels began to stammer he hardly knew what. Her aggressive composure disconcerted him. Then, with a great effort, he used her name. "Clara . . . won't you dress and come down?"

Her light, silvery laugh answered him. It sounded perfectly easy; but a strange quality in it betrayed even to Niels that in this woman, too, the nerves were in tension. Then, after a pause, "Why should I?"

"But . . . You don't understand . . . They are the first callers we've had . . ."

"They call on you, not on me," she said, the laughter dying out from her voice, the smile from her face. And, with a distinctly hostile note, "Leave me alone."

He was thunderstruck. Once more he began to stammer "Clara . . . Do me the favour . . ."

"Do you a favour?" the voice answered, low but strident. Then a brief laughter. And again the voice, vibrant with pent-up excitement, "You . . . you . . . you skunk!"

Niels turned.

"Do *me* the favour," the voice was now loud and ringing so that Niels thought it could be heard throughout the house, "and close my door . . ."

Neils had to stop on the stairs to steady himself. His knees shook . . .

Then he went down. In the hall he hesitated again before he entered the dining room.

"What perfectly lovely furniture!" Olga greeted him as he entered.

He looked at her and nodded. "You'll stay for dinner, of course," he managed to say after a while.

"That's what we were figuring on," Nelson said. "Indeed we were. If you've got a bite in the house?"

There was an air of immense embarrassment in the room.

Niels went to the dumb-waiter in the corner and picked up a table cloth. Then he inserted a leaf in the table. And at last he went to the kitchen door.

"You'll have to excuse me once more," he mumbled.

The children were crowding about their mother: they were afraid of him.

In the kitchen he started the fire, sliced ham and bread, and broke eggs into a frying pan.

His guests had been conversing in whispers. When he appeared, they went silent; and again that air of embarrassment settled over the room.

Then Nelson said, clearly with the intention of breaking the silence, "Bobby away?"

"Bobby's gone to call on his mother."

"I'm so glad," Olga threw in, "mamma's got that splendid place at the judge's. She says it's just grand. The judge is such a lovely old man."

Niels returned to the kitchen. Nelson followed.

"Look here, old man," Nelson said, "anything wrong?"

"No," Niels replied without looking up.

"I mean with the wife . . ."

"She isn't feeling well . . ."

"Child coming?" Nelson whispered slyly, nudging Niels with his elbow.

"No."

Suddenly Nelson became serious. "Look here. We came to do you a good turn, old man. We know that we're the first to call. You know the reason, of course, why nobody has ever come. We thought we'd break the ice. But, if we're not welcome . . ."

"You're welcome enough as far as I'm concerned," Niels said quietly.

"That's enough," Nelson took him up very quickly. "As far as you're concerned . . . We can take a hint."

Niels faced him. "Nelson, what is the reason?"

"The reason for what?"

"That nobody comes near us."

"You don't mean to say you don't know?"

"I don't know." Niels' voice carried conviction.

"Then *I* won't tell you," Nelson said. "Never mind about dinner. We're going."

"Nelson," Niels tried to plead. Then, shrugged his shoulders, "All right."

Olga was already in the hall, putting the wraps on her children. Nelson helped her into her coat. He took his own; and they went out.

In silence Niels led the horses from the stable, watered them, and helped to hitch them up.

Nelson lifted the children into the cutter, Niels standing by, facing the house.

And as he stood there, he saw the curtains of the window in the woman's bed-room move. She peered down at the scene in the front of the stable, furtive, smiling . . .

Nelson and his wife climbed in.

"Mr. Lindstedt," Olga said, tears in her eyes as she held out her hand, "I'm terribly sorry. I hope you'll believe me."

"By-by," Nelson nodded, laughing lightly. "Buck up, old hoss . . ."

Niels stood and looked after them, conscious that he was being watched from above . . .

Towards evening Mrs. Lindstedt came down, dressed more daintily, made up more carefully than ever, and surrounded by an enervating aura of scents.

Silently, but with smiles flitting over her face, her eyes dancing as of old, she went to the task of preparing supper for herself in the most leisurely way.

Niels sat in the dining room over a book. He had sent for a volume on National Economy which he had seen advertised; he was struggling with its abstruse phraseology. He had forgotten about his wife. Now he followed her with his eyes wherever she went.

She took no notice of him. But when, half an hour later, he got up to leave the house, she confronted him with an open, seductive smile. "Well," she said; and her voice was quiet, sympathetic, compassionate, "did your guests have a nice call?"

Involuntarily Niels had stopped to listen. Now he shrugged his shoulders and left the room without a word.

On New Year's Eve, Mrs. Lindstedt, coming down after supper, remarked casually that her teeth still seemed to give trouble; she would return to the city for a short stay.

Niels looked at her, silent, and nodded.

"I suppose Bobby can take me to town to-morrow morning?" she added, speaking sharply, with the unmistakable intention of avoiding the impression as if she were making advances.

"Sure," Niels said.

He took his cheque-book from the cupboard in the hall where he kept his papers, sat down, wrote a cheque for two hundred and fifty dollars, and tossed it across the table.

She ignored the slip of paper and got up.

But when Niels came down during the night to feed the fire in the big stove, he took note of the fact that the cheque was gone.

More even than before, Niels brooded over his relations to his wife. He thought, during the drives which he made, from bush to town, from farm to bush, of all the married couples he knew . . .

He could not puzzle it out.

On the other hand, whether Nelson and Olga approved, whether the world approved, mattered very little. If only . . .

He, Niels Lindstedt, a skunk? . . . Mean? . . . If any one had reason to complain of unfair dealing, it seemed to him it was he.

Her life was a horror. True.

As soon as she was absent, he was able to see her side of it. If only she would utter wishes! He realised with a shudder that she had become physically repulsive to him. But even . . .

What did it matter?

He became aware that this phrase – what did it matter? – occurred more and more frequently in his thought. Did nothing really matter?

Why had she gone to the city again? The matter of dentistry was the merest pretext . . . Yet, she had felt it incumbent upon her to use a pretext. But . . . let her go! Let her go! If that made life bearable for her . . . Let her go as often as she cared to. He would offer the next trip to her, at Easter . . .

Winter went. Mrs. Lindstedt returned; no change; or if any, a slight change for the worse; all things a little more pronounced, with a little more of an edge to them . . .

Niels had not sent Bobby to get her. He had gone himself. He had thought it might please her. She had all but ignored him at the station: handing her baggage, not to him but to the obsequious operator who stared at her. "Perhaps you are hungry," he had stammered. He had been hungry himself.

"I had my dinner on the train," the answer had come, icily, distancing. He had not even known you can have dinner on the train . . .

Two and a half months followed, after that two-hour drive during which she had carefully avoided touching him . . .

Niels did all the housework now, cooked three meals a day for himself and Bobby, washed the dishes, shook up his bed, swept the floor . . . Sometimes he did not see his wife for days at a stretch, leaving as he did for the bush before sun-up, and returning after dark, often to find the house cold and still: only a cup or a plate would betray that she had been downstairs at all, snatching a perhaps hurried meal while he was away from house and yard.

Easter came. She did not give him a chance to offer that trip. She merely announced that she was going, giving no reason whatever this time. Niels did not give, she did not ask for, any money. Three weeks later she returned with a livery team which she had hired in town.

During this absence Niels did no longer form any good resolutions. He was immersed in gloom.

Vague, disquieting suspicions invaded him: what was she doing in the city? What was she doing?

A dull, menacing feeling grew up in him, was on the point of flaring into hatred. She hated him, of that he was sure. He hated her. Why had she come back?

He felt as if he must purge himself of an infection, of things unimaginable, horrors unspeakable – the more horrible as they were vague, vague . . .

The thaw-up came. New settlers moved in: two young Canadians, brothers, the Dunsmore boys people called them; a German who squatted down along the creek, north-east from Niels' place, Dahlbeck by name.

The spring work began and was finished. The farm was a law unto itself . . .

Summer.

Often now, during Sunday afternoons, Niels was sitting in the back seat of his democrat, under the forward-slanting roof of the implement shed, with his book, the Elements of Political Economy. He entered his house only when it could not be helped . . . But he stared across at it, with unseeing eyes, at that big house which he had built for himself four, five years ago . . . For himself? No, of that he must not think . . . That way lay insanity.

Sometimes, during week-days, he took his meals in Bobby's shack instead of going to the house . . .

Bobby never said a word about all these troubles. But Niels knew that he knew all about them. Once or twice Niels thought things might be easier if he could talk them over . . . Yet, could he? Bobby was like a son to him . . . But, after all, he was not his son . . .

The crops grew well; they promised a bountiful harvest in June; but in July the drought came: the first drought Niels had ever experienced. What did it matter?

Sometimes clouds sailed up, obscuring the sky; and with a big bluster of wind they blew over, not a drop coming down from their bursting udders. The grass parched in the meadows; the cattle bellowed on the Marsh; the grain ripened, so light that there was hardly any difference between straw and ear . . .

And then the hail-storm came, like a sudden catastrophe . . .

When the hail had melted away – it lay three, four inches thick in places – Niels and Bobby went out to look at the damage. Water stood in the furrows; the ridges in between looked like black sugar, melting . . . The crops had disappeared.

Bobby exclaimed again and again, "Gee whiz!"

Niels strugged his shoulders with something like a chuckle. "And to think," he said, "that on the advice of that fellow Regan in Minor I insured against hail! Why, that hail-storm means money in my pocket! Eight dollars an acre . . . I could never have threshed eight dollars out of that dry straw . . ."

"I hadn't even thought of that," Bobby laughed. "Gee, Niels, you're a wizard. You make money even out of hail . . ."

But Niels' eyes had gone steely again.

What had she gone to the city for? What had she been doing there? . . . It was an obsession . . .

Niels thought and thought as he sat in his implement shed and watched his house. It was a Sunday afternoon, the last in August.

Hahn's revelations came back to him. "They're from the city." Eyes peered at Niels, alluring, provoking, from under fashionable, expensive hats . . . hats like his wife's . . . set in faces powdered and painted . . . "One of them will be your wife . . . for an hour . . ."

Niels whipped himself up and walked back and forth, back and forth, behind that array of his implements: wagons, plows, binder, seeder . . . He walked there because he could not be seen from the house. And every now and then he bent down and peered from under the low, jutting roof across his yard at the windows of that house.

In this hour of torture there was born in him a great determination: no matter what happened, his wife was not going to go to the city again. Three times she had gone. What had she been doing there? Never mind what she had been doing. She was not going to do it again! . . .

The week went by. Niels was aware of unusual activity in the house: in that room which he never entered any longer; and one day, when the door, now usually closed, was ajar, it opened under the tremour of his heavy tread on the landing. He saw enough to know that his wife was packing up . . .

She was making preparations to go on a fourth trip. She was not going to go . . .

Not a word did she say to him. But she spoke to Bobby, asking him to be ready to take her to town on a certain day.

She had waited till Niels was away to speak to the boy. But Bobby told him as soon as he returned.

Niels, in sudden blind rage, went to the house at once. It was in the middle of the afternoon, at a time when he hardly ever entered the place.

She was in the dining room, engaged in collecting some trifles which she intended to take along . . .

He had entered through the front door, thereby cutting off her retreat; of a set purpose he turned the key behind his back and drew it out, in a single motion.

He crossed the hall and stood in the door of the dining room, almost filling it with his huge frame.

"What are you doing?" he asked, quietly, but with a vibrant note which would have warned the most unobservant.

She turned; slowly, as if recalling her absent thoughts to some unimportant business which thrust itself in her path. On her lips, which were brilliantly, exaggeratedly rouged, lay a smile. In her eyes – couched behind lids, lashes and brows which also bore the marks of the make-up for artificial light – lay the remnant of a happy dream. Her dressing gown, of filmy, white, Japanese silk, showed every detail of her undergarments: lacy things of pink crepe-de-chine. Her chestnut-red hair surrounded her face like a flaming cloud. Her bare arms and soft white hands, issuing as they did from wide, flaring sleeves, were the very picture of allurement and temptation. The room was heady with heavy scents . . .

Niels looked with distaste at the scene; he felt a loathing for the woman. Had he obeyed his impulse, he would have given her all the money he had and sent her away. But it was a peculiarity of his nature that, having thought out and laid down a plan, he must go on along the demarcated line and carry out that plan even though circumstances might have arisen which made it absurd.

Thus he had broke his land, thus built his house, thus made himself the servant of the soil . . . It was his peasant nature going on by inertia . . .

She felt the approach of a catastrophic development. The smile faded from her lips; the dream died in her eyes. She focused them on the man in the door who thrust himself into her visions, standing there, huge, implacable, like doom. As this change took place, her whole appearance became, in a moment, from a picture of all that might in a physical sense be alluring, something pathetically artificial: as if a small animal at bay, a mouse perhaps, were looking out from some large shell, beautiful in its iridescent colours; or as if some old, old dignitary, a pope maybe, clad in gorgeous regalia that not he wore but that bore him up, had suddenly forgotten the part he played as the personification of some time-honoured institution and had become a frail, mortal man, shaking in fear . . . From behind the mask, the woman peered out, helpless, at bay, mortally frightened.

If at that moment Niels had struck; if he had gone straight to her and torn her finery off her body, sternly, ruthlessly, and ordered her to do menial service on the farm, he would have conquered . . . But he merely frowned . . .

Then, as if she awoke from a nightmare, she rallied and shrugged her almost bare shoulders: it was as if she shivered. Slowly a smile returned into her face. Two human natures had measured each other; and the woman had realised her power. The smile was new: it held a note of contempt.

"I?" she said slowly, languidly. "I am getting ready to leave."

"For the city?"

"Yes," she replied in a tone of great indifference.

"You have been to the city for the last time. You won't go again. If ever, you won't go alone."

For a moment she stared. Then she laughed. "I might

go into the bush instead . . ." And with a swift motion she swept towards the kitchen door.

Niels forestalled her, barring the way.

She turned to the front door.

"That door is locked," he said grimly.

Her arms sank helpless.

"Do you mean to say," she gasped; and for a moment her woman's nature overwhelmed her so that she sank into a chair. Then she rose again. "Do you mean to say I am a prisoner here?"

"Just about."

A silence of several minutes ensued, she standing by the table, he in the kitchen door.

She became calm, extraordinarily, dangerously calm.

"Why?" she asked in a voice cool, measured, almost impersonally enquiring, as if she were solving an intricate problem in mathematics.

That voice carried a sting. It roused red anger. "What have you been doing in the city?" he snarled.

She faced him, looked at him, laughed contemptuously. She measured him with her eyes, from head to foot and back again. When she spoke, her voice was ice-cold.

"Look at the fellow!" she said. Then, inner fires breaking through for a moment, bursting into flame, smoke, and ashes. "Look at the contemptible scoundrel! How he stands there and sneers, secure in his brute strength, abusing a woman! If only I had a revolver, a knife . . ."

She stopped, realising that she was becoming theatrical, raging, hardly able to prevent herself from breaking into a sob of impotence . . . Again she rallied, searching for the sharpest sting in her quiver.

"Why do you ask?" she said. "Is it jealousy? I know it is not. I'll tell you what it is: it is that ridiculous man-nature in you. You married me. You don't want me any longer. But I am not to belong to any one else. I am to be your property, your slave-property . . . Since you have no further use for me, you want to fling me on this . . . this manure-pile here." With a comprehensive sweep of her arm. "But let any one come and want to pick me up because I may still be of use to him, and at once the dog-in-the-manger instinct that lurks in every man pops up, and you put me under lock and key! . . . What did you marry me for, anyway?"

"That you know as well as I."

"No," she said, curiously. "I don't. I know why you married me, for what reasons; I don't know what for. The reason is clear enough. You married me because you were such an innocence, such a milk-sop that you could not bear the thought of having gone to bed with a woman who was not your wife. You had not the force to resist when I wanted you – yes, I wanted you, for a night or an hour . . . and you had to legalise the thing behind-hand. That's why you married me. You wouldn't have needed to bother. I had had what I wanted. I did not ask you for anything beyond. I'm honest. I'm not a sneak who asks for one thing to get another. I did not know all this at the time, that goes without saying. I know it now. Had I known it then, you would never have snared me. At the time I thought you were really in love with me, you really *wanted* me, you really wanted *me*! Not only a woman, any woman. Do you know what you did when you married me? You prostituted me if you know what that means. That's what you did. After having made a convenience of me. When you married me, you committed a crime!"

She paused. Once more her pose was theatrical.

Niels' thoughts were in a turmoil. That woman was right! That was why he had married her! Not she, he stood indicated. For a moment he was helpless. Then he felt that she was evading the question. Anger overmastered him once more. "What have you been doing in the city?"

She remained perfectly self-possessed. "You want to know? I'll tell you. I amused myself. I had a good time.

In the company of men who appreciate me. Men who are not dumb brutes. Men who seek me for the sake of what I am . . . That they incidentally desired my body also . . ."

Niels had been listening almost with curiosity. But now a tormenting agony invaded him; his joints were loosening, as if he must pitch forward. "Which you gave?"

She shrugged her shoulders and laughed. "That's it, is it? All the rest does not count; but that one thing . . . That's where the sting lies, is it? . . . Now I'll tell you something that will really sting when you come to think of it; provided that I've ever been anything to you at all; and provided that you have brains enough to understand it . . . Yes; which I gave the last time I went."

"What do you mean?" he stammered.

Her attitude changed. She spoke very quietly, as to a child. "I'll tell you . . . But let's sit down. I'm getting tired. There isn't any use in yelling at each other, either. I can tell you this in perfect ease. It's all past history for me."

She sat down; the man in the door remained standing.

"There was a time," she went on, "when I was in love with you. Even such as I do fall in love, you know. I admired your strength of body, your build, your steely eyes, your straight mouth. I admired the energy and determination with which you learned English and went to work. I thought you were a man. The class of people I had associated with – artists, writers, newspaper men – are mostly weaklings. Business men are dull. I had been married to one for altogether too long. I wanted you for years before I had you. Love is a fleeting thing with me. Desire is not. Love has to be conquered again and again. A sense of duty does not exist for me. But so long as I had not had you, I wanted you. I might have gone on wanting you, tempting you, if you had not been weak. I felt sure that you would marry that Amundsen girl. If you had married her – as, by the way, you should have done – I should have been unhappy for the rest of my days: if I had not had you. Once I'd had you, I should not have cared. Well, I had you . . . You proposed marriage to me. You will remember that I hesitated; that I did not at once consent. All kinds of thoughts went through my head. I came to the conclusion that, like the floorwalker, you really loved me. That you would reconquer me from day to day as he had done. I was tired of being a bird of passage. There were horrible things in my memory of the past. Money had often been scarce. What the floorwalker had left was too much to starve on; not enough to live on. As I said, I thought you were a man. You would steady and hold me. I thought I could waive my need for stimulants. I could spin myself into a cocoon with reading. I thought I could force myself to do the work which is indispensable in a house. I told you I never could be a farming woman. You insisted. It never occurred to me that you might be weak enough to want marriage on moral grounds. I gave in . . .

"Then I came out here. I did what could not be left undone. It was slavery; it was a horror. To wash dishes, to sweep a house . . . to do anything on time, regularly, as a routine, day after day: all that is a horror to me. But I did it. I was in love with you, continued in love with what I thought you were. I bore the rest. I still admired your simplicity, your energy, your power and steadiness in work . . .

'But then, during the latter part of the first summer, I became conscious of the fact – I was for ever brooding – that it was always I who came to you . . . never you who came to me. A suspicion took hold of me. I began to doubt you. I began to doubt your love. More and more life became a drudgery. I thought of a test. That was why I went to the city. I needed a recreation, it is true, a change. I sought my old company. It seemed hard to return to this place in the wilderness. Yet, I longed for you. But I made up my mind, when I did return, to withdraw, to wait for you, not to go to you again. You did not come. You let me drift, no matter where. Half from resentment, half from a desire to test you further, I stopped the work I had been doing. I waited; oh, so anxiously I waited for you to scold, to get angry, to beat me if need be . . . Just to show that you did care, that I was not simply a nothing, a figure-head, an encumbrance to you . . .

"You did nothing of the kind. It left you indifferent . . .

"I was not needed. Why was I here? Why was I sacrificing everything I had valued: the colour, the gayness, the zest of life for a man to whom I was nothing? Who perhaps hated me, had hated me ever since I had been his wife? And I became aware of the possibility that perhaps one day I might come to hate you.

"When the Nelsons came, my resentment grew too strong for me. As yet, even then, it was half done on purpose when I insulted you. The insult glanced off.

"I made another test. Again I went to the city. I wanted you to say no, then; that I could not go. I wanted you to be surprised that I asked for Bobby to drive me to town. You agreed to everything; as if it were the most natural thing for me to travel alone all over the country. I stayed away much longer than could possibly be necessary to have any number of teeth attended to. I wanted you to question me; or to get angry. You met me with a grin. My heart froze against you. When I got back, I shut myself up in my room.

"Yes I made still a third test. I went to the city at Easter. I used no pretext. I simply announced I was going. For half a year I had been living like an unmarried woman that has never known a man. What did you think I was made of? Did you think mine was the nature of a fish? You stirred neither hand nor foot. You did not say a word. You did not even object to my going.

"I went; and I threw myself away in the city. So far the men had been courting me; now I courted them.

Some of them were poor. I had plenty of money from the first two trips left. I had never been inside a dentist's office. My stay had not cost me a cent. I had lived with friends. I entertained men this time, with your money . . . I threw myself away, body and all. It was nothing to me. I thought it would mean much to you. I revelled in my revenge . . .

"And yet, Niels, even then I could not get rid of the thought of you. I still saw you when I was in the arms of another. . . .

"I might have stayed away, then. I came back. I still hoped . . . Nothing. Nothing.

"And now, Niels, will you let me go? My feeling for you is dead; you are nothing to me any longer, not that much . . . You are only a husband whom I married by mistake, somewhat ridiculous, and very hateful . . . Yes, I hate you, I hate you . . . Will you let me go?"

The man at the door had listened aghast. He did not understand. He felt as if he had been walking along an abyss, blindfolded. He shivered. Fever burned in him. Sweat broke out on his brow. He stared . . .

"Niels," she went on once more, "will you let me go? This time I shall not come back. I want to live, not to stagnate. I want to feel that I can go from this house as I used to go from my cottage in the bush. I want you to be a memory only. I want you to be the past . . .

"I do not ask you for money. I have money of my own. If you want a divorce, I am willing. You can throw the guilt on me. But then I demand to be paid for it. You have no proofs. I am willing to furnish them, for a consideration.

"If you don't want a divorce, I have a hold on you. I may ask for money at a later time. You are well-to-do. You are getting richer every day because you have no wants . . . I have known too well what it is to be without money not to appreciate it . . .

"All this I intended to write to you. Don't think that I do not want you to see the whole of the situation.

"And now, once more, will you let me go?"

All this went past Niels. He did not catch a word of it at the time: much later only did some of the things she had said come back to him as out of an evil dream. One fact stood out: she had given her body . . .

As in a spasm he answered, "I will not."

She looked at him, questioningly, almost curiously. Then she shrugged her shoulders.

He saw her dimly. In this conflict of two human natures such trifles as her appearance, the exaggeration of her make-up - too absurd to be taken notice of - angered him. He would have liked to strip all that costly tinsel off her, with one rough touch to wipe paint and powder down, so she would stand there, the bare, ugly, life-worn specimen of humanity she appeared to him to be under her mask. He might have pitied her then.

Her face hardened. "Niels," she said, "I warn you. It will go hard with you and me. I cannot stay here, a prisoner, condemned to a life-sentence. I won't."

"You are not going to leave this place if I can help it," he said doggedly.

"Listen," she flared up, "I have tried to make you understand. I have failed. I wanted to show you a last mercy by leaving. You prove to me that you are mean, brutal, revengeful. You think you have power over me. I'll show you that you have not. For the last time, will you let me go?"

"No."

"Then listen." She stood up. "From now on I shall live to get even with you. I don't want to leave any longer. I shall stay. I can hit you harder here. You don't need to lock doors. You have made me live through hell. I shall give you a taste of the same thing now. You don't know yet why people have not called. You will know one day. I, too, have powers. I have borne what I could. I can bear no more. People here are coarse and vulgar. They are not to my taste. I'll overlook that for the sake of revenge. You have made your bed. You must lie in it.

This house, the White Range Line House as they call it, is going to be a famous house on the Marsh; its name is going to be a by-word ringing through the countryside; and you are going to be the laughing-stock of the settlement. Mark my words, you will rue this day!"

With that she ran out into the hall and up the stairs, leaving him alone.

CHAPTER FIVE

Bobby

AGAIN THERE were drives, drives, drives; for Niels started work in the bush right after plowing . . . As always when he was driving, there was time to think, to brood . . .

At the very first, when his wife's revelations had hit him like so many hammer-blows, he had been stunned. Then, in life's first reaction against injury and death, he had been subject to sudden fits of rage, sudden wellings-up in him of primeval impulses, of the desire to kill, to crush . . .

At such moments he had indulged in horrible imaginings. He had felt as if he could have looked on while the woman perished under frightful tortures; as if he could have laughed at her contortions; as if he could have revelled in her agony.

But those had been no more than impulses, comparable to brief eruptions of a volcano which yet show what is hidden underneath.

He had kept away from his house when his wife was about, entering it only in the early morning and at night. He and Bobby were "baching it" in the shack, living as once they had lived together in the house. Meanwhile they worked at what had to be done: they dug potatoes, replaced rotting fence-posts, squared logs for a smoke-house and a larger granary; they went together into the bush.

Niels was watching his house . . .

It never occurred to him yet not to blame his wife for doing what it was her nature to do; not to judge her and to find her guilty . . .

But, as soon as the driving started, he went to work, unconsciously, at finding a new path through the tangled labyrinth of his life.

What was the problem?

He came to see that the real problem was very complicated. Judging her guilty, he demanded repentance and atonement. But he could not demand anything of her because she did not acknowledge his right to demand: he had no authority over her.

She was planning revenge. Revenge for what? No doubt for a wrong she thought had been done her.

Had he, Niels wronged the woman, intentionally or not? That was the great question.

She was right in reproaching him with weakness: he had fallen. But, once he had fallen, Could he have acted otherwise than he had done? Could he have simulated feelings which he did not have?

The whole marriage, the whole antecedents of this marriage were immoral . . .

So it all came back to this that he should not have fallen . . .

But suppose a man had fallen, what was he to do?

Suppose he had simulated feelings which he did not have . . . Suppose – unlikely as such an outcome must be – he had succeeded in deceiving the woman into the belief that he really loved her . . .

He would have had to bear the burden of that deceit to his grave!

Could he have stood up under such a strain? He could not. His marriage would have been worse than concubinage: it would have been prostitution on his part!

What had his resolutions amounted to, his good intentions of a year ago? To this that he had intended to buy her off.

He had strongly, forcibly realised that he was not the only sufferer. But he had not been willing – because he had been unable – to give her what she wanted, what she was looking for in him. He had been willing, instead, to give her money to go to the city with, provided she remained faithful to him . . .

He had been fool enough not to see as he saw it now that no man can afford to let his wife go anywhere alone unless he can trust her; and, of course, he can trust her only if he knows that she can trust him, in everything, absolutely: he can trust her only if not only she loves him but if he loves her, and if she knows it, of positive knowledge . . .

To make the best of a bad bargain! What folly! He saw clearly now that nobody, in this relationship of marriage, can ever make the best of a bad bargain. It is all or nothing. Give all and take all. If you cannot do that, stand back and refrain.

But then, he had not refrained. He had taken her . . .

No matter where he turned in his agony, he saw no help for it; he saw no way out.

Once more, when this utter hopelessness of the situation became clear to him, he hardened his heart. He could not help himself; he was he; he could not act or speak except according to laws inherent in him.

What must happen would happen. He had sinned. He saw no atonement. None, nowhere.

And what about his life? What was its justification? No justification existed . . . Except perhaps, perhaps in helping others? . . .

On one of his first drives to town he met the ox-team of the new German settler, Dahlbeck by name.

On the wagon-truck drawn by the slow, plodding beasts rested a sand-box without a seat. The man sat on the edge of the box, his feet dangling between the wheels.

In front, on a little pile of straw, reposed a woman. The back of the low box was piled with bundles holding her belongings.

It was the big, strapping girl of the first farm to town; the one that had once looked at him when she had stood at the pump . . .

She was lying down as the two teams approached each other; but she sat up as Niels drew near.

Somehow, at his sight, a change took place in her expression. She recognised him. Her nonchalance dropped; and though she remained sitting, she seemed to rock herself on her hips. A provoking, challenging quality crept into the open smile with which she stared at him . . .

The man's stern face, narrow, hatchet-shaped, also underwent a change, discernible in shadings only. In that change there was betrayed a feeling of restraint, almost of shame. It looked as if he would have liked to interfere, to call the woman to order; as if he felt embarrassed at his own failure to do so. His nod, in answer to Niels', was almost forbidding.

Niels liked the man for that nod. He read his mind in it.

This man was a slave of passion. He would have preferred freedom; but he was a slave. The woman dominated, swayed, attracted, repelled him as she pleased. The woman was his evil genius . . .

All that Niels read in a glance and a nod . . .

Slowly, slowly, a new development traced itself out in the White Range Line House.

It was not often that Niels even saw his wife in the early part of the winter. Still more than before Mrs. Lindstedt led an indoor life. It seemed she never left the house any more . . .

Niels provided for everything she might possibly need to carry on a purely animal existence. He saw to it that there was bread – Mrs. Schultze baked it; he gathered the eggs and skimmed the milk; he watched the flour-bag, the potatoes, the smoked meat. He carried wood and water in.

All this he did either before day-break or after night-fall.

He knew that upstairs, in that room on the east side of the house, there lay or sat a woman, his wife, spinning off her hours, her days, her weeks . . . For a long time he did not even hear her.

The only signs of her life consisted in the slow, slow dwindling of the supply of flour; in the disappearance of an egg or two a day from the colander on the kitchen shelf; in the fact that at night there was a little less water in the pail on the bench by the door . . . Only once or twice – very rarely – there was a light burning in the room upstairs, in the morning or at night . . .

It would almost seem as if she watched for his appearance on the yard to extinguish even her lamp.

The only intercourse between the two, and that an indirect intercourse, consisted in this that once a week he took her mail which continued to arrive with great regularity and deposited it on the deal table in the hall whenever Bobby brought it from the office. When he looked for it the next time – as he never failed to do – it was gone. Whether she answered any of the letters or not; and if so, how, Niels did not learn . . .

Then, shortly before Christmas, a chance meeting came about in the kitchen.

Niels entered, rather later in the evening than usual, carrying a pail of milk to take it down into the cellar. It was quite dark inside and outside. Yet Niels knew that he had left the lamp burning on the table. Perhaps, when he went out, the draft had extinguished it. He set his pail down by the door and felt for matches. As he did so, his hand touched the hot glass of the lamp. A gasp escaped him; and the same moment there was the swish of clothes, quite nearby, as of somebody running. Then the crash of a falling chair and a half-suppressed cry.

He found the matches, removed, still in the dark, the chimney from the burner, struck his match, and lighted the lamp.

As he turned, he saw his wife in the corner behind the door. Apparently she had come down, thinking that he had finished the evening chores and had left the light burning by mistake. When she had heard him approaching over the crunching snow, she had blown the lamp and tried to escape without being seen. In the dark she had missed the door . . .

He looked at her; and she, with a defiant toss of her head, gathered her wraps which had half fallen about her and fled. He heard her passing through the dining room, into the hall, and up the stairs.

It was a meeting of no more than a quarter minute. But in those few seconds Niels had seen a number of things.

She had been in her nightgown, with a dressing gown thrown over her shoulders. The dressing gown was of light blue silk; the nightgown, of pink organdie or some other light, filmy material, profusely adorned with lace.

But the face!

For the fraction of a second he had thought it was the face of a perfect stranger. It had been that of an aging woman, yellow, lined with sharp wrinkles and black hollows under the eyes, the lips pale like the face . . . She had been without her make-up . . .

After Christmas, one day, while he was attending to his chores, a second meeting took place.

This time the mere fact of the meeting was hard to explain. The first time it had been accidental; this time there could be no doubt that it was intentional. Since their first encounter Niels had made it a point to give ample warning of his presence whenever he entered the house.

On this particular night he had gone down into the cellar, carrying the kitchen lamp and rattling the tin pails which he had previously scalded in the kitchen.

He was dipping the cream off the morning's milk when she, too, came down, carrying her own lamp in one hand and a little dish in the other. She took no notice of him but passed him by as if he did not exist.

Again she was in undress for the night, with a gown thrown over her shoulders. Again her face, that of an aging woman, aged by God knew what, stood in strange contrast, an incomprehensible, almost uncanny contrast, to her appearance; it was so yellow, lined . . .

Neither said a word. When she returned upstairs, Niels finished his work in the cellar, feeling guilty, down-cast, despondent. He took the skimmed milk to the kitchen to leave it there, ready for the morning when it would be fed to the pigs. Then he went out to bring in a few armfuls of wood for the heater in the dining room. He noticed, before he went out, that there was a light in that room; yet he never thought anything but that she, knowing he would come back, had simply left the lamp burning when she went upstairs.

As soon, however, as, in returning, he opened the door, he saw her standing by the stove, her dressing gown thrown back, warming herself in the heat that radiated through the mica-panes of the feed-door. For a moment he hesitated, looking at her. Then she spoke.

"Just put the wood down," she said, perfectly cool. "I'll see to the fire."

Her voice was that of a person speaking to a servant whose presence is in no way considered as embarrassing or as imposing restraint.

Yet she stood there as no woman could show herself to any man but her husband . . .

Henceforth the same thing happened often: soon it became the regular thing . . .

Whenever Niels entered the house, at least at night – for it could not be but that she watched for the time when he would come; never before had she been downstairs with such regularity, not even in the first few months of their marriage – she went about as if either everything were perfectly harmonious between them, and they perfectly secure from the intrusion of any stranger, or as if he did not exist, as if he were a being of air, a spirit ministering and bound to minister to her wants.

Niels did not know how to take it, what to think or to do.

Sometimes he waited till a later hour before attending to his chores in the house. It did not make any difference. Once he waited till midnight.

That time, when he entered through the kitchen door – the milk was frozen solid – the whole house was dark. But when he returned from the cellar, the dining room was lighted by the big floor-lamp; and there, by the stove, stood his wife.

He could not doubt any longer: there was a purpose behind her conduct.

What was that purpose?

He could not see his way through her psychology. He had no means of reading the mind of a woman driven to extremities.

It never occurred to him that this was a last attempt on her part to bring about a reconciliation . . .

She displayed herself to him; but to save her pride, she made it hard for him to find her attractive . . .

Had he made a single motion towards her, had he said a single word, even though it had been a word of forgiveness instead of desire, perhaps the worst might still have been averted; fate might have been stayed . . .

In him, however, all sexual instincts were dead.

. . .

The work in the bush went on . . . Day after day there was time to ponder, to brood. Matters were getting on Niels' nerves.

He employed quite a crew in the bush now. He was being watched. He was the boss . . .

Harder and harder did he drive himself. His "hands" took it that he was setting an example for them. Naturally, he wanted to make money . . . When he told them to "take their time," all but Bobby saw in that mere hypocrisy . . .

Niels drove, as he had always done, the "old Percheron team," Jock and Nellie – there was another such team on the farm now, bred and raised there.

Once he had been considerate in the highest degree wherever these two horses were concerned.

That was no longer the case.

Once, not so long ago, he had never neglected to pat them when he fed them in the stable. Now he roughly shouldered them aside when he entered their stalls.

When Jock, as of old, in the beginning of the winter, had once or twice turned his head to scrape his master's hand with his teeth, Niels had, with an impatient movement, declined his familiarity . . .

Horses know as well as dogs whether their masters feel friendly towards them or not. Unlike dogs, they do not cling to or fawn upon him who does not deserve their love. They cannot but do the work demanded of them; but they are henceforth mere slaves.

Towards the end of winter Niels' relation to his horses became completely demoralised.

One day, when he entered Nellie's stall, carrying hay, while she was eating her oats, he roughly hit her with the handle of the fork because she did not sidle over fast enough.

She turned her head and bit at him.

He flew into a towering rage, got a short stick of wood, returned into her stall, took her head by the halter, and brought the stick down on her flanks so that she reared and nearly crushed her colt which had whisked over to her other side.

Ever after she was nervous, almost vicious when he approached her.

As it happened, Bobby had come in just when Niels was punishing her. Instantly Niels felt ashamed of himself. But he muttered, "I'll show you," as he went out.

Back in the open, on the yard, he felt crushed by the weight of the consciousness that he was losing his hold on himself; so much so that he could not bear to face Bobby at once. He went into the implement shed, ostensibly to look for something or other; in reality, to hide from the boy.

There, in the dark, he sat down on the seat of the binder; without any thought at first; but with a feeling of such unhappiness as he had never felt before. How could he, how could he let things get the better of him that way? He, Niels!

Are there in us unsounded depths of which we do not know ourselves? Can things outside of us sway us in such a way as to change our very nature? Are we we? Or are we mere products of circumstance?

He felt like a rider on horseback who tries to control his mount when it is under the influence of an uncontrollable panic . . .

Was he, Niels, going insane?

If so, what could he do about it?

What was that woman doing to him? Was she taking the revenge she had threatened?

What did that revenge consist in?

Spring came. A hundred acres were seeded.

And in the house the woman awoke.

The dreaded next move was being made.

So far it consisted in nothing more but that she began

to take walks in the bluff where the soil was dry and clean, consisting of the matted roots of grass, low-growing plants, and trees.

For these walks she dressed in the most elaborate way, combing her hair in the latest fashion, and "making up" with all her art.

Niels could not help spying upon her sometimes. He found work that would take him into the cow-lot; or perhaps he had something to do in the garden, east of the house.

She would walk about in the bluff, sometimes dreamily, sometimes almost gaily, a smile on her face, lost in thought.

Or she would take a chair out, or a rug which she spread on the ground, and sit down and read: to a stranger it would have appeared a very idyl . . .

Only, had that stranger by chance seen the change in her look when she caught sight of her husband, he would have shuddered at the sudden expression of hatred that came over her face . . . It was not a mere dislike, not a fleeting aversion: it was the chilling insanity of revenge . . .

Niels never saw her like that; but somehow he, too, shuddered at her mere sight.

He would go to some corner of his farm, perhaps to the grove at the south-west corner, where he was cutting poles to replace rotting fence-posts. And he would sit down and brood. He would then almost wish that something decisive, something catastrophic would happen.

The fact was that he began to live under a fear: the inactivity of the woman began to unnerve him.

What was he to do? Bobby would leave one day. He was growing up. He was twenty years old. But Niels needed Bobby: Bobby was the last link that connected him with the world of living men: the last barrier between him and insanity . . .

The Sundays were the worst. Then Bobby went out . . .

Niels, too, began to go out on Sundays, using his drivers: then he could be seen, driving furiously and aimlessly over the Marsh, his hair growing longer and longer on his shoulders, his beard flowing over his breast. People shook their heads . . .

Think, think . . .

A ray of light. Perhaps if he threshed the whole thing out once more, from beginning to end, being all alone, he would find some solution . . .

He heard of a certain hay-meadow. A store-keeper in Poplar Grove looked after it for the owner. He could always think best when driving. He would go there to-morrow and see . . .

He started out very early in the morning, at sun-up. Whenever he approached farm or homestead in the bush, he galloped his horses.

He would not have needed to fear. If he avoided people in this settlement, the people also avoided him. Nobody knows how rumours spring up in the wilderness; spring up they do. The story went that Lindstedt was insane; that he was a hermit; that he kept his wife a prisoner on his place . . . Nobody would have come to the road to exchange a greeting with Lindstedt . . .

Gradually a definite line of thought evolved.

It was almost a year now since the final break with his wife. But he could have reconstructed the whole course of the argument. He had a knack of viewing things most clearly in retrospection.

His wife had intended to leave him. He had refused to let her go. Why? Why had he not simply agreed? Would it not have been best for both of them? Of course, it would.

Had she asked him now to let her go, he would have been glad; he would have welcomed it as a great deliverance.

True, it was no longer possible to realise old dreams.

His marriage had killed them. His dreams were dead. What if they were?

What would life be without her? Not happiness. Not what he had once dreamed of as his life. But there would be peace: he could drown himself in work. And the fruits of work? Well, at the worst he could give them away . . .

Why had he refused to let her go? Slowly that summer arose before his memory. Last summer. Last summer only?

And the whole year before it!

Three times she had been in the city.

Slowly, out of his brooding over those absences, a question had arisen. This question: What had she been doing in the city? It had disturbed him, gnawed at him, and finally whipped him into the determination not to let her go back to the city. "No matter what she had been doing, she was not going to do it again!"

He understood. During that interview in the dining room he had been blind, he had been inaccessible to any reason. He had unthinkingly held on to that decision.

He understood. He was glad he could interpret his action so clearly, so accurately. And suddenly the solution of the whole problem flashed up before him: he saw a way out of his labyrinth. Why, it was all clear. There could be no doubt.

What he was going to do, what he must do was this: he must offer to send her away; he must offer money; he must bribe her to leave him alone . . .

He did not go on. He turned his horses and drove home, furiously. He reached the farm shortly after noon.

It was still early when he saw his wife leave the house for her now accustomed walk in the bluff. He had been waiting about at the stables.

For a moment she stood in the door of the house, looking out to the right and the left. She was dressed in a light summer frock of striped zephyr; and she held a parasol of pearl-grey silk over her head. Her face showed a perfect make-up: lips of glowing red, dark brows over dancing eyes, cheeks of pallid smoothness . . .

If she was aware of Niels' presence on the other side of the yard, she did not betray it.

His heart sank.

She looked the picture of contented happiness – so much so that he began to doubt of the success of his scheme. He wondered what might be going on in that head.

He turned and went into the stable. He stopped at the little square window which, curtained with cobwebs in which dust and chaff were caught, looked out to the north. From there he watched.

After a minute or so the woman, adjusting, with an almost convulsive shrug of her shoulders, a light shawl about her neck, turned to the east and passed through the lane that separated the kitchen garden, now become a potato-patch, from the wall of the lean-to. She disappeared from Niels' field of vision.

For a while he busied himself about the stable, irresolutely. Bobby was far away in the south-east corner of the farm, disking. Niels had sent him there on purpose. Now was the time to do what he intended to do.

A strange hesitancy took possession of him. Again he was going to carry out a preconceived plan. He had done so before; and what he had done then was the exact reverse of what he should have done . . . Perhaps it might be best to wait, to think matters over more fully . . .

He stood and brooded. No; think and then act on the decision arrived at; that was the law of his nature. He could not help himself. It had to be done.

For the first and last time in his life he was conscious of deliberately composing his features for the occasion . . .

He found his wife sitting on a rug which, at the northern edge of the bluff, was spread on the ground, in a little natural glade shaded by a thicket of plum trees.

As he approached, she looked up at him, with the old expression of half mocking friendliness and interest. It disarmed him for a moment. Then he became aware of an uncanny element in that expression.

A question arose: whom did she see? Surely, it was not he whom she looked at that way?

As if to confirm his thought her features underwent a change as if she were, by an effort, recalling her eyes from a distance. She focused them on him: a steely hardness entered them. Her features became hollow under her mask. Haggard she looked out from behind a screen.

Niels' mind worked feverishly. He recalled various things: how he had first seen her without her mask, one morning when he had entered her bed-room before the usual hour: how another face had looked out at him, like a death's-head almost: the coarse, aged face of a coarse, aged woman, aged before her time . . . Other sights rose, full of revelations. But above all that of how she had stood in that dining room of hers, on that fateful September afternoon last year. Then, too, the smile had faded from her lips; the dream had died in her eyes . . .

Niels stood and hesitated. He felt chilled to his very bones. Whatever he might wish, she would for that very reason decline . . .

Just then, after a minute of allowing this air of hostility to do its work, she moved and spoke.

Her movement consisted in a raising of her head while, with the point of her folded parasol, she tapped the toe of her shoe; her eye looked straight at him, or rather through him.

Her speech was a single word, freezing in its coldness. "Well? . . ."

Niels cleared his throat. Then, haltingly, awkwardly, as he had always spoken to this woman, "I have thought this matter over . . . Something has to be done . . . I am going to pieces . . . So are you . . . If you want to go . . . I am willing . . ."

And there his speech gave out as a runnel of water gives out in a sand-hole.

Her eye had flashed up. A smile had returned to her lips. It was an evil smile.

He looked at her aghast.

Then she burst into an artificial laugh. "No," she said, still laughing.

And suddenly she was on her feet, whipped up, as if a steel-spring had sent her up with enormous power.

The laughter had died. She was fury personified.

Niels had already turned and was leaving her. With his shoulders bent as he might bend them in a beating, lashing rain, he walked off with long, almost furtive strides.

She followed him. "No," she yelled after him, "that favour I won't do you! No longer! You're going to pieces, are you? . . . Well, let me tell you . . . I'm not through with you yet. I'll go when I'm ready to go. You're only going to pieces . . . I won't go till you've gone to pieces . . ."

Niels went faster and faster; but she ran after him, stumbling, gathering herself up again, falling, rising, losing her parasol, and finally breaking down and lying there, on the yard, just at the corner of the kitchen, where the lane between house and garden came to an end.

Niels did not look back. He went straight across the open and into the stable whence he had watched her a while ago.

Bobby was there. Some accident had brought him back from the field. He was looking for some piece of harness to replace another which had probably broken. He had heard all or part at least . . . What did it matter? . . . Niels paid no attention to him. For a moment the boy, having found what he was looking for, hesitated at the side door which led to the horse-lot. Niels waved his hand at him to be gone . . .

Then he stepped back to the little window.

There, at the end of the lane, the woman that was his wife was picking herself up from the ground. In stumbling, she had stepped on the hem of her frock and torn it so that it was hanging about her feet; and she stumbled again. She raised her head and looked dazedly about. Her face was bleeding. Earth and chaff, such as gathers on farmyards, were sticking to the make-up of her cheeks. She reached for the corner of the building to steady herself and groped her way along to the door, stumbling once more, bending down, and picking up the torn edge of her gown. At last she disappeared inside.

Niels' first impulse had been to go to her aid. But he thought better of it. It would not do. He waited ten minutes, went to fetch rug and parasol, and dropped them into the entrance of the house.

Still he hesitated.

No; to go upstairs was useless. His mere sight would irritate the woman . . . It was best to leave her alone . . .

Spring passed by; summer came.

The hay had to be stacked in the slough, then hauled to the yard and restacked there. Showery weather during July doubled and trebled the work . . . Niels was aging, decaying . . . Yet, the energy and circumspection with which he furthered the work and repaired the damage done to the hay – as far as it could be repaired – were still those of his best years: his care for the farm was almost passionate.

But it was the last flicker of a dying flame. Hopelessness and indifference began to show more and more even in his physique. His shoulders stooped; his features began to sag. He never shaved any longer, his hair hung low. He felt old, tremendously old, centuries old. He felt as if he carried the experience of a world, carried it as an actual load on his shoulders.

In daytime he drowned thought in work; at night he read.

But even his reading was restricted to one book, the Bible; and in the Bible to one chapter of the Old Testament: Solomon's wisdom. He intoxicated himself in the rhythm of its sentences. He read the same thing over and over again till he knew it by heart. In the field he muttered detached phrases, repeating them a hundred times. "This also is vanity and a striving after wind." "And he who increaseth knowledge increaseth sorrow." "All the rivers run into the sea, yet the sea is not full; unto the place where the rivers go, thither they go again."

When he came to the sentence, "That which is crooked cannot be made straight," it seemed a comfort. The phrase, "There is no profit under the sun," seemed to echo his own conclusions. "And there is no new thing under the sun." No; others had arrived at the same truths as he, Kings and High Priests . . .

Yet right by his side Life was lived: the life of children who do not look beyond the hour. The child was Bobby.

Bobby was getting restless. When he tried to talk and saw that Niels was not listening, he went out and sat on a stone or a block of wood, frowning, dissatisfied. He was a man now, twenty-one years old. Niels had been more than an employer to him: he had been an idol. Still, he had his own life to make. He could not for ever be looking after Niels . . .

But time went and revealed its secrets. Things that were hidden came to light.

Bates, a neighbour of Niels', on the south-east quarter of the same section, "burned out." He wanted to leave, to give up: he was a city man, drifting back to the city . . . Niels bought his quarter, bought it for Bobby, to be farmed by him for himself, beginning with the next year . . .

Niels had arrived at something like composure again. It was a dark, pessimistic composure, it is true; but it seemed as if it might last forever . . .

Then that composure also broke down.

One afternoon, in cutting time, Niels forsook his binder. Something, he knew not what, prompted him to do so. It was no suspicion; it was hardly an uneasiness. Bobby was stooking.

"I'm two rounds ahead," Niels said as he let himself down from his seat. "I'll be back before you catch up."

He crossed the stubble and disappeared in the grove which bordered his farm in the west.

He came to the fence and climbed over it.

On the road, he looked about. As if it were the first time he saw it, the size of the settlement struck him which had grown up on the Marsh. For a moment the sight of all the farms recalled him to reality. He passed his hand over his sweaty brow, sighed, and was on the point of turning back. But the moment he faced his field again, an invincible disinclination to ride that binder took hold of him.

He went north, along his fence.

When he came to the gate, he did not open it, but stepped over the stile which he had built by its side. On the yard he stopped and looked about.

All was still, so still that he heard the fluttering of the wings of a bird flitting by. He stared at the house. The door stood wide open.

Suddenly his heart began to beat like a sledge-hammer; he could hear its thud.

Under an irresistible compulsion he slunk over to the door and stood there, listening.

Not a sound.

He went to the corner of the house.

This time he heard something: whispers and laughter, half suppressed.

He went to the corner of the house.

This time he heard something.

He went all the way back to the entrance of the yard. There he turned south into the bush, almost running over the sun-dappled soil between the trees. He went on till he was beyond the stables, and then turned east, circling the whole clearing of his yard. At last he turned north again, along pig-pens and milk-house, till he reached the garden. He vaulted over its pole-fence and crossed the potato-patch. North of the garden a thicket of plum trees had developed into a dense screen since the lot had been cleared.

Niels crouched. Slowly, carefully he invaded the bush.

Suddenly he stood as if frozen in his attitude.

There, right in front of him, not more than twenty, thirty feet away, unhidden by intervening shrubs or trees, sat his wife, just as he had found her two months ago. But by her side sat a man, the younger Dunsmore, his right arm about her shoulder, holding one of her hands in his left. They were whispering and laughing. The man bent over and kissed her on the mouth, long, fervently, with the kiss of a sensual lover.

Niels moved; a dry twig snapped under his foot. Then he stood arrested again.

The woman's right hand came up and grasped the head of the man from behind, holding it; and beyond and above the head her eyes appeared, staring straight at Niels.

She had heard the crackling of the twig. She knew he

was there; and she perpetuated the attitude in which she had been caught, enjoying his dismay, perpetuated it for his leisurely inspection . . .

Her eyes held him, looking at him, derisively, looking at his shrinking figure and drooping head . . .

Thus the two, man and woman, stared at each other for half a minute . . .

That woman in front of him, in the arms of her lover, was insane . . .

Then the head of the man was lifted and obstructed the woman's look.

During that fraction of a second Niels withdrew into the denser thicket behind.

He heard a laugh: the light, silvery laugh, not at all artificial, which had rung in his ears for days, years ago. It sounded so sane, contented, so natural that, for a moment, he doubted the very testimony of his eyes: what he had seen could not be reality!

Then he returned the way he had come. But he did not run this time; he went as if lost in thought. In truth he was not lost in thought: there was no thought in him; he was merely stunned.

He went past his farm, on to wild land, and sat down. He remained for hours. He was barely conscious . . .

It was late, after nine, when Niels appeared at the shack. He declined supper. But he attended himself to all those of the chores which necessitated entering the house. All else he left to Bobby.

. . .

Once more Niels was a changed man.

True, he rode the binder again: he drove the sheaves to the yard: he plowed the land.

But it was Bobby who did the farming. It was Bobby who planned and suggested, directed, instructed.

It was Bobby, too, who, when winter came began the work in the bush.

Only one single part of what had to be done on the place Niels attended to without being reminded of it: the part that had to be done in the house.

There, nothing betrayed that anybody was living in it: nothing except that the wood-box became empty, that the water in the pails sank lower, and that eggs, potatoes, meat were slowly, slowly getting less.

Niels watched this with fascination: he counted the things which thus disappeared.

Apart from that, the decay in Niels consisted more in a gradual disintegration of will and purpose.

He became indifferent to everything, even to his comfort. That he went on with the work, under Bobby's direction, was merely because it was the easiest thing to do; it required no thought, no decision, no break with the past.

Winter went by; life went its way.

Bobby seeded his own farm, the quarter section that was to be his. He picked a four-horse team from among Niels' colts, bargained for them with his employer, and paid in cash: he had the accumulated earnings of years. As for the farm, he would pay in half crops.

Bobby was loyal. Seeing that Niels was doing this for him, he would not leave him while he was what he was. But Bobby wanted to get married, to establish himself . . .

Well, even for that there would be a way pretty soon.

Haying time.

It was Bobby who rented a meadow where the two had never cut before. He was not working for wages in haying; he was working on shares with Niels.

The quarter next to the one he rented had been taken by Dahlbeck, the German settler on the bank of the creek.

Thus it came about that, whenever Bobby and Niels went out to the slough, in the early dawn, both sitting on their hay-racks, taking six horses, in front of them or behind them a third hay-rack would be moving along. On it sat Dahlbeck, pale, slim, and wiry; and by his side, the Dahlbeck woman, flashy, handsome in her coarse peasant way, and using her eyes to establish a bond between herself and Bobby or Niels . . .

Now it happened that Bobby – in an impulse of impatience at Niels' lethargy – one evening when he was shaving turned about on him where he was sitting in front of his shack, in the dusk, and said jestingly, "Come on, Niels, let me give you a trimming, too."

Niels looked at him, silently, with an almost forbidding disapproval of his jocularity.

But Bobby had already taken a pair of clippers. "Come on," he repeated, "let me, eh?"

And Niels let him do as he pleased.

"The beard, too?" Bobby asked when he had finished the hair. And he laughed. "Come on, now. Be a sport. You look like Methuselah!"

Niels raised his chin. What did it matter? It was not worth while to resist. Besides, there was a feeling of physical comfort in the proceeding.

"Gee whiz!" Bobby exclaimed when he looked at his handiwork. "You're a young man yet, Niels. I'd almost forgotten. I thought you were old enough to be my granddad by this time."

Absent-mindedly Niels guided his finger-tips over his chin and nodded. He got up with a sigh and went about his chores.

There was one person who noticed the change at once next morning: the Dahlbeck woman as everybody called her. She glanced at Bobby and laughed; and Bobby smiled back.

It struck the boy that there was a resemblance between Dahlbeck and Niels: not in appearance or anything concrete; but in their outlook on life . . .

Niels and Bobby stacked in the slough; but Dahlbeck took all his dry hay home. The woman raked whenever he was gone; they had no horse-rake yet.

In the afternoon it so chanced that Bobby wished to draw a load home to be put in the loft of the stable. He and Dahlbeck started at the same time . . .

Niels was on the far side of the stack and never noticed the coincidence. He turned to the mower. That mower, Bobby had said, needed oiling; he knelt down to his task. The horses were standing north of him, their noses to the hay.

Suddenly the shadow of a figure fell across the grass in front of him. He winced; and as he looked up, there stood the Dahlbeck woman, laughing at his startled glance.

She said nothing. She merely looked at him and let herself down to a squatting posture.

Over them stood an almost cloudless sky. The summer had been that typical prairie season in which settled weather is broken only by swift, violent storms in which the equilibrium of the atmospheric forces is speedily re-established.

The slough about them was fragrant with the hot exhalations of the hay.

Niels had stopped in his work and was staring at her, the oil-can in his hand. At last he spoke, "What do you want?"

The woman laughed. She threw herself back in the loose hay that littered the ground. As she did so, her hat fell from her head, baring tightly rolled tresses of abundant, dark brown hair. Her skirt slipped up; the full, strong calves of her legs protruded.

"You!" she said in a whisper from which the heat of passion breathed.

Niels still knelt motionless. Pictures of the past flitted through his mind: the first that had come to him through many months. The frown on his brow deepened into a scowl.

"You ought to be ashamed of yourself," he said with distaste.

Once more she laughed; and she rolled over in the hay, closer to him, so that she nearly touched him. "Joseph!" she whispered mockingly.

That note of mockery called up the almost forgotten memory of her who was his wife as she had been one time and as she had had power over him in years gone by. A feeling of shame swept through him, unnerving his strength. His head sank down on his chest. He had no right to upbraid the woman . . .

He got up, threw the oil-can into the tool-box, and went over to where the horses stood. He picked their lines up and guided them to the mower. Nellie stepped over the pole. He hooked the traces into place.

The woman whose laughter had died away followed every one of his movements with her eye. It was she who was scowling now. And when he clicked his tongue to pull away from her, she sprang up and ran after him, catching hold of his shoulder. She was beside herself with rage.

"You hypocrite," she hissed, "are you better than other people? I know you, you devil! You can't play the innocent with me! No man can! You least of all! You married the district whore . . ."

And for several minutes she went on, pouring abuse from pent-up stores as foam boils from a brimming vessel.

But Niels did not hear. He had stopped. His knees shook under him. Lightning had struck him; and the flash had illumined the past as a flash of real lightning illumines a forest trail for him who travels in the dark, making every detail spring out of the night at once.

What, in the fraction of a second, he saw like a panorama, with hundreds of details, all simultaneously, was this: the hesitation of the woman when he had first mentioned marriage to her; Bobby's silence when he had opened the gate for her and him; the atmosphere of a hollow void which had surrounded them when they had come to the Marsh to live; Nelson's words, "You don't mean to say that you don't know?" and again, "Then I won't tell you;" Hahn's remark, "There's one in every district. There's one in yours;" and, much later, the woman's words, "I gave myself, body and all . . . It was nothing to me!" Ellen's "How could you? . . ."

All that and much more Niels saw and heard in that illuminating flash.

For a moment he felt that he must pitch forward and faint. Instinctively his trembling hand reached for the machine to steady his swaying body . . .

The woman saw it and stopped in her rush of words. Her eyes became wide. She realised what she had done: she had swung an axe into a great, towering tree; and the tree had crashed down at a single blow . . .

She let go of the man; and he dropped the lines and stumbled away . . .

When Bobby returned to the slough, sitting on his hay-rack, he found Dahlbeck and the woman at work.

The sun was setting.

He drove to the stack. Jock and Nellie were hitched to the mower; the lines were trailing behind; they were grazing, their heads bent low. The Clydes still stood at the stack, half asleep, one leg drawn up.

Niels was nowhere to be seen. The landscape presented the picture of evening peace.

Slowly Bobby went to the other side of the stack and called over to where Dahlbeck was working, "Seen anything of Lindstedt?"

Dahlbeck stopped his team. "No, not a thing."

Bobby stood undecided. It struck him that the woman who was pitching the last of the day's cutting into cocks did not even turn to look at him.

There was nothing to do but to load his rack as best he could alone.

He whistled away for a while as he went about the work. Then he became silent.

Soon after, the Dahlbecks left the slough on top of their load.

Bobby was by nature companionable. The great, hollow night that rose about him made him feel lonesome.

What was wrong that Niels should be gone?

It had never happened before . . . Yet, come to think of it, it had happened before: when they were cutting and stooking the grain in the harvest field . . . Niels had walked off; then, too, Bobby had been puzzled and worried. Niels was going to pieces, there could be no doubt. He was getting to be very queer . . .

A slow, numbing dread took hold of Bobby . . .

There was a memory in the boy's mind, of his own foster-father, Lund, who had disappeared in the bush . . .

He began to hurry. He had only half filled his rack when he stopped. He pitched his fork up into the load and went to get the other horses. He tied them behind, all four, took his lines, climbed up, and drove through the slough to the road.

He had six miles to go; but the horses stepped briskly along.

What could be wrong?

The bush stood silent, motionless. Not a breath stirred. The creaking and rattling of the wheels echoed back to the driver who sat hushed on the load.

Now and then the horses snorted; they were wide awake; horses are watchful, scary at night.

At last they came to the east-west road leading to the corner of the bluff. There was the Dunsmore shack ahead, to the left; Dahlbeck's place to the right. On the yard man and wife were pitching off their load.

Even here no sound except the desultory, almost hesitating bumps and screeches of the rack . . .

Then, ahead, against the paler sky of the west, the bluff loomed up, like a huge bowl inverted over . . . what?

To dispel the feeling of oppression Bobby began to whistle once more. He stopped at once: the sound jarred on the silence.

He turned the corner and came to the gate. He slipped from the load and stood, listening. Not a sound. Low in the west, the waxing sickle of the moon was hanging, a mere wisp, a little curve of light, about to set. There was no wind: but the leaves of the aspens in the bluff were rustling softly: they were never still . . .

On the yard, white buildings stood outlined against the sombre bush, some looming high: house, barn; some squatting low: pig-pens, cow-shed. Nowhere a light . . .

Bobby shivered.

He turned to the horses. They, too, listened to the silence. Their ears moved back and forth, jerkily.

To defend himself against the feeling of dread, the boy began for the third time to whistle. Again he stopped. The sound seemed like a profanation of something . . .

Quickly he opened the gate; the horses pulled at once, as if afraid of being left behind, alone . . .

A few minutes later Bobby had lighted a lantern; he unhitched and untied the horses. He opened the door of the stable. They knew their stalls and for the moment needed no further attention.

He picked the lantern up and ran to the shack. It was empty. The dishes and the stove had not been touched since dinner time. The alarm clock showed a quarter past nine . . .

"Well," he muttered with a phrase of his mother's, "I'll be jiggered!"

He returned to the yard.

Once more he looked about and listened . . .

Incomprehensibly, uncannily, he was aware of a new accession of dread. A single, horizontal line of light showed in the upper east window of the house. During the past two years the house had often seemed spectral to him: never before as now.

Where was Niels?

Bobby shuddered. A feeling took hold of him as if from somewhere in the dark eyes were looking out at him.

A cow lowed on the open marsh . . .

Bobby awoke to life. The herd was coming home.

He went about his chores, pumped water, fed pigs . . .

The pigs knew the routine: when he entered the milk-house to stir shorts and barley into the milk, they ran along their fence, squealing . . .

In the cow-lot, after he had lighted a smudge, the swishing sound of the milk in the pails sounded like company, like a re-affirmation of the common work-aday sanity of country life, shutting out the horrors that lurked somewhere . . .

Yet, where was Niels?

The moon had set; even the pallour in the north-west of the sky had darkened. It was night . . . Where was Niels?

There was the possibility that he might have gone to the shack meanwhile. No. The shack was empty as before. It was eleven o'clock.

Was he to look for him? Was he to give the alarm to the neighbours? . . . His foster-father had been help-less, half blind, half lame. He had been out of his senses . . .

Should he enter the house? . . . No. He could not face the woman . . .

He was hungry. He went to the shack again and lighted the stove. As he sat there, with the door open, the light of the lamp on the table falling slantways out on the little clearing and, beyond, among the white glistening boles of the young aspens, he, too, began to review what he knew of the woman in the great house, of her who had been the curse of the place . . .

He thought of the shock it had been to him when she had smiled down at him from the seat of the wagon, saying what she had said . . . He had never known much about her; but he had heard whispers, seen looks exchanged between grown-ups . . .

For a moment then, Niels had fallen in his esteem; till he had spoken to him in front of the stable . . . The tone of his voice as he had spoken to him! . . .

If only Niels would come home . . . Now . . . Quick . . .

He, Bobby, had sometimes felt harshly towards him, of late, when he had become so queer . . . He would never do so again if only . . .

He rose and busied himself with pots and pans.

Niels had been a father to him. He thought of a Sunday, years ago, when Niels had refused him a horse. "Not if you want to go to bad places . . ."

Once more Bobby went out on the yard, looking, listening . . . To the gate, peering along the road, north, south . . . Nothing . . .

It was after midnight when he returned to the shack. He was so worried he did not even enter; he merely glanced at the clock.

Then he squatted down on the ground, by the door . . .

Sleep must have overcome him at last. He was suddenly conscious of starting up. For several minutes he sat stock-still. He thought he had heard something. The first grey of dawn was hovering over the world. His clothes were damp with dew; he shivered . . . The stillness of death, except for the chirping of some bird . . .

He rose and went into the shack to lie down . . .

Then, just as a few minutes before, in his sleep, the sharp report of a shot . . .

With a jerk Bobby straightened, every muscle taut; drowsiness had fallen from him like a cloak.

He hurried back to the yard. He saw the stable door open, ran, and looked in.

There, in the cold, grey morning light stood Niels, the smoking gun still in his hand. And Jock, his horse, was convulsively kicking his last at his feet . . .

. . .

When Niels had left the slough, he had lost himself in the bush. He went blindly, with unseeing eyes, unthinking brain.

Like the bell of doom the woman's words seemed to reverberate within a hollow vault of brass . . .

There had been thoughts, suspicions, almost certainties half faced. There never had been unescapable conviction . . . From all about him there was only one voice of the woman, "You have married the . . ."

He went blindly, stumbling over roots and stumps. He was bleeding from nose and forehead. He had lost his cap . . . He picked himself up again, fell again, tearing his clothes, bruising his limbs. He went on as an animal goes, wounded to death, seeking his lair, to hide himself . . .

He was in a trance. Three, four times he came out on the road. Instinctively he stopped, trying to focus eye and mind on it, swaying from side to side like one drunk. Then he turned back into the thickets behind.

Two, three hours went by that way.

Several times he sank to his knees, bending his body low, crouching in an agony of misery.

Had anybody met him and asked him, sternly, "What is that thought which is lurking beyond the edge of your world, ready to rise above the horizon?" he would have searched in his mind, sincerely, honestly; yet he would have found nothing but a painful, raw void to face, to probe into which without encountering anything was baffling, infinitely tormenting. He would have groaned as the man groans on whom a painful operation is being performed while he is under the influence of an anaesthetic. Although the onlooker is, perhaps, from past experience, fully aware of the fact that he who lives in that body feels nothing, the groan sounds all the more pitiful, all the more enervating . . .

After hours of such somnambulism Niels found himself stopped by his own fence. Again he stood, one of his hands resting on the wire, as, with an infinite exertion, he tried to comprehend, to concentrate his mind on the thing that had stopped him.

And as soon as it entered his consciousness that these sloughs, these rising ridges, that bluff half a mile away were his, he turned back.

Behind him were other sloughs, swampy hollows, their soil churned up, trodden and trampled by wandering cattle into little hillocks tufted with grass, hardened by drying, with muddy holes in between where the feet of the heavy beasts had sunk deep.

Over these foot-traps he tottered, stumbled, fell headlong, picked himself up again . . .

Once more he was stopped by a fence. Again that slow, painful process of concentration began; again the fact filtered through the defences of his mind that the fence was his . . .

His lip curled in a physical sense of distaste; he turned back again. Dusk was rising . . .

When, an hour or so later, the fence stopped him for the third time, he did not turn back. For a while he stood like a man broken by a lifetime of work too heavy for him, bent over, one hand on the post, one on the wire . . . Then he tried to straddle the fence, stumbled back, and finally went down on his knees, thus crawling on to his own land where he lay, exhausted . . .

But some impulse was at work in him. Slowly he drew his legs up and raised himself on hands and knees; and at last he got up on his feet.

Within half an hour he found himself in a bluff of poplars. He felt his way from tree to tree, supporting himself by his hands, feeling up and down the ridged trunks as if searching for something.

In another half hour he was south of his yard; and then, behind the granary. Around its corners he groped his way . . .

When he reached the front, he attacked the door: it took several minutes to open it: his hands seemed to have lost the knack of lifting the latch.

It was a high step to take; and in attempting it he fell headlong. There was a pile of bags hung over the partition between bins. Niels pawed at it till they came down. Then he turned on his back, pushed the bags into a heap, and leaned against them . . .

There he sat, his knees drawn up, his forehead resting on them, his hands lying on the floor . . .

Occasionally he lifted his head, like an enormous burden which swayed on his neck, with that re-awaking and astonishment with which he who, having gone to sleep in his own bed, finds himself in a strange place would look about for something to recognise . . .

At first there was nothing but darkness.

At last a tiny speck of light stood out, just by the door, halfway up the jamb. It was reflected by a highly polished object hanging there: that must be the butt of the big-game rifle which he had bought for Bobby . . .

After many attempts to rise he crawled forward.

He had heard a noise: the creaking of a hay-rack, the slow step of horses, a snorting, the dull thud of the gate swinging against its stop.

The door had swung almost shut; he pushed it half open and lifted his legs over the edge of the threshold till he sat there, in the crack of the door.

Far out on the yard – the granary stood in a recess of the bush – the light of a lantern moved to and fro, about the stables, to the east. The lantern burned dimly: its glass was smoky . . .

A curious interest awoke in Niels. Unseen, he saw.

The lantern, bobbing up and down, crossed the whole length of the yard, moving quickly. Its dim light illuminated the running legs of the boy till the door, half shut, closed out the view.

From Niels' throat came a sound as if he were chuckling.

The light returned. The boy was standing, looking, listening . . .

Niels' eyes were fastened on him, out of the dark that screened him. The little dome of visibility ensphering the lantern did not reach to the granary.

Niels fought with himself to supress his laughter. He was playing a prank. He saw, he was not seen . . .

The cows lowed. Bobby returned . . .

Niels began to dangle his feet, like a child, or like one who has been sick and has unlearned the art of walking: he delighted in the sense of the motion.

But when his heel struck the stones of the foundation below, he started and covered his mouth with his hand: a movement of childish mock fright . . .

Then, after many more comings and goings, Bobby left the yard not to return . . .

Long, long Niels sat and stared into the dark. There was just starlight enough to show the outlines.

It was all there, the whole picture of the yard, dim and quiet: without its details. His eyes were gradually, automatically adjusting themselves, so that, when they were called upon, they saw.

The call that came consisted in a change of the picture. It was long past midnight.

The line of light disappeared from the crack between blind and frame in the upper east window of the house . . .

Instantly Niels saw. He did not move. The change did not at once release any conscious reaction, any thought.

The next moment the light reappeared at the lower window, in front of the staircase, throwing a dim glow over the sward of grass on the yard. For a moment a figure appeared in the frame of the window; a woman in flimsy, gaudy undress. An arm, almost bare, reached up to draw the blind so that it intercepted the light.

Utter darkness fell, darker than before. But after a minute or so, very dim, almost divined, the light fell into the lane between kitchen and garden.

Niels sat very still, frowning.

A whole, forgotten world came back to him: a distasteful world, not in keeping with his animal comfort.

He wanted to put the thought away as it tried to emerge. He was tempted to brush it from his brow with his hand. But he did not move. His hands rested alongside his thighs, on the threshold of the door. His body was bent forward. His muscles were tightening, slackening, in reflex action . . .

He stared and did not move.

In his mind, in the background of his memory, proceeding from the faintest adumbration of some great fact dominating his life, a question crystalised . . .

What had all this to do with him?

With that problem he wrestled for an hour.

Again a change in the picture of the yard. Once more the light went on its progress downward in the house.

And this time, what he saw connected itself with the past, suddenly, without any slow development or unfolding. The whole antecedents of the present moment stood before his mind as if he were living them within fractions of a second: it was like a dream which, retrospectively, motivates a sound or other perception received in sleep.

His muscles tightened and remained tight. It was as if a powerful spring inside of him had been tightly wound and then arrested by some catch, either to snap under the strain or to unroll itself in the natural way by setting some complicated wheel-work into irresistible motion, grinding up what might come in its way or attempt to stop it.

Wave after wave of hot blood went through his body, lapping up into his brain, breaking there, flooding his consciousness with an opaque, scarlet flood . . .

He raised himself on his feet, without swaying, and stood. Then it was as if a cruel wrench had been given that spring inside of him, tightening it to the breaking point. And as that point was reached, he moved.

He moved with tremendous speed.

The next moment he stood at the door of the house and threw it open.

Voices from the back room; laughing voices.

"Sh-sh!"

"Nonsense! Who'd come at this time of night?"

A third voice, whispering.

A roar of laughter . . .

That released the tightly wound spring. Irresistibly a clockwork began to move. There was not a spark of consciousness in Niels. He acted entirely under the compulsion of the spring.

He remembered later, much later . . .

He was back at the granary and reached into the door for the gun. He made sure it was loaded.

Again he crossed the yard and entered the house, noisily, without taking precautions.

He went through the front room and threw the door to the dining room open.

There, consternation had done its work.

A man's figure, half clad, was vaulting through the open window to the right; a second one was fleeing through the door into the kitchen.

At the left, the woman was sitting, her face made up, her body wrapped in silks . . .

On the table dishes, plates, cups, a biscuit-bowl, a tea-pot . . .

The woman rose, a half frightened, half triumphant smile on her face. She sought his eyes; but she looked into the barrel of the gun.

The shot rang out.

She screamed and ran for the kitchen door, upsetting a chair on her way. But before she reached it, she fell, flinging her arms and kicking her feet so that a silken slipper fell in the centre of the table.

Then she went quiet and lay in a heap.

Niels had already turned, slamming both doors as he went. Again he crossed the yard. He entered the stable. He could never remember why he had done so. He went through the driveway and east, towards the horse-lot.

There, in this short aisle, in neighbouring stalls, stood Jock and Nellie, just visible in the dim light of dawn.

Niels, swaying again, came very near to the rump of the gelding.

Jock, as the door was opened, had turned his head. When his master swayed near him, he, expecting a blow, kicked out.

Niels raised his gun and shot the gelding through the head . . .

All that day Niels slept: a deep, sunken sleep.

Bobby had pulled the dead horse out of the stable, putting the chain around his rigid hind legs and hitching the Clydes to the chain. It would have seemed a sacrilege to use the young Percherons for such a purpose.

Niels slept.

Bobby did the chores. He milked the cows, watered the cattle, and let them out on the Marsh. He brushed the horses, untied them, and opened the door to the lot.

Niels slept.

Bobby manoeuvred the hay-rack against the door of the stable and pitched the hay into the loft.

Niels slept.

Bobby was now convinced that he had heard two shots. He looked Jock over. He found only one bullet-hole.

He went to the shack and fetched the rifle. Its capacity was five shots; it had been fully loaded. There were three shells left.

Bobby looked at the house that stood in the morning sun as it had stood there on every day since he had known it. There was something uncanny about it.

He shuddered. What was he to do?

He could not go to the hay-slough alone this morning.

Niels had not said a word. He had thrown the rifle over his shoulder and gone to the shack, slowly, steadily, soberly. There, he had flung himself on the bed, in his clothes, vouchsafing no information, inviting no question, answering no enquiring look . . .

"Don't you want breakfast?" Bobby had asked.

Niels had already been asleep.

Bobby went all around the house. The east window of the dining room, on the north side, was open.

Should he look in? He could fetch the saw-buck or a truss from the milk-house to stand on.

He did not go. He was afraid to look in.

He returned to the yard, picked the rifle up where he had left it leaning against the stable, broke the barrel, and emptied the remaining shells into his hand.

Something frightful had happened. What?

He felt disconsolate.

Niels had never owned shotgun or rifle.

But one day, in winter, a year or two ago, Bobby and Niels had been coming from the shack; and there, in the first, frosty light of the morning, they had seen a moose standing at the far corner of the garden-lot, head thrown high, mobile nostrils aquiver to catch a scent . . . Both men had stopped in their tracks. Then Bobby, bending down, had picked up a stick and sprung forward, levelling it like a gun at his shoulder, shouting, "Bang . . . Bang!" Whereupon the noble animal, all nerves and trembling muscle, had reared up and disappeared in long, graceful bounds. "What a pity," Bobby had exclaimed, "that we haven't a gun!" Niels had shrugged his shoulders. But the next time he had gone to town he had brought back this rifle for Bobby. It had never been used except for practice and in fun . . .

If it had not been for him, Bobby, there would have been no fire-arms on the place . . .

Many times, during the forenoon, Bobby went to the shack. Niels never stirred.

Bobby became hungry. But Niels needed the rest. He merely fetched some bread and a cup, went to the pump, drew fresh water, and sat down to munch his crusts . . .

Bobby had no education. If you had asked him what a tragedy is, he could not have answered. But he felt that a tragedy had been enacted in the house . . .

Niels had been young, strong, enormously strong, handsome, clean, competent . . . yes, and good! Bobby had seen his decaying, slowly, steadily, irrevocably. Now that he came to think about it and looked back at what he had been during the last few months, he felt profoundly shaken; he felt shattered in his belief in the firm foundations of life . . . His own life would have to be lived under the shadow of what had happened to Niels, of what would happen to him . . . He could never be the same carefree boy again . . .

He had often, of late, heard Niels mutter certain words. On this summer day they took a meaning for Bobby. "And he that increaseth knowledge increaseth sorrow . . ."

He had been happy, constitutionally happy. He would never be quite so happy again; but he would be more thoughtful . . .

More thoughtful? Had he not been thoughtful enough in the past?

On the contrary, *had* he been thoughtful in his relation to Niels? Had he not often, of late, been impatient with him? Had he not shrunk from the careless, untidy habits into which he had fallen?

Bobby, young as he was, came to know the bitterness of regret and repentence . . .

Several times he rose, walked about, fought down his sobs . . .

Niels lay like a log.

All life on the Marsh would be changed . . .

Slowly the sun rode on and finally sank to the west.

At last, late in the evening, when his rays came almost parallel with the ground, Niels awoke.

He raised himself till he was sitting on his bed, his feet on the floor, his shoulders curved forward, his hands lying by his sides. As Bobby darkened the door, he looked up. His eye was clear; but his look came from another world.

"It's evening, is it?" he asked. His voice, too, sounded as from an infinite distance.

Bobby nodded, a lump in his throat.

"Get something to eat," Niels said without stirring.

Bobby began to work as if a great deal depended on his speed. His hands shook. He dropped this, spilt that. He started a fire, fried eggs, made tea.

Niels got up, slowly, heavily, stretched himself, and went out to where the wash-basin stood on a homemade bench.

There he washed, slowly, painstakingly, splashing and brushing for fully five minutes.

With the same painstaking care he dried face, neck, arms.

When he re-entered the shack, he sat down at the table, heavily, as if his weight had increased tenfold.

Bobby, too, sat down. But he could not eat for the dull, numbing excitement that was in him.

Every now and then, while Niels satisfied his appetite, eating slowly, but in great, enormous bites, his eye rested for a moment on the boy.

He finished and made an attempt to rise: the attempt failed or was given up. At last he pointed over the table, with a sweep of his arm.

"Clear that off."

When Bobby, working feverishly, had done so, Niels

added, "Bring pen and ink. And the bundle of papers from the cupboard."

Niels lifted his arms on to the table as if they were weighted with lead.

He tore the string that held the bundle of papers and picked out his cheque-book and a large, folded parchment. He tried to remove the stopper from the ink bottle. Failing, he said, "Open that."

He dipped the pen and began to write, in large, stiff, unwieldy scrawls. When he had finished, he wheeled about on his chair, nearly falling.

"Bobby," he said as if speaking, too, were very difficult, "there's the patent for my land. It's yours. With all that's on it. Here's a cheque. There's something owing on the other quarter. It's the full amount. I won't be back."

"Niels," Bobby cried, almost choking with sobs, "what have you done?"

"I?" Niels said with a sudden flicker in his eye. "I have killed my wife."

"O God!" Bobby groaned. "I was afraid that was it."

"Afraid?" Niels said slowly and sternly. "What have you to be afraid of? You've been a son to me. I leave you my property."

"Niels," Bobby cried. He would have liked to throw himself on this man, to hold him, to shield him with his body.

Niels waved him back.

"Niels," Bobby cried again, "what are you going to do? You must hide . . ."

"Hide? No. I am going to town."

And slowly, heavily he rose and went to the door, Bobby was beside himself.

Niels turned back, swallowing two, three times.

"Bobby," he said at last, "you've been a son to me. I want . . . I want to thank you . . ."

"Don't!" Bobby cried, flinging his arms up. "I can't stand it . . ."

"Stand it?" Niels repeated. "I am going to town to hand myself over." He took a step or two till he stood in the middle of the little clearing. "Don't try to hold me. Don't follow me."

Bobby did not move. He stared at the man.

Niels stood for another few minutes, his lips muttering words.

Then, mastering his refractory body, he pulled himself up; and for a moment his voice became articulate and distinct, though not loud.

". . . Hanged by the neck until dead . . ."

Everything seemed to turn about Bobby.

Then, when he looked again, the man on the clearing was gone.

CHAPTER SIX

Ellen Again

IN DUE COURSE of time a trial followed, conducted in a small city of the prairies.

The prisoner at the bar had refused to engage a lawyer for his defence. Nor did he utter a word which might throw light on the crime or on his motives. In plain, unequivocal terms, given in writing, he pleaded guilty to the charge of murder.

During the preliminary investigation a doubt had arisen as to his sanity. He protested strongly against that suspicion. He was perfectly sane, perfectly responsible for his actions, so he asserted, when he shot the woman; he would do so again should the occasion arise . . .

But the court appointed a lawyer for him: in capital cases a plea of guilty is valueless.

The lawyer felt that this trial might be the making of his career. He went himself into the Marsh and questioned a good many people: neighbours of the accused, Bobby, Mrs. Lund, Ellen Amundsen, Hahn, Nelson.

Thus, on the day of the trial, there appeared some twenty persons subpoenaed by the defence. The crown had only one witness as to matters of fact: Bobby Lund who had heard the shots and seen the prisoner with the gun in his hands. Apart from that it rested its case entirely on circumstantial evidence which was, indeed, amply strong enough.

The prisoner showed considerable impatience while his counsel conducted the defence. The indictment read for murder. He admitted his guilt. What more was there to be said?

But the case went its course as prescribed by law. The court, seeing that the prisoner appeared to be almost anxious to incur the maximum penalty, that of death by hanging, was all the more inclined to be exceedingly careful, to weigh every testimony: as to the prisoner's antecedents, his character, the many good deeds ascribed to him, and the character of the murdered woman . . .

The young lawyer made the most of every favourable circumstance.

By the time the case was ready to go to the jury, no onlooker could have any doubt any longer as to the outcome. An acquittal was impossible; but so was a conviction on the charge of murder. The jury found the prisoner guilty of manslaughter with attenuating circumstances and recommended him to the mercy of the court.

The verdict read for ten years in the federal prison, with hard labour . . .

A few miles north of the great city of the plains there rises abruptly, out of the level prairie, the brow of a hill. It does not look imposing from a distance.

But as, coming from the city, you approach it, driving perhaps in a car, and as the hill rises before you, it is apt to take on, in the impression it makes on your imagination, much larger proportions than its natural dimensions would warrant.

That impression is due to the sinister suggestiveness of the work of man. For the brow of the hill is crowned with a group of buildings of truly Titanic outline.

A perpendicular wall rises up, fifty feet high, many feet thick: a smooth wall, built of limestone blocks, stretching for several hundred feet from east to west, and forming, behind, a perfect square by its enclosure. In the centre of the south end there is a gate, wide and high, but completely closed by steel bars four inches apart. A man, armed from head to foot, always paces the arched gateway behind.

On top of the walls, at every corner, there stands a small tower from which, also on top of the walls, there stretch two parapeted walks at right angles to each other, reaching halfway to the centre of each side of the square. Each of these towers offers, when such is needed, shelter to two men who, armed with rifle, revolver, and sword, walk back and forth, back and forth on their beats. Every few hours they are relieved, others mounting guard, day and night.

Yes, when you approach that hill, you cannot get near it without being challenged. Men on horseback patrol every possible approach; their mounts being swift and strong. If you are alone in your car, you may be allowed to pass unquestioned: a single person can hardly be the bringer of any danger. If there are two or three of you, you will have to state your business before being allowed to proceed on the last half mile of the journey. If a crowd is with you, you will be turned back or at least detained. Should you, by any chance ignore the challenge, your car, disabled, will run into the ditch. In any case, before you reach the walls, every eye is watching for you; every move of yours is being followed. The report of your coming had preceded you, no matter how fast you may have travelled.

Altogether, the impression these precautions make is that of a terrible, implacable grimness, like that of doom.

Inside the huge enclosure which is thus protected against any unauthorised approach, you divine more than you see: half a dozen buildings which harbour the prison, the shops annexed to it, and the offices of the administration.

Outside, nestling against the talus of the hill, there are two, three large houses, brick-built: the residences of warden, physician, chaplain.

Behind it, north of it, a little town grovels at its feet . . .

Some two hundred outcasts spend from two to thirty or forty years of their lives within that enclosure, at labour which brings them no return.

As, in the morning, they file out from the dormitory – tier upon tier of steel-barred cells where they have spent the night alone between three walls, for in front of the steel-bars which form the fourth wall a guard paces up and down – you are apt to shudder at sight of these unfortunates who walk along in single file, in groups of ten or twenty, silent, accompanied by a guard.

When, at noon, they return from the shops, silent again, in groups of ten or twenty, and in single file, they pass, in the huge kitchen which occupies the basement, along heated steel shelves on which a bowl waits for each one of them, filled with food to be taken to the cell and to be eaten there in silence, in solitude, and yet not in privacy . . .

After an hour or so, they file out again to the shops . . .

And yet, even here a human heart beats, human sympathy plans the welfare of others: the heart of the warden.

There was a time when the prisoner trembled or scowled at sight of an officer: that time is past.

To-day, when the warden appears, most of the prisoners – those for whom there is hope, hope of a future outside, or of manhood in some form inside – most of them smile.

The warden is a fearless man; he goes unarmed. He is the friend of the unfortunate. He has a way with him which gains their confidence.

It was long, very long before he gained Niels Lindstedt's confidence. But he did not give up; and gain it he did. He spoke to him often during the first two, three years . . . After that, prisoner number 187 often, as often, spoke to him.

It was the warden who made him think, remember about the past. It was the warden who slowly, slowly made him see that he was not an outcast, a being despised for what he had done. It was the warden who told him that he, too, placed in the same circumstances, might and probably would have acted as Niels had acted . . . It was the warden who held out hope that perhaps within another two, three years . . . It was the warden who corresponded for him with Bobby Lund . . .

No, said the warden, Bobby Lund would never dream of accepting the farm as a present; he had his own farm; he was looking after Niels' stock; after his land; he was holding it in trust against his return . . . It was his, Niels', duty to go back to this land . . .

It was the warden who spoke to him of Ellen . . .

After the fourth year Niels attended evening classes conducted by the schoolmaster of the village: high school classes. He learned something of French and Latin, of Algebra, Geometry, Science . . . He acquired a vocabulary which would enable him to read real books. He was often puzzled by the abstruseness of it all. Finally he was amused. He learned to laugh at man's folly in puzzling out such curiosities of the mind . . . What had it all to do with the real problems of life?

But he kept at it. He even passed examinations.

And one day in his sixth year, the warden entered the blacksmith shop where Niels, at his own request, had been employed and told him that he had succeeded in his intercession with the minister of justice: the end of Niels' term of confinement had been fixed for the spring of the following year, limiting the total time he had to serve to six years and a half . . .

Once more, during the latter days of April, Niels was on his way from Minor to the farm in the margin of the Marsh, walking. It was daytime. He had dropped off the train at noon.

Four or five miles from town he found things so changed that he could no longer follow the old-time trail athwart the sand-flats. An almost continuous settlement covered the formerly wild land over which the trail had angled. He had to go straight east, to follow roads or road allowances. Where they were not sandy, he sank to his ankles in mud. The thaw-up had just been completed.

When he reached the Range Line, he was six miles south of his farm. This was the middle of what had been the northern part of the Marsh.

The Marsh itself was also changed. Formerly the Range Line trail had followed a sandy, gravelly ridge swinging east and west. The road followed a straight line now, being graded wherever it led through lowlands, flanked by ditches which were drained by huge master-ditches running crosswise and carrying the water to the Lake.

Right at the corner, where once there had been nothing but swamp, lay two prosperous farmsteads close together; and nothing but the hedgerows of swamp alder which bordered the fields reminded of the Marsh as it had been. They, too, being deprived of the water they needed, would soon disappear . . .

Half a mile north another prosperous farmstead: a new farm house, with porch and sleeping balcony, and a huge, up-to-date barn which dwarfed the landscape round about . . .

Still further north the hovels of German and Icelandic

settlers had been replaced by new buildings, some of them painted, some unpainted, but all of them bearing the imprint of truly Canadian settlements.

Niels felt intimidated. This prosperity which had invaded the Marsh was unexpected; the old pioneers had receded to the margin of civilisation; a new generation had taken hold. The change was not entirely welcome: he was of the old generation which had been evicted. On almost every farmstead he saw a garage: cars had always been his pet aversion . . .

The old familiar bluffs had been cleared away. Fields stretched in their places. About the yards straight-lined plantations of imported trees framed the clusters of buildings.

This was no longer the bush land he had loved . . .

He came to the corner of the section on which his own land lay. He stopped and put his bundle down to look about. For a moment he was not even sure it was the section . . . And yet, a lump rose in his throat: there, in the evening sun, ahead of him, stood the bluff, still bare of leaves, but towering and dominating the landscape all about. No barns could dwarf it . . .

Beyond, the cliff of the forest still fringed the creek.

He looked east.

A mile away, in the very margin of the bush which, many miles wide, bordered the west shore of the Lake, a smaller farmstead became visible to his searching eye: that was the old Bates place, the place he had bought for Bobby in the long-ago past . . . Yes, there was a small house, log-built so it seemed, a little stable, and two or three other small buildings, all of logs . . . That would be Bobby's establishment. Bobby was married.

And ahead: where the small grove of second-growth aspens had marked his own line to the west, big, towering trees stood, a narrow strip of them, between road and fields, quiet in the evening sun . . .

He picked his bundle up and went on.

To the west, too, there were farmsteads, two in the open sand-flats - log buildings, these - how could any one make a living there? One, in the margin of the bush that fringed the creek - this one a large, ambitious establishment. That must be the old Sigurdsen place? . . .

He went on and came to his corner.

He looked at the fence: it was in good order: here and there rotting posts had recently been replaced.

Again a lump rose in his throat: he had come to a gap in the young bush fringe which he had spared when he cleared his land: through it he saw horses grazing along the edge of the field which lay black, ridged, duly fall-plowed. They were Percherons, pure-bred; he knew the breed . . . And . . . and . . . was not that aged mare there . . . that lifted her head and gazed at him . . . was not that Nellie?

Putting down his bundle, he climbed the fence. Tears were trembling in the corners of his eyes as he approached the horse, his hand outstretched. But she eyed him warily; and with a sudden motion which fully betrayed her identity - a peculiar throwing of the head, chin upward, while her ears flicked back flat on her head - she scampered away, ten, twelve younger horses breaking cover, out of the bush, and following her.

Niels laughed; his laugh was shot with tears . . .

He returned to the road and went on.

There, ahead of him, was a small gate in the fence. He did not know it; it was new.

Curiously he approached. A white sign was fastened to the gate-post by its side - a sign with blue letters . . . It bore the words "Post Office" as its legend.

He saw that a path led from the gate through the bush fringe, up to a little house . . . Should this . . . should this be the shack in which he and Bobby had lived in the past which was now so remote - the shack that had first been built for old man Sigurdsen, dead and buried these ten years and more? And who might be living there now?

But that remained to be cleared up later . . .

He went on.

Yes, there was the big gate that led on to his place; with the stile by its side; just as he had left it. His heart began to beat faster, faster . . .

Then the vista opened on his yard . . . There stood the buildings – granary, stable, cow-shed, implement shed, pig-pen, milk house, and . . . dwelling . . . There was the horse-lot, the garden behind the house, the cow-enclosure north of the entrance, in the bluff . . .

Yes, there was one thing he felt sure of: no matter what else the future might hold in joy or sorrow, this would be home: his refuge, his hermitage . . .

Slowly he stepped over the stile.

As of old he went all about the place, looked into the granary where grain – oats and barley – was stored; into the stable, empty but for one old, old horse, a Clyde that stood, blind and lame, in his stall; into the pig-pen where half a dozen pigs came grunting and sniffing to meet him; into the milk-house where tin pails were inverted over stakes driven into the earthen floor, scoured and shining . . . All was as it used to be.

He looked at the house . . . should he enter? There were new curtains on all the windows; on the lower floor the blinds were drawn.

His heart pounded like a hammer as he touched the door knob and turned it. It was almost dark inside. He entered . . .

The hall was empty. From it the staircase led up, without banisters, into the upper story where there was still a little light.

A shudder ran over him as he thought of entering the north room. No; he would go upstairs instead . . .

He climbed the steps: the door to the east room was closed; that to the west room open; the reverse of what it had been in his time.

In the west room stood his old bed, made up as if to receive a guest. The curtains were of scrim which he recognised.

Slowly he turned back to the landing . . . Slowly, hesitatingly, he opened the door to the other room: it was empty except for crates and boxes stored there . . .

From that sight Niels took courage and went down again. There, in the hall, he stood for a moment. His huge frame seemed to shrink. But at last he raised one of the blinds, went to the rear of the room, and turned the knob.

The first object that struck his sight was the old tin heater of his bachelor days.

The second one, the deal table, covered with oil-cloth.

The third, a piece of cardboard lying on it, inscribed with a blue pencil, "Welcome Home."

He sank down on a chair, overcome with a strange feeling it was almost happiness . . .

Lastly, he went into the kitchen. There, everything looked as if he had just left it. There were eggs in the colander on the shelf where they used to be; a smoked ham lay on the table, with the butcher knife beside it; the water pail stood on the bench by the door, filled to the brim.

Everywhere on the lower floor, too, scrim curtains were hung in the windows.

Who had put them there?

Well, who but Bobby? . . .

Bobby had tried to wipe the past out as far as Niels was concerned. He had removed whatever might remind him of it. Bobby was like a son . . .

It was chilly in the house, the season being still early. So, after a while, Niels lighted a fire in the little stove . . .

Then he sat again and mused.

It would be a lonely life . . . a life like that of his first winter in the north, in Nelson's shack . . . Still, it would be home. He remembered how that little shanty of Nelson's had first seemed like home to him: there he had felt anchored for the first time after his wanderings: he had played with, and rejoiced at, the thought that he had already money enough to put up such a shack for himself.

This house – a big house; but no longer the largest or best-built house for many miles around; it was over twelve years ago now since it had been built . . . Just how long was it? Yes, it must be thirteen years – this house could never be what a little shack would be . . . It would always remind him of, always oppress him with, the thought of the years which he had lived here, not alone . . .

There was that other shack on this very place. But it was occupied . . . And for the first time he wondered by whom . . .

Just then a commotion arose outside on the yard.

A voice was calling, a strong, almost masculine voice which he yet recognised as that of a woman, Mrs. Lund.

He went into the bare front room and looked out through a crack between blind and frame of a window.

There, in the darkening dusk, Mrs. Lund stood in the horse-lot, the southern gate of which she had opened. She stood upright, her hands raised to her mouth as a megaphone, calling, calling. "Come on!" she called, "come on, come on, come on!"

And the horses obeyed. They knew her. They knew her voice . . .

Slowly, through the bush beyond, they approached the gate; and when they had reached it, they tossed their heads, shot past the strong, grey-haired woman that stood there with a brief spurt of a gallop, drank at the trough, and filed into the stable, one by one. His horses . . . Percherons all . . . There were twelve of them, of all ages, with Nellie, the oldest one, following last . . .

Mrs. Lund was closing the gate; and when she had done so, she, too, went after them into the stable.

It was getting dark.

Niels felt that he should go out; but something held him back.

Yes, of course, it was Mrs. Lund who was looking after the place: it was she who lived in the shack: it was she who was keeping the post office as in the past . . .

Once more thoughts flooded in on him: he visualised things that had happened long ago.

One day in the past he had gone to Odensee to get Mrs. Lund so she would cook for the threshers on his place.

"They've sold me out now," Mrs. Lund had said with reference to her little store in the village.

"Couldn't Nelson have done something?" Niels had asked.

"Oh Nelson! He's getting to be altogether too big for the likes of me. He has no time to be thinking of his poor mother-in-law . . . Nelson, the big cattle man. Olga, of course, would like to help . . . But there are the children; and I suppose she has her own worries, too."

"Have you a place yet?"

"Yes," Mrs. Lund had answered, "yes; and a good place, I think. At Judge Cameron's, at Poplar Grove . . . But to think that at my time of life I must still go again and hire out to do housework!"

"In a few years," Niels had suggested, "Bobby will get a place."

And Mrs. Lund, with suddenly renewed animation, relapsing into her grandiose manner, had fallen in with him. "Yes, Mr. Lindstedt. What's true must be true. Bobby's a good boy. Bobby's a clean boy, Mr. Lindstedt. Thanks to you. Bobby's the hope of my old age. We took him from the children's home. We gave him what we could. We kept him as if he had been our own. . . . He will remember. He'll do the right thing by me when the time has come . . ."

Had Bobby done so? No doubt he had . . .

And here she was taking care of his, Niels' place . . .

Again Niels sat and mused . . .

"No," the warden had said to him, one day, in the prison; "how you stand with God, I cannot tell. God keeps his own counsel. But let me remind you of the great sinner who had been a bad man all through his life; but on the cross he repented; and Christ forgave him . . . Niels, though you have sinned, I don't think you've been a bad man . . ." And searchingly he had looked into his eye.

And Niels had answered, after a silence of thought, slowly, hesitatingly, "No; I believe I have tried to do what was right, in most things. I've been self-seeking when I was young . . . I have too often thought of my own life only . . . As for the thing that has sent me here. I don't blame myself . . . Not for that immediate thing . . . But for what preceded it . . . For what led up to it . . . For the very beginning of it . . . Many years before it happened . . . I have long since seen that I had sinned . . ."

"Niels," the warden had gone on, "if I'm any judge, God has forgiven you . . . The killing . . . That, too, was in the atonement . . . But as for men, you have been judged by your peers, and you have paid the penalty. You have taken life. Yet they have judged you fit to live on. What I'd like you to feel is this. When you go out of here, you can hold your head up. You must hold your head up. As far as human justice goes, you have paid the price . . ."

And yet it was hard: out there, the woman went about doing the chores on his place . . . Could he face her? But face her he must . . .

Then the front door of the house was opened.

"Anybody in here?" Mrs. Lund's voice called.

Niels rose and stood silent, a lump in his throat, his heart pounding fast. "Yes, Mrs. Lund," he answered at last, "I'm here, Niels . . ."

"Mis-ter-Lind-stedt," she sang out and came running in. "Where are you? We didn't know just when to expect you . . . I saw smoke coming from the chimney . . . It's so dark. Where are you?"

"No," Niels said, "don't light a lamp yet . . ."

"Oh?" Mrs. Lund said. "Well, I won't, then . . ."

And they shook hands in the dark.

"Sit down." Niels said, "sit down . . ."

And Mrs. Lund sat and cried. "Excuse me, Mr. Lindstedt," she said. "Excuse an old woman. You've been our benefactor when we were poor. . . . We've been worried about you . . ."

"How's Bobby?" Niels asked after a while.

"Bobby? Fine. Bobby's a farmer, Mr. Lindstedt, thanks to you. He's doing fine. Considering, you know . . . He's only a beginner. But he's going to give me a home as soon as he can. It was he who thought of putting me here for the time being, so we could be together at least. I've got the post office again, you know. It relieved him of so much work to have me here. I'm an old farmer myself, you know. You remember how we worked on the place in the edge of the slough . . . Poor daddy, he couldn't do much any longer. Oh, Mr. Lindstedt, he was the best husband, the very best; God have mercy on his poor soul . . . But it all went to smash; you know that, too . . . Bobby's fine, thank the Lord . . . Not that he's rich. He's married. You've heard about that, I suppose . . . She's a daughter of Henry Kelm, George Kelm's brother. She's a good girl, I can assure you, Mr. Lindstedt . . . She's a fine girl . . . A real helper . . . And they've five children by now . . ."

"Five?" Niels echoed.

"Yes, sir. Five. Five little Bobbies on the place . . . Two pairs of twins, all boys . . . and one girl . . ."

Niels smiled in the dark.

"That's as many as Nelson's got. He's got only five, you know. But Nelson, of course, has a car, a big one, a . . . oh, I don't know what you call them, an Underground or something. And he's got a new eight-roomed house, of brick . . ."

"Well, well," Niels said. "And now, Mrs. Lund, I don't think I'd mind any longer if you lit the lamp. You know so much better where to find it than I . . ."

Mrs. Lund bustled about excitedly; and when she came back, the two looked at each other by the light of the lamp which she was carrying in her hand.

"Well, I declare!" Mrs. Lund exclaimed. "You're looking younger . . . younger and better than when I saw you last . . ."

She stopped; for, when she had seen him last, there had been a woman in this house, sitting in the corner of the kitchen, gossiping with her and Mrs. Schultze; she had been clad in a silk dressing gown; and she had been smiling ironically from morning till night, smiling at such trivialities as thresing . . .

But Niels merely nodded.

Mrs. Lund, on the contrary, looked older, much older than she had done at the time; though, on closer scrutiny, the impression arose perhaps chiefly from the fact that her hair was light-grey, almost white.

In Niels' mind, far back, there hovered a question: a question which he did not dare to ask . . .

"But the changes," Mrs. Lund went on, "the changes, Mr. Lindstedt! You won't recognise the Marsh any longer . . . Nearly all the old settlers are gone: the Dahlbecks are gone; the Schultzes – Mr. Schultze was frozen to death the year after . . . well, you know; the Bakers, the Wagners, the Smiths . . . They proved up and sold and went . . . That's the way it's been going in this settlement, Mr. Lindstedt. Bobby and you, and Kelm and Ellen Amundsen. That's all that are left of the old bunch now . . ."

Niels closed his eyes. Then he smiled.

The was one thing left for which he had to atone. He had doubted and worried, worried and doubted about that one point . . . He had come to the conclusion that, if he found the girl still living in the bush, he would take it as a sign that once more there would be peace, once more there would be some semblance of life left for him in the future . . .

Mrs. Lund saw, divined, and kept her peace . . .

At last Niels rose. "Mrs. Lund," he said, "would you mind helping me once more with my chores? I'll be awkward, I'm afraid. I've lost the knack of things. There's the milking still to do, I suppose. And the feeding. And when we are through, we'll go and call on Bobby . . ."

"Sure," Mrs. Lund replied. "I'll hustle up . . ."

There was hay in the loft of the barn, crushed oats in the bin . . . The cows came home . . .

It was eight o'clock when the chores were done. Mrs. Lund went into the house and lighted the kitchen stove . . .

Niels remained on the yard, going here and there . . . In the farthest corner, on the east side, behind pig-pens and milk-house, he came across a pile of squared timbers; timbers which he had cut and squared with Bobby in years gone by. They had been meant for a smoke-house . . . They were dry and sound . . .

He stood and mused . . .

Would he ever be able to establish a routine again? Would he ever be able to do the work on the farm? . . .

And yet, already the place was home . . .

He, Niels, forty years old . . . forty years! . . .

Mrs. Lund called for supper . . .

An hour or so later they crossed the farm, following a foot-path worn into the soil no doubt by Mrs. Lund, by

Bobby, his wife and . . . his children . . . That footpath suggested that there were neighbours, friendly neighbours. There had never been any before . . .

They approached the place in the dark. Two dogs came running and barking to meet them.

They sniffed at the woman and wagged their tails; they sniffed at the man and growled.

"Down, Mickey," Mrs. Lund called, "down! . . . The house is all dark . . . They must have gone to bed."

In front of them a little shanty squatted low, with a lean-to, tar paper tacked to the walls all around . . . On the north side a little snow lingered, a frozen pile, showing grey in the black of the shadows about. The shanty looked hump-backed, one-eyed, crippled . . .

Mrs. Lund sang out, "Bob-beee!" It sounded like an echo of ancient memories through the night . . .

"Yes," a voice answered from within, "just a minute."

And a few moments later the door of the lean-to opened, and out stepped Bobby.

He was in shirt and overalls, barefooted, his hair rumpled: he looked lean and wiry even in the dark.

"Hello, mother," he said, "come in . . ."

"Bobby," she said, "I'm not alone . . ."

And only then Bobby noticed the broad, dark figure of the man by her side.

"Gee whiz!" he exclaimed. "It's Niels . . . Come in."

And he ran back into the house to light a lamp.

Niels entered the kitchen. It was a small, bare room with an old table, a bench, and three or four boxes for seats. On the east wall there were a few shelves; in the centre, a cook-stove. The joists showed; the walls were single-boarded, of box lumber tacked to scantling; the floor, of raw planks, rough, splintered, but clean, strewn with sand.

Bobby was so excited that he did not even think of properly greeting Niels nor of making excuses.

A moment later a woman entered, blinking in the light, barefooted, young, strong, but over-worked . . .

"That's the missus," Mrs. Lund said.

And Niels, looking at her out of kind, searching eyes, shook her hand which she gave without answering the pressure and without looking into his face.

"We'd expected you, of course," Bobby said. "But we didn't know the exact date . . ."

Niels looked at him. He was thin, his face not as merry as it used to be: he was older, maturer, ripened by worries, thoughts, regrets . . .

"We'd gone to bed," Bobby went on. "To save oil, you know . . ." And he laughed.

Niels listened to that laugh. No. There was no harshness, no bitterness in it . . . He had not expected to find the poverty he saw . . .

"You'll stay overnight?"

It was Mrs. Lund's turn to laugh. "Nonsense, Bobby, Mr. Lindstedt has a good bed at home. Why should he sleep in your bunks? . . ."

"Well," Bobby replied, "that's true, too. We have no bedsteads yet," he explained to Niels. "Or any longer, I should say. You know, four boys tear a lot of clothes. We sold our own bedstead last winter to buy shoes for the kiddies . . . But if the bunk isn't too hard . . . We've got the room . . ."

Again Mrs. Lund laughed her broad, hearty laugh. "Room! It's some room all right . . . There aren't even panes in the window. The dogs jump in at night . . ."

Niels had been looking from one to the other. The young woman . . . yes, she was a mate . . . She had no doubt been pretty, with the prettiness of youth . . . Now she looked helpful rather . . . But was not that what was needed? . . .

He turned.

"Never mind, Mrs. Lund. I'll stay . . ."

The young woman, clad in a thin gingham house-dress, had busied herself at the stove. She was shy, bashful in the presence of the stranger.

"Tea or coffee?" she asked Bobby, not caring to address Niels directly. And Bobby turned to Niels with an enquiring look.

"Tea," Niels said, understanding her at once. And, to Bobby, "And now let me see the children, will you?"

They tip-toed into the adjoining room.

All five were sleeping in one of the two bunks; the other was empty . . .

For a while Niels stood and looked, by the light of the little lamp that was burning there. The boys were red-faced, fat-cheeked youngsters; the girl, somewhat thin and pale . . .

The bedding consisted of blankets, grey, none too warm; in lieu of a mattress a layer of hay was spread on the boards.

Niels looked back in his memories, on that room of Lund's where a second-hand, defunct gentility had prevailed . . . The same poverty. But here the poverty of a beginning . . . There it had been the poverty of the end.

"We're none too well fixed," Bobby said.

"Well . . ." Niels pondered.

"We've only thirty acres so far. We'll get things as soon as the land is paid for . . ."

"The land? . . ." But Niels broke off and turned to go back into the kitchen.

There, Mrs. Lund received him in quite her old manner. "Mr. Lindstedt," she said, "all this does not look very prosperous yet . . . But one day . . . One day we are going to have everything as it should be. A large, good house; a hot-bed for the garden; real, up-to-date stables; and . . . Everything!"

And Bobby and Niels both nodded.

During the next few days there were many things to be discussed. Bobby had for seven years looked after the field-work on Niels' farm. He had never touched a cent of the proceeds. He had banked it all in Niels' name . . .

Niels insisted on a half-crop arrangement. Bobby, declining at first, had to yield in the end. Thus the rare thing happened that a pioneer farmer passed from a stage of great necessity without any transition to that of comparative affluence.

Mrs. Lund, too, was entitled to a substantial remuneration. She had taken care of his stock and yard. She accepted, as a gift, duly deeded, an acre of land on Niels' place, to be fenced, with a three-roomed house, fully furnished, to be built in the fall . . .

In spite of these arrangements Niels found that his wealth, in money as well as in chattels, had more than doubled during his absence. Some of his horses, the drivers, for instance, Bobby had used and stabled entirely on his place. Some of the cows had been lent to neighbours, so they could milk them in return for their feed . . .

These things settled, Niels went at the work of seeding his field. And now, for the first time, he faced the day alone . . .

It was not an easy task. To drown one's thought in labour is very difficult on the farm: everything is conducive to contemplation. No high ambitions lead you away from the present; and yet those ambitions which are indispensible, the lowly ones, are really the highest on earth: the desire for peace and harmony in yourself, your surroundings . . .

But there were no surroundings – there was no little world, no microcosm revolving within the macrocosm. There was the duty to the farm, the country, the world: cold, abstract things devoid of the living blood . . .

There was still another difficulty. Since life could be borne only if the immediate past, the last ten years, were covered with a half artificial oblivion, the past to be faced in memory was the past of his dreams . . . It was almost as painful to face as the later one . . .

So long as Niels had to avert his eye from old desires, visions, dreams, there was no foundation for his life.

One day, Mrs. Lund brought the topic of certain furniture up. She had insisted on doing the milking, in return for what little cream and eggs she needed daily. She was going from the cow-lot to the house, carrying two foaming pails, and stopped in the middle of the yard.

"Mr. Lindstedt," she said, "what are you going to do about that furniture from the house?"

Niels winced and stopped in his tracks. He had just come in from the field and was watering his horses.

"Where . . . where is it?" he asked at last.

"It's all piled in a little shanty in the bluff over there," she said, pointing east. "Bobby and his wife put it up between them. It's a mere windbreak. The rain can get in. The stuff will spoil there . . . After all, it's worth money . . ."

"I'll see," Niels said slowly. "Who . . . Who suggested taking it out of the house?" For the mere fact that Mrs. Lund mentioned the thing proved that it had not been she.

Mrs. Lund laughed. "Oh," she said, "that was an idea of Ellen Amundsen's. The last time she was over . . ."

Niels said no more.

Next day he went into the bush and searched till he found the shanty, well hidden in willows; and, piling some brush against the wall, he set fire to it without ever looking inside . . .

Ellen!

Henceforth, while he was doing his work, not now with that passionate intensity of former years, but slowly, carefully, weighing his every move, his thought reverted more and more often to her . . . She had been over here . . . She had made suggestions . . . She had thought of him while he was away . . .

Ten years or longer ago he had left her alone . . .

His life, her life: two vessels which he had shattered at a single blow . . .

As for his life . . . there was only one thing left which he could do: gather the shattered fragments and fit them as best he might be able to do.

The nightmare of ten years he had atoned for, perhaps. But there, in that remoter past which, in his thoughts, now became more vivid, more real than the years immediately preceding the present he had done a great wrong: he had left alone a human being that had been in need of him: had left her alone because he had thought he could never be as little to her as a brother. And that human being had been she, the woman of his dreams, his vision, his love . . .

When the huge steel-gate of the prison on the brow of the hill had swung shut behind him, not many days ago, he had felt inwardly balanced; he had felt at peace. Scar-tissue had grown over his soul. It had been the peace of resignation, but it had been peace . . .

He felt himself plunged back into unrest, chaos . . .

Once more he was a stranger on his place; he was eating the bitter bread of exile . . . .

There would never be any rest for him unless the girl in the bush forgave him . . . He must try to be to her now what she had wanted him to be to her then: a brother . . .

Was he able to do so? Were all those things that had once disturbed him and her, were they dead in him? Could he face her quietly, without desire? . . . Even though she might not hold it against him that he had left her for ten years or more . . .

He tried to visualise a meeting. It never occurred to him to take into account the fact that they were both more than ten years older than they had been. Himself – like all people to whom vanity is constitutionally foreign – he did not see: he was he; the one who saw; not the one who was being seen . . .

Ellen . . .

As he tried to see her with his mind's eye, he saw her as she had been, not ten years ago, but seventeen . . . Yet, not like that altogether, either . . .

Her body, her movements he could not bring into clear focus at all. Sometimes he had a glimpse of them: a blurred glimpse, through vapours and seething mists of passion: but a glimpse nevertheless as she had stood with him in that room of her house where she had told him her story. And whenever he caught that glimpse, even to-day, his heart beat faster . . . He reached for that vision as if he wished to hold it, to grasp it with all the tentacles of his mind. But the very next moment he realised that it had eluded him; it had vanished like a spirit into the air . . .

Her face, on the other hand, her expression, he saw very clearly, just as he had seen them on the very first morning when he and Nelson had arrived on her father's place . . .

There it was: her eyes light-blue, her features round, her complexion a pure, Scandinavian white. Again it was her expression that held him: hers was the face of a woman, not of a girl. There was a great, ripe maturity in it; and a look as if she saw through pretences and shams and knew more of life than her age would warrant. No smile lighted her features; her eyes were stern and nearly condemnatory. But somehow, as Niels looked at her, with his mind's eye only this time, a great desire came over him to see her in the flesh and to make her smile . . .

His throat tightened; his heart pounded as of old . . .

To think he had lost her: not as a mate – what did that matter? Had lost her as a guiding influence in his life, had lost her as a sister, a friend . . .

He, he had gone astray; had left her alone . . .

Would she want him to come back? Would she accept him now? Would she forgive him?

Yet . . . she had been here; had been thinking of him in his absence.

For a week he pondered the question, musing, probing himself, probing her . . .

. . .

Then, one day, late in the evening, when he had just finished the last round with his seeder and as he stood ready to bend down and to unhook the traces of his horses, he had a vision. He closed his eyes and stood still to see it more clearly.

The vision he saw was that of the homely face of his mother. Yet, her features were strangely blurred; as if, superimposed on them, there appeared those of another; and at last he recognised these as the features of the old man, of Sigurdsen, his neighbour whom he had loved.

Long, long ago, in another such vision, his mother had looked at him reproachfully, seriously, warningly.

And the old man, in the wanderings of his decaying mind, had betrayed to him some corner of his subliminal memories . . .

These two, in vision and memory, seemed to blend, to melt together. Both looked at him, in this new vision, out of one face in which, now his, now her lines gained the ascendency . . .

The wistful face of his mother relaxed in a knowing smile: yes, such was she who had born him . . .

The old man's face took her place: he was moving his lips and muttered, "Hm . . . tya."

One Sunday at last he went north, afoot.

It was a warm spring day; the leaves on the trees still dormant; tassels hanging from the aspens, grey and red . . .

Slowly he crossed the corner of the Marsh: this was the only trail that was left as it had been years ago.

For a while he stood on the bridge, a new concrete bridge which had taken the place of the old, wooden structure . . .

A mile from the creek he passed a large clearing to the right: Kelm's place which he had helped to clear. A huge barn with a hip-roof glanced over the trees; a small, well-built frame house nestled in a bluff . . .

Farther on another farmstead, to the left, quite new: a square clearing, bare, with the house in the centre; the other buildings of logs . . .

Then bush, bush, as of old . . .

Once, Niels reflected, the settlement of the Marsh had been an out-post of the settlement in the bush: that was now reversed. The settlement on the Marsh was so much denser . . .

All seemed unchanged.

He came to the corner of Ellen's yard. As soon as the view opened up, he stopped and stood.

Yes, it was the old place entirely: house, granary, stable, implement shed. One single change: the well which he and Nelson had dug had a pump; and the pump was connected up with a windmill.

All about reared the bush . . .

Even that small change spoke of years that had run down the river of time . . .

For a long while Niels stood and waited, trying to calm the turmoil in his heart . . .

He came like the prodigal son . . .

At last he went on.

He came to the gate, opened it, and entered the yard which was still covered by the short, clean sward of chickweed.

A dog sprang out of the barn, barked, and ran back; out again and in once more. It was a young dog, a bitch; and when Niels could look into the open door of the stable, her strange, fierce behaviour was explained; a litter of pups played there, in the drive-way . . .

He knocked at the door of the house.

A voice. "Come in." Ellen's voice.

He opened, entered, stood . . .

Their eyes met. Niels lowered his.

What he had seen, shook him like an invisible hand; it hit him like a hammer blow at his heart. He could not bear it. He stood like one accused, like one pleading guilty . . .

What he had seen was this.

Behind the table – the same table at which, seventeen years ago, one winter morning, he had eaten his breakfast – on a straight-backed chair, sat a middle-aged woman, knitting, with shell-rimmed glasses on her eyes. Her features were no longer round; they were square; but her complexion was still that pure, Scandinavian white: her hair, straw-yellow, streaked with grey . . . But now as then it was the expression that held him: hers was the face of a girl, not a woman; it was stern, to be sure; but in this sterness lay hidden the dream, the unfulfilled, uncompromising dream of a virgin child . . . No smile lighted her features. Her eyes looked searchingly out from behind her glasses: searchingly, questioningly, expectantly. There was nothing in them that seemed to condemn; they seemed to wonder and – what was hardest to bear – they were full of sympathy . . .

Then her voice, clear, high-pitched, not quite steady, "You have come . . .!" as if awed.

She had risen. Without looking, Niels was aware of her figure. A somewhat flat bust; wide, round hips . . .

When he did look, she had removed her glasses; her eyes, light-blue, were fixed on him, probingly, with infinite pity . . .

"Yes," he said, falteringly, "I have come . . . as a brother . . ."

She came forward, leaving her work on the table, and moved a chair.

"I've been waiting," she said, her voice still unsteady. "I've been waiting, Niels. I've waited twelve years . . ."

At that Niels broke down. He sat on the chair she had touched, his head bent, fighting for composure. And after several minutes, "Ellen . . ."

"I know," she said and nodded. "No need to tell me. You've suffered . . ."

Silence.

He sat; she stood, very near.

"Shall we go?" she said at last, steadier now. "Behind the house, where we used to sit?"

Niels rose, took a chair, and turned to the door.

She picked her knitting up, adjusted her glasses, and followed.

When they arrived in the little natural bower formed by hazel brush and plum trees, he squatted down on the grass as he had done one day in haying time, ten, twelve years ago . . .

All about reared the bush. Tremulous stood the aspens, their buds just breaking, tasselled in grey and red. The plum trees, too, had the white buds of their blossoms just bursting. The air was spring-cool . . .

They sat in silence, a long, long while . . .

Once Niels tried to speak. His first attempt failed. His voice was hoarse, husky: it sounded so strange.

He tried again. "Ellen," he said, "can you forgive?"

She looked up; he went silent.

"You came," she said softly. "No need to speak . . ."

And so they sat on, now and then scanning each other, sometimes furtively, sometimes openly. They were feeling their way into a changed present; what they found in each other was the past. . . .

They sat for hours; till, under the westering sun, the air became chilly.

Ellen spoke. "Come," she said. "Let's go to the house. I'll get supper."

And once more Niels sat silent, in the corner of the room this time, behind the table, in the shadow of the wall. That shadow, too, was the shadow of the past.

Happiness almost ancient and a sense of infinite sorrow which was new were mixed in the mute abandonment to his feelings in which he sat there. The sorrow was at the lapse of time; the old, never ending sorrow that what was is no more; the happiness, at the bridging of the gulf of years, accomplished without words, without explanations . . .

As Ellen moved about, laying the cloth, heating water, breaking eggs – doing the small, trivial things of life, in the dusk: not with her former quick grace any longer, but with a pensive, quiet deliberation – his memory re-awoke: he saw her again as she had been in the years of their intimacy, their brotherhood: she was she, after all: the only woman . . .

He lulled his heart with a dream that was new: the dream of the restful perpetuation of this state of dusk, of mutual wordless comprehension, of dispassionate friendship, brotherly love . . .

The evening passed. Not many words were interchanged. Words were not needed.

Then, in the still early night, they went to the gate. There, separated from each other by the fence, they stood for a moment.

Ellen spoke. "Niels, I've waited for you. I knew you would come. Life will be bearable after this; it has been bearable the last ten years only through expectation . . . I want to say one more thing, Niels. I have been to blame towards you . . . Can you forgive? . . ."

Niels threw his hands up, a vague gesture to silence her. "Don't . . . Don't . . . If you speak that way, I cannot bear it . . . The wrong that was done was all on my side. I have repented . . ."

"Not all," Ellen said, her voice shaking, "not chiefly, even . . ." And after a short silence, she added, "You will come again?"

Niels nodded silently, unseen. But in a chance motion his hand touched hers; and they knew . . .

Once more, during the week, Niels tried to drown his dreams in work. Once more he did what he had done many years ago: he worked passionately, as if his very existence depended on doing more than he could.

The smaller trees in the bluff blossomed forth: clouds of white blossoms: the leaves were hanging from the poplar twigs, weak, as if tired; young, helpless; before them the whole of summer lay, the summer of life.

In Niels' heart there was a strange struggle, a readjustment of many thoughts, feelings, anticipations.

It was a painful process: as if the parts of a broken limb were being fitted together, slowly, tentatively, by a skilled but callous physician who did not seem to succeed. It was as if some part were missing; or rather as if a superfluous part were there, preventing the perfect joint. And that superfluous part which prevented the past and the future from fitting together was a strange, new hope – a hope which it was almost painful to feel and altogether forbidden to face.

It was a mere adumbration of the thought of a possible outcome, a mere foreshadowing of a state of things that might, might come about like a miracle hardly to be visualised. It was at once suppressed with a beating of the heart, a scarlet flooding of the brain . . . To face it seemed equivalent to precluding it: it was such a tender, delicate thing of a hope . . . .

Niels felt like a convalescent who has, for many weeks and months, been forbidden to move and who, tentatively, first stirs a finger and then a hand . . . furtively, almost ashamed of the realisation of powers in him returning, re-awakening . . . He felt as if he must hold still so as not to frighten away what was preparing in him: a new health, a new strength, a new hope, a new life . . .

He saw the week going by, sometimes impatiently, sometimes in fear, always with pulse beating faster, with heart a-flutter, articulate thought blurred out, eye clouded.

And yet he said to himself, once, twice, a dozen times, "I am her brother . . . Nothing must interfere. I am her brother and nothing else . . ."

The days went by: the marvel of passing time.

Another Sunday, with white clouds sailing: a Sunday in June.

Ellen stands at the gate, looking along the road which is still no more than a bush trail.

They look at each other as they meet; and they blush.

Ellen swings the little gate open and turns; he follows.

Both know; and each knows that the other knows . . .

A new, strange thing has happened between them. Expectancy is in their eyes, emotion. They see that coming which makes their hearts beat – that which is like a memory of old times, long past. But it is not with fear that their pulse is quickened . . . It is with an anticipation which neither of them is unwilling to prolong; for behind that anticipation there stands a certainty . . .

Again, as they cross the yard in silence, going to the accustomed place – that natural bower in the fringe of the bush – imponderable things, incomprehensible waves of feeling pass to and fro between them: things too delicate for words: things somehow full of joy and disquieting though not unpleasurable expectation.

Spring breezes amble through the bush; a meadow lark sings on the nearby clearing; robins chase each other in the grass.

And as the silence lengthens between them, between man and woman, the consciousness arises in each that the other knows his inmost thought: that both have secretly, almost reluctantly, faced the same hope . . .

Colour comes and goes in their faces, imperceptible almost – not seen by either, for they avoid each other's eyes – yet divined.

And as they stand there, by the chairs which the woman has provided, a memory rises, flushing her face with a scarlet flood . . .

She speaks as if she would ward it off; she speaks hurriedly, like a girl, precipitately; and her words are the same as they were ten, twelve years ago. "Shall we sit here?" she says. "Let us have a walk rather, shall we?"

Niels nods. Her words are expression of his thought or his desire unformed; he does not think in articulate terms . . .

"The bush hides," she says. "It shelters, protects. It has served me well . . . But sometimes I wish I had a vista through it, out on the plains, to the horizon. I want to see wide, open, level spaces. Let us go to the slough . . ."

Again Niels nods. He does not trust himself to speak. His voice would seem so strange: it would break a spell. There is no barrier between them which would need to be bridged by words. They are not looking at each other: they are one.

"Wait," says the girl. "I will get my hat."

And she slips past him, into the house.

He idles back to the yard. The blood sings in his veins; he stands, strangely aglow.

Light-green, virgin, the bush rears all about. Aspen leaves shiver, reflecting little points of light from their still glossy surface.

"I love spring," says the girl as she rejoins him, her hat slung by its ribbons over her arm. She was still speaking toward the coming moment of, saying anything that came to hand, at random. "I wish it were always spring . . ."

They pass through the gate and on to the bush road, turning north, side by side.

Again, between them, the tension grows less. What has happened between them is a beginning; it is not the end . . . What must come will come; there is much to follow. Why tremble? Why hasten it? To be merely alive is joy enough . . .

First they follow the bush road; then they leave it, threading a cattle path that branches off to the left where the road bends eastward.

Birds flutter up as they touch the bushes. They flit away, looking curiously at the intruding pair . . .

The cattle-path forks: the girl follows one branch, the man another. They do not flit and run: they go quietly, sedately. Still they avoid each other's eye; but each knows that the other is flushed, that his face smiles, with a strange, almost otherworldly smile. Whoever arrives first at the rejunction of the trails waits for the other: the other is coming . . .

Thus they reach the little school and look about. The yard is cleared; no brambles cover it any longer. Around the building the ground is bare, vegetation being worn down by many feet. They stand and look, their feelings half joy half sorrow . . .

They go to the windows of the school house and peer in. They do not laugh; but they smile at sight of benches and blackboards.

Then they go on, quietly, reminiscently. No need for words. Between them there stands the past; not as a barrier now; as a bond.

These two have been parted; and parting has opened their eyes. They have suffered; suffering has made them sweet, not made them bitter. Life has involved them in guilt; regret and repentance have led them together; they know that never again must they part. It is not passion that will unite them; what will unite them is love. . . .

They are older. Both feel it. Older than they were when they threaded these thickets before. They are quieter, less apt to rush at conclusions, to close in a struggle with life . . .

They come out to the slough and see the horizon, far in the north. They stand and look. Both think of a hay-stack that stood in the meadow, a few hundred yards in front. There is no hay-stack there now: it is spring, not autumn.

"Shall we sit?" says the girl.

They find a place in the grass, with a fallen tree for a back-rest.

They sit and look out, as if in resurrection of what was dead.

The man has turned. He was conscious of something in the girl by his side . . . of something disturbing or perhaps disturbed. He looks at her face which is held straight ahead, almost rigid. Something works in her features; and between the lashes of her light-blue eyes – white, sun-bleached lashes – there quivers a tear.

"Ellen," he says, his voice a-tremble.

"Niels," she replies, "it is time we make up for what we have done in the past . . . I have something to say to you, Niels. I should have thought of it twelve years ago; but I did not know it then. Yet I knew it the moment you had left my yard. Only I did not trust my own knowledge. Niels, I, too, am a woman. I, too, need more than mere brotherhood. The years go by; we both are passing through life. There is nothing that will remain when we are gone . . ."

"Ellen," he says again and presses her small, shapely, calloused hand in his own large one . . .

"I know," she says. "Don't speak. I have more to say. I have been to blame . . . I should not have said at the time, what you wish can never be. I should have said, what you wish cannot be so long as I live under the shadow of my mother's life. But if you can wait . . . For, Niels, I knew then as I know now that it is my destiny and my greatest need to have children, children . . . And I knew then as I know now that there is no man living on earth from whom I could accept them if not you . . . I thought I could live my life as a protest against the life my mother had lived. I had loved her and she was dead . . . I should have known . . . Had she been living, the mistake would never have been made . . ."

Again the man by her side presses her hand. Their shoulders touch. Not with the fleeting touch as in the bush. They are leaning against each other, quietly, trustingly, in peace with the world.

The man speaks, slowly, softly, his head bent low. "Do you think we can live down what lies in between?"

"Niels," she says, "I've had more than six years time to think that over. I believe we can. And whether we can or not, we must try . . ."

An hour or so later they rise and walk home through the dusk. They do not kiss. Their lips have not touched. But their arms rest in each other; their fingers are intertwined . . .

As they go, a vision arises between them, shared by both.

Afterword

BY KRISTJANA GUNNARS

SETTLERS OF THE MARSH is a Canadian Prairie novel. It has all the characteristics of the genre, insofar as that can be a genre. The setting is the Prairie. The characters are immigrant homesteaders, mostly of Scandinavian origin. Some themes typical of Prairie literature are immediately evident: people live far away from each other in rural areas and they do not often get together. Consequently a sense of isolation and silence sets in. One of the main conflicts posed by the novel is the tension between voice and silence, and therefore between community and isolation. Family takes on great importance: to have a family means you have a community at home and people to talk to. Family may mean the difference between sanity and insanity, and ultimately life and death. For people who are too isolated and wrapped in silence are, in Prairie fiction, often reduced to suicide or even murder.

The conflict at the centre of this novel – between voice and silence – gives rise to further tensions. Urban and rural elements; sophistication and naiveté; love and friendship; home and exile; going astray and finding one's way: all these are pitted against each other in a whirlwind structure of circles on circles revolving around a great silent centre. While voice and silence – presence and absence or community and isolation – are focal aspects of Canadian Prairie literature, the conflict is heightened by the cultural temperament of the characters. The central figures in this story are Scandinavian – Swedish or Icelandic – and Grove somehow knew that the great conflict in the Northern European soul is traditionally voice and silence. The Scandinavian story is often a suppression of voice into an enforced silence that eventually explodes, usually into some reprehensible act.

We usually think of *Settlers of the Marsh* as another prairie novel. We rank it with Martha Ostenso's *Wild Geese*, Sinclair Ross's *As for Me and My House*, and even Laura Goodman Salverson's *Viking Heart*. All these novels are works of their time: the traditional English novel of sentiment, as inherited from Jane Austen and Charles Dickens, is concentrated, confined, and pressed, both linguistically and narratively, into more poetic experiences of frustration. The changes brought on by Ernest Hemingway and the new writers of the early twentieth century placed greater emphasis on the reader. Internationalism set in. Taboos of the past were violated. *Settlers of the Marsh* appeared in 1925, at a time when readers could expect more than a good story and a confirmation of an assumed value system. At that time reading had begun to take on the air of risk. Literature was expected to look a little like the forbidden fruit.

It should therefore not surprise us to find that when we open this Paririe novel we hear echoes of D.H. Lawrence, Gustave Flaubert, and even Theodore Dreiser and Henrik Ibsen. Themes found in D.H. Lawrence's novels are rampant here: the relationship between parents and children and the effect that has on the children's ability to relate to other loved ones. Niels Lindstedt is unable to get close to women, and this presumably has something to do with his mother, a single parent who, he senses, pitied him and found him wanting. Ellen Amundsen is unable to accept the responsibilities of womanhood because her mother was mistreated in marriage by her father. When Ellen and Niels get together, they are outside, in nature, as usually happens in Lawrence, with the intention of drawing forth the primeval nature of man's desires and pitting it against the misguided pressures of society. Similarly, Flaubert's *Madame Bovary* is replayed in the story of Clara Vogel, who marries a country man to whom urban society is foreign and who knows nothing about more sophisticated matters of culture, education, and polite society. In the prairie scene, a woman like Clara Vogel has only one description: the district whore. She may in fact not be a "whore;" her type is celebrated with veneration in French literature down through the decades. But she is totally out of place in the Canadian prairie among Scandinavian settlers. She reads books we now think of as cultured – among them *Madame Bovary* – but which were then and there simply considered decadent. We may even find echoes of Ibsen here, to whom the conflict between the genders was a major issue. In Ibsen men and women do not understand each other: their goals and ambitions differ. In Grove as well, Niels cannot understand either Ellen or Clara. Though they are vastly different women, they are equally strange to him. He is puzzled about their presumable idiosyncrasies: either they will not work like a man or they will not live like a woman. Nor do the two women understand Niels. They both grossly misapprehend his intentions and personality, and though he is the gentlest of souls who refuses to do them harm, they both see him as a potential abuser.

In spite of such apparent reverberations from the outside world, Grove was no doubt trying to write a novel specifically for and about the Canadian prairie. When Niels Lindstedt is influenced by his wife to do some reading of fiction, he finds he is unable to relate to these European creations. We are told that "in vain he searched for something that might enlighten him as to his mentality, that dealt with problems which were his. . . ." This concern is at the centre of Canadian literature, particularly in the west, and in 1925 it was still not easy to locate human drama in the prairie. It meant writing about people who, like Niels, struggle in silence with unmentioned dreams and unfulfilled desires. There is no flamboyance in this scene, no ready source for comedy in the grim reality of life in the Northern Manitoba bush. To write about this time and place meant to relocate our interests: in other words, to be successful with prairie novels required a cultural overhaul. Publishers were not as convinced as Grove was that it would work. Now we are in a better position to see the value of what he had done.

Niels's more enduring questions revolve around the purpose of life. Within the conflict between voice and silence, the question of will is supreme. He is not sure whether he can control his own fate, and he suspects the opposite is true: that he is controlled by fate. When he finds the attentions of Mrs. Vogel oppressive and he feels powerless to withstand them, he muses that "he was a leaf borne along the wind, a prey to things beyond his control, a fragment swept away by torrents." Indeed, the whole novel, until the end, seems to be a demonstration of the idea that man is only chaff in the wind. Niels is at the mercy of circumstance, origin, and time. All he has to go on is brute strength and an impaired sense of judgement. If he succeeds, he is simply lucky. The same can be said of Ellen, although she has greater willpower than Niels. Throughout the book, Niels is strangely at the mercy of others. Yet he has to take responsibility for his fate. "If, for what had happened to him, anybody was to blame at all, it was he," he reflects. Thus the sense of guilt becomes entangled with will. Silence, that great oppressive force that maintains a person in exile and isolation, becomes harmful. Yet it is also the source of Niels's strength. What gives his life meaning is the hope that Ellen will marry him. Silence about this hope makes it possible to secure the illusion that she might. Nothing is fulfilled. Life is a continuous state of expectation and hope. As Dante announced so early in literary history, when you abandon hope you are in hell. Without his hope for Ellen's companionship, Niels's life is hell – with Clara at home, and later in prison.

Underneath the apparent desire for silence, therefore, there seems to be a desire for ignorance. To live in the prairie requires an ability to dream and harbour illusions. If that is taken away, it is impossible to carry on with any great degree of sanity. Realism becomes an enemy of prairie life. If the Russians at one time discovered, through Tolstoy and Dostoyevski, that suffering gives life its meaning, then the Canadians discovered, through Grove and Ostenso, the opposite: that suffering renders life meaningless. Unlike the prison scenes of earlier Russian literature such as *Crime and Punishment*, Niels's prison term in the prairies contains no pathos and no sense of greatness. Ellen does not visit him there. He is alone, and he comes to his understanding through taciturnity and mindless determination. In this element at least, *Settlers of the Marsh* appears to draw from Scandinavian literature. There the gods are in control; they waft you about and you can only blame yourself. Man is not inherently good and fails only because of one Greek tragic flaw. Instead, man is inherently ignorant, at the mercy of greater forces that also appear mindless, and there are tragic flaws all over the place. At one point Niels wonders about the cosmic mindlessness he sees himself in and whether breaking the silence could be an alternative: "Was it really best not to question and just to live on?" he asks. That question is central to the whole book.

The concerns of human voice and silence here have a universal significance as a result. It is possible that not only Niels, Ellen, Clara, Bobby, and Nelson are silent with each other about what is on their minds and what they know. It is probable that the universe in general is silent about its secrets. There are no religious elements to this book of a Christian nature. Instead there is something pagan about the cosmology that is assumed and realized. Within voice and silence, fear is pitted against faith. Much of what maintains the silence is fear – fear of causing harm both to oneself and to others. The result of causing harm is isolation and loss of community, which turns out to be the worst evil in the book. Niels articulates this position to himself: "The highest we can aspire to in this life is that we feel we leave a gap behind in the lives of others when we go." It is a grim achievement: to inflict a sense of loss on others by our passing. Niels lives with the loss of his mother, a gap he delays trying to fill by asking Ellen to take her place in his life. He asserts to himself that his mother lives on only in his sense of loss. If he were to overcome that absence, he would in effect be erasing her memory. This is a pagan notion that is very Nordic in flavour, When Ellen at the end of the book asserts to Niels that the worst loss – the worst oblivion – for a person is not to have children to "live on in," she is making a similar claim for eternity. Faith becomes simply faith in other people and nothing else.

Niels's solution to the prospect of never achieving fulfilment in life – never coming to a satisfactory end – is to make life a continual series of beginnings. He fantasizes, once he has abandoned the hope of marrying Ellen and of finding any purpose to his life, that the only thrill for him lies in clearing new land: "A dream rose: a longing to leave and to go to the very margin of civilization, there to clear a new place; and when it was cleared and people began to settle about it, to move on once more, again to the very edge of pioneerdom, and to start it all over anew. . . . That way his enormous strength would still have a meaning. Women would have no place in his life. . . ." This must be an especially Canadian prairie dream: the dream of beginning again; of starting over with a clean slate perpetually.

Assuming a godless and purposeless universe, nothing happens unless man makes it happen. Work is done for the sake of work. Life is lived for its own sake. "What was life anyway?" Niels asks. "A dumb shifting of forces. Grass grew and was trodden down: and it knew not why." That is the bitter world view of this novel.

Given such a dark outlook, Niels and Ellen may well question the necessity of breaking the silence. Perhaps there is virtue in the great silence that keeps us from facing such a picture. There is something even more bitter to be gathered from this book: the view of the young country, of which the prairies are a part. Canada is still, at the time of this book, a new nation being cleared for habitation. This nation is comprised of people from a host of other nations. Something about this fact leaves Niels with a heightened sense of purposelessness. He reflects: "He looked upon himself as belonging to a special race – a race not comprised in any limited nation, but one that cross-sectioned all nations: a race doomed to everlasting extinction and yet recruited out of the wastage of all other nations. . . ." This is perhaps the strangest statement in the whole book. The immigrant as "wastage" from other nations is a low view indeed, and says a great deal about Niels's view of himself and his fellow settlers. He adds that "it was only the dream of the slave who dreams of freedom. . . ." He sees himself as a worthless slave, yet here he is, in the very place where he can own his land and be master of his fate. If freedom is represented as slavery, illusion as reality, we are viewing what Milton's Satan discovers as he comes to Paradise: that it is possible to carry a hell within and never get out. Indeed, Niels realizes himself that "the wind that bore him whither it listed came from his innermost self."

Settlers of the Marsh, therefore, not only proposes a grim view of the universe and man's place in it, but a grim view of the self. The only person who is really moved to tell her life story is Ellen. On two occasions she explains herself to Niels, and unlike Clara Vogel, Ellen is trying to articulate the truth. That "truth" is her reality, which is that life is inherently not good; women especially suffer; and perpetuating life is a form of suffering. Most people in this novel simply bite their lips and struggle on, some nobly like Bobby and Ellen, and some not so nobly, like the Lunds. It is a world of harsh blizzards and impersonal chance meetings. In such a setting, devoid of will, the self turns out to have little importance. Consequently there is no reason to tell a story: no reason to write. Grove is therefore engaged in the difficult task of writing fairly traditional narrative about people about whom there may be very little to say, for they have little to say themselves. If this is a quality of prairie fiction, then Grove has hit on something interesting. Perhaps the lesson that Niels learns from his experiences – the lesson that you cannot hope for fulfilment in this place – is something that has been with prairie literature for a long time. Certainty this is so in Sinclair Ross's *As For Me and My House*, which also has a lot to do with isolation, silence, and family, and where human desires are thwarted and people go astray.

Yet it must be acknowledged that Niels and Ellen do get together in the end, and there seems to be a benevolent hand holding the reins of fate after all. *Settlers of the Marsh* turns out to be no Shakespearean tragedy where everyone dies in a conglomerate of ironies. There are only a few corpses in this book, and they only serve to clear the way – the Amundsens, Lund, Clara Vogel – and we end up with a comedy. But it is a grim comedy, and we can echo Margaret Laurence in saying this must be a jest of God – or of the gods. If they are laughing, it is because the suffering the two main characters have undergone is purposeless and could have been avoided. The poignancy involved in thwarted or star-crossed love found in the traditional English novel, such as George

Eliot's *Middlemarch*, is somehow absent. Instead of pathos we have an odd sense of uselessness.

The journey Niels and Ellen have taken has been a journey through fear of themselves to faith in each other. Union between them is only possible when Niels accepts that he must remain her friend, have her as a brother, and not become her mate. He articulates what he has learned at the end: "he had done a great wrong: he had left alone a human being that had been in need of him: had left her alone because he had thought he could never be as little to her as a brother." Ultimately, his story has been a story of "going astray." Ellen, on the other hand, has learned that not all men are brutes, and procreation is a desirable thing after all. It is good to have children, and women need not be powerlessly at the mercy of their men. Here Grove has presented a rare insight which is worth noting. The idea of romance – which is not the same as love – has hindered friendship when sex cannot be a part of it. The romantic novel would come down on the side of Niels. The realistic novel would side with Ellen, whose suffering is due to her loneliness after all the men who proclaim to love her do what Niels does, and abandon her because she will not marry. Especially in this instance do we see where Grove breaks with the romantic tradition. His realism is grim. His world view holds no comfort. All we have, in *Settlers of the Marsh*, is a few ignorant people who need to have faith in each other regardless of their ignorance and fears. And this, after all, turns out to be enough.

BY FREDERICK PHILIP GROVE

AUTOBIOGRAPHY

In Search of Myself (1946)

ESSAYS

It Needs to Be Said (1929)

FICTION

Settlers of the Marsh (1925)
A Search for America (1927)
Our Daily Bread (1928)
The Yoke of Life (1930)
Fruits of the Earth (1933)
Two Generations (1939)
The Master of the Mill (1944)
Consider Her Ways (1947)
Tales from the Margin (1971)

SKETCHES

Over Prairie Trails (1922)
The Turn of the Year (1923)

LETTERS

The Letters of Frederick Philip Grove [ed. Desmond Pacey] (1976)